CW00823178

UNTIL PROVEN INNOCENT

UNTIL PROVEN INNOCENT

Nicola Williams

HAMISH HAMILTON
an imprint of
PENGUIN BOOKS

HAMISH HAMILTON

UK | USA | Canada | Ireland | Australia
India | New Zealand | South Africa

Hamish Hamilton is part of the Penguin Random House group of companies
whose addresses can be found at global.penguinrandomhouse.com.

First published 2023
001

Copyright © Nicola Williams, 2023

The moral right of the author has been asserted

Set in 12.5/17 pt Fournier MT Std
Typeset by Jouve (UK), Milton Keynes
Printed and bound in Great Britain by Clays Ltd, Elcograf S.p.A.

The authorized representative in the EEA is Penguin Random House Ireland,
Morrison Chambers, 32 Nassau Street, Dublin D02 YH68

A CIP catalogue record for this book is available from the British Library

ISBN: 978–0–241–56271–0

www.greenpenguin.co.uk

To the oldest and youngest members of my family: my mother, Waveney Williams (born 1931) and my great-niece Niylah-June Feliu-Watson (born 2001).

And to my friend Tony Laforce (1962–2022), who since we met nearly twenty years ago became one of my best friends ever. He loved books, and writing, and read more across a wider range of genres than any person I know, so it is fitting that wherever this book goes his name will be in it. At the time of writing this his loss is very recent, so this is hard. He is much loved and missed by all who knew him, and he was, quite simply, one of a kind.

I

Walking alone in Peckham on a dark, wet, wintry night, the last thing you want to hear is footsteps behind you. JT had been hearing them for somewhere between a minute and forever. During that time he had done everything he could to shake them off. He had walked as quickly as possible without running – too conspicuous – until he reached the yellow-orange glare of the street lights on the semi-deserted road near where he lived. He had alternately picked up then slacked off his pace, only to hear a corresponding variation in the footfall behind him. But there were two things he wasn't going to do: stop and look behind him, or run. No point, if they were going to do for him. He'd never outrun a bullet.

For a Friday night, he couldn't believe how empty the streets were. Just his luck. But as he approached the bus stop he saw a large woman in her late fifties under the shelter, clearly just off the night shift. It seemed a miracle she was standing there at all. But she might just be the miracle he needed.

'You got the time, love?' he shouted as he approached, trying and failing to hide the nervous edge in his voice. Out of the corner of his eye he could see a bus slowing down. Maybe he could jump on that. Or others would get off. Either way, at least there would be witnesses.

Instinctively the woman clutched her bag to her body. She peered at him, first with guarded curiosity, then, as she recognized him, with open contempt.

'Me? I know who you are, Jimmy Thomas. I wouldn't piss on you if you were on fire!' She jerked her head forward, to a point in the distance somewhere behind his shoulder. 'Ask him!'

The man was gaining. He knew it. The bus was still too far away. 'Fucking bitch!' he muttered, as he hurried past.

'Think I haven't been called worse?' she shouted after him.

Behind him, he could hear the swish of the bus doors opening and closing. Then silence. He buried his hands deeper into his jacket and felt the comforting cold metal in his right-hand pocket. Even though she was a neighbour, he'd been surprised when she gave it to him. He didn't think her type had anything to do with guns. But he didn't ask any questions. No one did, round here. Besides, in his line of work he should have had one long ago. He wished Ray had been with him. He'd have known what to do. But he'd needed to make a quick decision – take it, or not. So he took it.

It was one thing walking around with a nine, though quite another to use it. He hadn't even taken it out yet and his hand was already trembling. He had known the day would come, that first time.

'Don't even think about it!'

JT had no idea how the man behind him had come so close, so quickly, but he recognized the voice even before he was spun round and pushed up against a high concrete wall.

'You'd better keep your fucking hands where I can see them, if you know what's good for you. What you got in there, then?' his attacker continued, right hand rummaging through his pockets as his fleshy left forearm pressed against his windpipe.

'Fuck off!' JT managed to splutter. 'You can't do that to me!'

'What do you mean, I can't do that to you?' he replied, mimicking the smaller man's choking, spluttering voice. 'It's *Sergeant* Jack Lambert, and I *am* doing it to you, you fucking little grass. Not even a good one, at that.' Still searching, he increased the pressure on JT's neck. 'Aha!' He pulled the gun out of JT's pocket. 'Look what I've found. And I thought I'd just find you running drugs for Tony.' Lambert slowly raised the gun. JT squeezed his eyes shut as he felt it pressing high against his temple, tasting vomit rising in his constricted throat. If he was lucky, maybe he would pass out first.

'So what's this about? I know you don't have the balls to use one of these. You know what judges are giving for possessing a firearm, what with "London's inner-city gun-crime problem" and all? Especially if you've been threatening a police officer with it. And you not long out of Pentonville. You know,' he added slowly, 'I could kill you right here for all the use you've been to me lately. Think anyone round here would care?'

'Jesus, don't shoot, Sergeant.' He could barely get the words out. He was crying now too, but he didn't care. 'I can't breathe . . .'

'You're still talking, though.' But suddenly Lambert loosened his grip and watched impassively as JT doubled over, gasping and clutching his throat. When he finally stood up, the red marks on his pale neck and the bruising on his forehead were as visible as the mixture of hatred and fear in his eyes. That was the look Lambert wanted to see.

'So, what do you know about Tony? What do you have that's fresh?'

JT looked sullenly at Lambert. It was always Tony. 'Nothing you don't already know. And don't bother hitting me again neither. I've told you before: it's different now. More fancy customers; less risk. Someone who wants some lines for their dinner party and who's always gonna pay, no questions asked.'

'But he hasn't stopped round here, has he? He's making it even more of a shithole than it already is.' Lambert clenched his fist, then tightened it further as if squeezing a lemon. 'You better start giving me something I can use, otherwise you're no good to me. Just how long do you think you'll last when I put the word out that you were my grass? And next time, don't try hiding – not from me. You know what I can do.' Lambert waved the gun in JT's face one last time before putting it in his pocket. 'And I'll take this. You can't use it anyway. Didn't even know the safety was still on.'

JT stared at him, genuinely frightened. 'But it's not mine.'

'Oh, I know. All the times I've nicked you, you've never had one. Besides, how many people round here can afford their own gun? You know how many robberies and shootings this has probably been used in? If you don't have anything useful for me next time, I'll nick you for this.'

Lambert watched as JT staggered away from the wall and up the street. The rain was spitting in his face, plastering what was left of his hair to his skull, but he waited until his informant rounded the corner. He'd have to work out what to do with the gun. He was a police officer, after all. But he didn't have time for that now. He had something else to attend to, and he was running late.

2

Anyone walking past the Church of God Ministry on that rainy February night would have been hard-pressed to notice the man lurking in the shadows by the side entrance, as big and burly as he was.

And that was just the way Jack Lambert wanted it.

The one thing the job taught you was to cover all the angles. If he had been spotted, as dishevelled as he knew he looked, no one would have mistaken him for a criminal; everyone knew that, round here, the criminals were the best-dressed people in the neighbourhood. They wouldn't have been caught dead in a glorified donkey jacket smelling of smoke and beer, and a pair of Doc Martens that had certainly seen better days. And even if designer stubble had still been a fashion statement, his wasn't. At worst, he would most probably be mistaken for an odd-job man, perhaps, or maybe even a vagrant looking for a handout; after all, he thought cynically, everyone knew the virtuous minister's wife never turned away anyone in need. Virtuous – what a fucking joke. But no one would have believed it was him, a police officer, anyway. Though he lived locally, few London coppers lived in the same area they policed, and the only time he had ever set foot in a church was for the disaster he used to call his marriage – so long ago he couldn't even remember where the church was, let alone what denomination.

The only thing he hadn't counted on was anyone else being around other than the person he had come to see. It was Friday, after all, not

Sunday — and it was late. He could hear music: some kind of singing and a piano, plus other voices, talking. Still, he knew he was expected. He wouldn't have to wait long.

He heard bolts being slowly pulled back, as if to muffle the sound, and a key turning, tentatively, in the lock. Then the door opened about three inches and a woman's face peered up at him, around a foot below his own.

'I can't speak to you now. There's too many people, and my husband's still here.'

'I don't think you want me to go away.' He bent down and put his face as close as he could to hers. 'In fact, I think you'd better invite me in.'

He watched her recoil, but, as he expected, seconds later he was standing just inside the doorway. The music sounded louder now. She looked nervously over her shoulder. They were both at the end of a long, dark corridor. At the other end was a door with a small glass panel. The faint light from beyond the door and a dim night-light provided the hallway with its only illumination.

'This is a house of God. We don't allow drunks in here!'

'Come off it, lady. I bet your husband likes a nip of the communion wine. Anyway, you're in no position to get all high and mighty with me.' Lambert deliberately leaned forward again so that she could get the full alcoholic effect. 'You know that.'

He watched as the woman flinched and turned away, affected either by his breath or his words. Probably both.

'What do I have to do to get you to leave my son alone?'

'Keep him out of trouble, for one. But you can't do that, can you? So you'll have to give me some money instead. Like we discussed.'

'And suppose I don't?'

That was an angle he hadn't covered; it had never crossed

Lambert's mind that she would have thought of doing something so stupid, not for a moment. The woman herself seemed surprised at what she had just said. From the look on her face, Lambert knew that she had already changed her mind even before he spoke again.

'Well.' He started counting off reasons on big, thick fingers. 'One, he'll go to jail again – and I can tell you, the longer you've been out, the harder it is to do more time. Two, everyone will know about the Reverend's thieving, drug-dealing son.'

'Most people already know,' she replied, embarrassment and regret heavy in her voice.

'You didn't hear me, Eloise. I said *everyone* would know. And they might get to hear about that other little matter – something I know you'd really want to keep secret. You have another son, don't you? Paul? How do you think he'd feel about his saintly mum if he knew?' Lambert looked her up and down, his gaze deliberately leering, sexual. 'Yeah, you were probably a tasty piece back then. Not really my type, mind.'

The woman's shoulders drooped. For long moments the only sound was that of the choir rehearsing as she struggled to regain her composure. The earlier flash of defiance had now completely disappeared. She was defeated, defeated in the one place where she would never have imagined this to happen to her.

'The amount we talked about, I . . . I can't get you that. I don't have it.'

'Ask your husband.'

'You know he wouldn't help. And what excuse would I give him?'

'If there's one thing I know about you people, it's that you lot are very religious. Always giving money to your churches like some good luck charm. Black magic, if you like.' He laughed at his own bad joke. 'Doesn't do you much good, though, does it? You're still at the bottom of the pile. Fucking Poles come in and even they're better than you.' He paused, relishing the hurt look on her face. 'You must have a church fund of some sort. Take it out of that.'

Even in the half-light, Lambert could see the horror on her face. 'I can't do that!'

'Not my problem, darling. Just get it. You know what'll happen if you don't.'

Suddenly, a light was switched on in the upstairs landing, not quite enough to light up the hallway but enough to make them more noticeable.

'Eloise, who's that downstairs?' a voice called.

'Ah, the good man himself,' Lambert hissed.

'No one, Desmond,' Eloise replied as she attempted to push Lambert out through the door.

'Thought you lot thought lying was a sin.'

He was openly mocking her now – her, and everything she held dear. Eloise stopped pushing and for the first time that evening looked him full in the face. Without taking her eyes off him, she continued, 'Just someone begging for money.'

'How many times have I told you, don't give them any money. Food, yes, but no money. Come upstairs, please. There's something I'd like to show you.'

'I'll be back at the end of the week,' Lambert said, under his breath. 'You'd better have it ready for me then.'

He had already turned away when he heard the door shut behind him. He looked around before he emerged from the shadows and slipped through the half-open gate, making sure no one saw him. Things were going pretty much to plan, but Eloise Matthews might not be quite the pushover he'd expected.

Perhaps it was time for some firmer persuasion.

3

It was a paean to conspicuous consumption, but Lee had to admit it was money well spent. If Maple Court was going to throw a barristers' party, it might as well be a good one. The venue was lovely. Not some cheese-and-wine embarrassment in the Chambers library, but a proper blowout. There was an expensive sheen of affluence that could only reflect well on Chambers. A live jazz band was positioned just in front of a waterfall cascading from ceiling to floor, the gentle splashing of the water blending smoothly with the sophisticated music. Uniformed waiters and waitresses glided expertly through the crowd like swans, gracefully carrying trays of wine and champagne, and platters of expensive canapés. The women in particular – girls, really – were remarkably attractive. Tom's doing, no doubt.

Each member of Chambers had to pay £1,000 towards it. This was described as a 'voluntary contribution', when in fact it was any-thing but. She suspected the flat rate had been Giles's and Tom's idea; as Head of Chambers and Senior Clerk respectively, that was nothing to them. Even she wouldn't feel it that much – not at the moment, anyway. But the pupils and junior tenants – some of whom, after Clerks' fees and Chambers' expenses, wouldn't make that in a month – had complained bitterly. Maybe that was why a gaggle of them were knocking back as much free champagne as they could – with unfortunate consequences. Under different circumstances, Lee would have been right there with them, but she was experienced enough to know that even though this was a party, she wasn't here to enjoy herself. This was a one-drink event, maximum. In spite of the Knightsbridge setting, live jazz trio and open bar, this was work.

She had spent a good two hours schmoozing – speaking to her regular solicitors, letting them know how important their continuing patronage was; cultivating new ones too because, as Tom was fond of saying, 'You can never have too much work.' Now her feet hurt. As tall as she was, she wondered why she bothered with heels at all. Leaning casually against the wall, she shifted her weight discreetly from one leg to the other and watched Giles and Tom separately working the room. From her vantage point, it was a silent study in power and influence. Giles Townsend KC, florid and oozing smug pomposity, was holding forth on some topic or other to a group of younger lawyers, seemingly oblivious to the fact that the numbers were slowly dwindling. One after the other they drifted away, gravitating towards Tom, dressed in sleek Italian tailoring, like iron filings to a magnet. They were no fools: they knew where the real power in Chambers lay.

Just at that moment she saw Tom glance in her direction. He whispered something to Dean, the Junior Clerk standing next to him, then excused himself and sauntered over. The mere fact of him doing so caused the group he had left to look at her with renewed respect.

'Ah, Ms Mitchell – the Michelle Obama of the Bar. Good bash, don't you think?' It was always Ms Mitchell with Tom – a formality he chose with every barrister in Chambers, rather than one that was forced upon him. 'Of course,' he continued, still scanning the room, 'I'd like it better if the juniors weren't drinking us dry. If they get pissed and lose us work, I'll have their balls.' Looking at her near-empty glass, he beckoned to a passing waiter. 'Would you like another drink? Better get it whilst there's still some left.'

'No thanks, Tom, I'm driving. Besides, I'll be leaving soon.'

'Oh!' He sounded more displeased than disappointed. 'Well, I saw you chatting to the head of Devereux Chambers. I know he's been very impressed with you since the Omartian trial. Not thinking of leaving us, are you?'

'You been spying on me, Tom?'

'Let's just say I take a very keen interest in all my – er, Chambers' barristers,' he corrected himself quickly, 'especially one of our rising stars. I'd like to think this was just the continuation of an already thriving career in Maple Court, one that I'm sure will become increasingly successful.' He paused. 'In fact, I can guarantee it.'

'Not even you can guarantee that, Tom. These things go in cycles. Two years ago I was just as good as I am now, and I was barely making ends meet.'

So far they had been standing side by side, looking for all the world as if they were having a genial social conversation between colleagues. Now Tom turned to face Lee.

'I'm surprised at you, Ms Mitchell. I thought you were too smart to underestimate me.'

'I was thinking the same thing. Now I've got a major win under my belt, and lots of new work coming in, we both know I'm an asset to Chambers. And if I go to Devereux or anywhere else, my practice will follow me.'

It was a while before Tom replied. 'Well, as you yourself said, these things go in cycles. I'll see you on Monday.' As he moved away, he looked her up and down. 'Nice shoes.'

Lee had had enough. She fished her mobile out of her evening bag and was just about to ring David when she heard, 'Well, at least he gave you a compliment!'

Lee looked around to where a seemingly disembodied voice was coming from behind a large potted plant. She would have recognized it anywhere.

'Mary? I thought you'd left. How did you manage to hide behind here without being spotted? Especially by Tom?'

'With my big pregnant bulk, you mean?' Mary Fisher said ruefully. Lee watched as she shifted her position in her seat slightly, resting her hands above and below her belly as she did so. 'No, just taking a breather. I'm staying until the bitter end. Once the baby comes, I'll be out of commission indefinitely. This is my last chance to make sure my solicitors don't forget me.'

Suddenly Lee was dying for a cigarette, but smoking indoors was out of the question. In any event, she had stopped smoking completely around Mary since the day she had announced she was pregnant. It was no small sacrifice, but she knew her friend appreciated it.

'Tom won't let them forget you, you realize that.'

'Why? Because of Ollie? Nice to know that being married to *very* minor aristocracy with no money will keep me a place in Chambers, but Tom wouldn't care if I got any actual work. I could come back to a shit practice – or none at all.' Mary's tone was now prickly and defensive. 'Would you want him to do that for you as the only Black woman barrister in Chambers?'

Lee stared at her. 'What's your problem? Any time you want to swap, Mary, just let me know.'

'Shit! I'm really sorry, Lee. I don't know what's wrong with me lately. I'm becoming a raging hormonal bitch. I feel fat and tired. My feet are so swollen I dare not take my shoes off in case I can't get them back on again, and I haven't had sex in what seems like centuries – a problem I'm sure you're unfamiliar with. How is David, by the way?'

'At home. You know he hates these things. I can be there in less than half an hour if I leave now.' Lee drained her glass. 'How are you getting home?'

'Ollie's coming to pick me up. He's being very protective. Sweet, really. But I'll definitely be in Chambers at some point next week – unless the baby makes an early appearance.' She paused, adding thoughtfully, 'Having kids is good for a family law practice: people see the pictures on your desk and think you know what you're talking about. What about you?'

'I'm starting an armed robbery on Monday. Should go three to four weeks if it doesn't plead or carve.'

'If my hearing is listed for Monday and it finishes early, I'll probably go straight home and ring the clerks from there. The Tube at rush hour is no place for a woman in my condition. Teenagers surgically attached to their mobiles; able-bodied men, legs akimbo – fuck the "baby on board" badge. I'll only get a seat if a woman offers it to me.'

Lee smiled. 'You're turning into a grumpy old woman, you know that? I'm going outside for a cigarette before I drive home.'

A member of staff opened the heavy glass door for Lee as she made her way out.

'Would you like a taxi, madam?'

'No, my car's here.' She retrieved her valet token from her bag and gave it to him.

'Right away, madam.'

The valet brought her car to a graceful stop at the foot of the hotel steps, remaining in it a fraction longer than he needed to. As he got out, he gave Lee a slightly puzzled look, and then handed over the keys with a polite, practised smile. As they walked to the driver's side together, he whispered, 'Excuse me, you a lawyer?'

Not someone else looking for free legal advice. For a minute, she thought about lying, before answering, 'Yes. Why?'

'I knew it!' His smile was big, and genuine now. He glanced over at the doorman, who was staring at them both. 'Not supposed to talk to the customers. You probably don't remember me. Mark? Mark Herbert? You got me off a TWOC-ing when I thought I was going inside for sure. Ray Willis recommended you. He was always bigging you up. That was my chance. Got this job and haven't been nicked since.'

Ray Willis. Lee didn't want to go down that memory lane. 'But you still like cars, I see.'

He laughed. 'Yeah, but at least it's legal now. It's not much, but I'm not going to fuck this up.' He opened the driver's door for her. 'Thanks again. Nice motor, by the way.'

Mark was right: even though Lee wasn't in love with it yet, she had to admit it was a nice motor. It had been hard to part with her old Saab convertible. Even with one previous owner it had been at the top of her price range when she bought it at the start of her career, but it symbolized where she wanted to go – in every sense. This new Audi spoke of quiet wealth and elegance; the car you get when you've made it. Plus she wanted a hybrid and this was the best on the market. From second-hand to brand-new luxury reflected her career at the Bar thus far.

As the driver's door was slammed shut, its heavy sound was reassuring. With the windows wound up and the music on, she felt as if she were in a steel-and-glass cocoon. She turned slowly into the usual late-night Friday traffic and headed south of the river.

London was becoming increasingly tribal. It was a short journey home, but the ethnic make-up and types of housing during the journey were like experiencing a world in one city — moving through areas dominated by different groups, from affluence to social housing and back again. Historically, the area straddling Brixton and Tulse Hill where she had grown up had been one of the poorest. Not any more. Nothing like an artisanal coffee shop and an expensive deli here and there to mark out gentrification. But there were still pockets of decay and neglect that remained. In some ways it was worse now. No matter how bad things got back then, gun crime, knife crime and stealing from your neighbours had been virtually unheard of.

The flashing blue lights up ahead, therefore, were, sadly, no surprise. However, the sheer number of police vehicles was. In this area, that could only mean one thing. A shooting. Cars that had been flowing freely up to this point slowed to a trickle as gawping occupants tried to see what they could. The closer Lee got to the crime scene, the denser the traffic became, until it was virtually at a standstill in both directions. Young police officers were gesticulating in vain, desperately trying to keep things moving. Some looked nervous, others tense. She could see half a block had been cordoned off to the left, the blue-and-white tape extending out, narrowing the road.

She inched forward until her car was level with the greatest concentration of police vehicles. It had started to rain, the drops on the side windows obscuring her view, but she could see two police vans parked nose to tail with each other, forming a barrier between the eyes of the public and the frenzied activity behind them. Two officers, presumably the drivers, were standing nearby. One looked slightly older, and, compared to his colleague, didn't seem particularly bothered by the commotion going on around them. He was behaving for all the world as if he had seen it before, and probably had.

She pressed a button, and the electric window on the front passenger side slid down.

'Excuse me, what's going on?'

'None of your fucking business!' the younger one snapped. 'Move on!'

Clearly all the training at Hendon didn't extend to civility. 'Well, officer, seeing as I live just up the road, I consider this *is* my business. And move where? I've driven about a foot in the last ten minutes. And nice to see community policing at work. Is that how they're teaching you to speak to people these days?'

'No. That comes from being on the street and dealing with people like you.'

Lee's calm evaporated like mist. 'What the hell do you mean, people like me?'

The older officer stepped forward. 'Come on now, Doug. Knock it off. There's no need for that.' He spoke mildly, but as soon as he did so his colleague stepped back.

'Suit yourself, Bill. You deal with it.'

Bill leaned into the window. It was raining more heavily now, spattering and bouncing off his yellow reflective jacket. 'Sorry about that, ma'am. He's a bit jumpy. We've had a very serious incident involving a youngster.' He shook his head. 'Not nice.'

'Is it a shooting?'

He nodded but didn't speak.

'Is he dead?' Lee tried to peer round his bulk, to see what she could observe in the sliver of space that separated the two vans. A siren wailed in the distance.

'I'm not at liberty to tell you that, ma'am. And you're not going to see anything like that, believe me.' He stood up and looked ahead. 'Traffic's moving now. Drive on, please.'

But Lee had seen something. A glimpse of a brilliant white box-fresh trainer on the right foot of a prone body partway down an alley, the beam of the street light picking it out and illuminating it, making it stand out between the legs criss-crossing in front of it. Just that, but it was enough. A sight thirty minutes – and a world away – from the glittering party she had just left.

As she opened the door to the flat, Lee could hear the faint sounds of a guitar strumming. David was still up. She didn't know which was more of a relief – that, or the fact that she could, at last, go barefoot. She took off her shoes in the hallway, feeling the cold polished wooden floor beneath her feet, and walked towards the living room. The door was ajar. Her boyfriend was concentrating so hard on the task at hand that it was at least a minute until he looked up to greet her. When he did, though, the smile he gave her was worth it. Oddly enough, he looked relieved.

'You're late. I was wondering what had happened to you. Thought your Chambers thing was finishing at midnight.'

Lee looked at her watch: 1 a.m. 'Why? Want to keep me safe from all the gangsters and carjackers out there?' She thought about what she'd seen earlier.

David stopped playing, put the guitar down and looked directly at her. 'I'm more worried about those sharks you work with. But there's nothing wrong with a man wanting to protect his woman, Lee.' He paused. 'So, what happened? You don't look like you had a good time.'

She leaned over and kissed the top of his shaven Black head. 'I wish you'd been with me.'

'You know I hate those things. The last time I went –'

'The *only* time you went . . .'

'– they asked me about music law. Music law! What the fuck do I know about that? That's what music lawyers are for.'

She shook her head. 'That's not what I meant, anyway. Something happened near my mum's house. A shooting.' She thought of the single white trainer, again. 'Someone young, I think. A teenager, maybe – right at the place that used to be a Caribbean grocer's when I was growing up. My mum used to send me round there once, twice a week for stuff you couldn't get anywhere else. It's derelict now, of course. Probably get redeveloped into some fancy flats.' She laughed, but there was no humour in it. 'Just like this one.'

'No chance. This is The Hill, not Ricketts Road. Different league, baby.'

He wasn't making things better. She sighed, got up and walked to the French windows leading on to the garden. The moon was struggling to fight its way out from behind a cloud, but at least it was succeeding. It was fast approaching 1.30 a.m., and still raining, but she needed the scent of fresh air and flowers to clear her head. Living, growing things.

She didn't hear David until he was standing right behind her. For a big man, he was amazingly light on his feet. Tall as she was, he made her feel protected and safe, both of which she needed right now. He put his arms around her waist and she leaned back against his broad chest. She traced the tail end of the tattoo snaking up his bicep, disappearing under the sleeve of his T-shirt.

'Speaking of your mum, she called earlier.' When Lee stiffened, David added, reassuringly, 'Don't worry, she's fine. She said it was important, but it could wait. And that was the longest conversation I've had with her in a while.' He was quiet for a moment, then said, 'So, what do you want to do? Sell up and move? You've earned this, Lee. Don't be ashamed of what you have.'

'*We* have,' she corrected.

'Come on. I could never have afforded this on my own. You could, though. But the point is, we're both from the endz. Moving back there won't stop gun crime. You know that.'

'So what will?'

'Honestly? I have no idea. But at least I'm not pretending to know, like half the politicians and so-called community leaders out there.' He squeezed her tight. 'It's late. Come on, let's go to bed.'

4

Earlier that night, Wallace had been off-duty, but the station had called him anyway. He wasn't angry – far from it. He would have given them a bollocking if they hadn't. It was a new posting for him, and he had to make his mark. It would be a long drive in, but, like most officers, he had long since given up the idea of living anywhere near where he worked. It was great in theory – until people realized who you were. Then, between little old ladies knocking on your door to report their cat missing and people slashing your tyres so often the insurers refused to pay up, your life became a misery.

In fact, he realized as he hit the M23 into London, he'd moved further and further out with each promotion; if he moved again, he'd end up living in the sea, not just near it. But it wasn't as if he had much family in London – or anywhere, come to that. And friends seemed to be getting fewer and fewer each year. He thought about those he still had sometimes – mostly fighting in hot, arid countries, where there was certainly sun and sand, but definitely no beach: as far removed from a holiday destination as you could get. He was still in touch with some of his ex-squaddie mates; occasionally they'd even get together to raise a glass to the Fallen. But that was it.

Without taking his eyes from the road, he selected a track on the car's audio system. He was becoming expert at doing this at 70 mph. As the sound of Miles Davis filled the car, it occurred to him that he was becoming the living embodiment of the jazz-buff loner who seemed to be the archetypal British TV detective. Except in real life they didn't usually come in Black.

Miles was good to drive to, though: a fluid, controlled fury which was just enough to keep him alert for what was to come.

For a Friday night, he made it up from the coast and into South London in good time. In fact, it was the last quarter of a mile to the crime scene that was the slowest. Up ahead, he could see his officers directing the traffic, trying to move it forward, even encouraging cars to mount the pavement in a desperate attempt to clear the bottleneck. Wallace tooted his horn sharply, twice. No luck – the cars in front of him didn't move an inch. He pressed down again on his horn, hard. The man in front of him, in a battered Nissan Micra, merely blew his own horn in response, turned round, looked at him and slowly, deliberately gave him the finger.

Wallace banged on his windscreen and wound the window down, holding up his warrant card. But the man in front just stuck his head out of his window, turned to face him and replied, in a heavy Eastern European accent, 'You think that scare me? Police here not like back home.'

Wallace sighed. He knew there was nowhere for the traffic to go, but he had to get through. If he'd had blues and twos, that would have done the trick: nothing like a police siren and flashing lights to make even the heaviest traffic part like the Red Sea. But he had come up in his own car. He looked around. He could have sprinted the last four hundred yards if there had been anywhere to park.

But then, mercifully, the traffic moved forward again – just a little, but enough for him to get within shouting distance of one of the officers standing next to two police vans.

'Oi! Bill! Over here.'

Bill looked round, frowning at the thought of a member of the public presuming to call him by his first name. Then he spotted Wallace. Even at that distance, Wallace could see the relief on his face. As he watched him approach, half jogging, but mostly walking, Wallace thought it was a good thing Bill Roberts was a police driver: with his bulk, he'd never catch anyone on foot. Good driver, though, and a solid, decent bloke. In the week since Wallace had been at the station, he'd already seen him demonstrate that. He would trust him with his own car, and that was saying something. Unflappable too, like most of the old hands; not cynical, though, which was a miracle. Was it because he was that rarest of creatures – a policeman with a happy personal life?

'Very glad to see you, guv,' Roberts said, mopping his brow – whether from the exertion or the first spatters of rain now beginning to fall, Wallace wasn't sure. He nodded in acknowledgement.

'All I've been told so far is that it's a shooting. That was,' Wallace looked at his watch, 'nearly an hour and a half ago. Fill me in on the rest. Is he dead?'

'Probably is by now, guv. Ambulance came earlier.' Wallace found some officers had a problem acknowledging his more senior rank, especially if they were older than him. He could tell by the way they addressed him – politely, but as if they had to force the words out, as if it somehow demeaned or diminished them to do so. Not so Bill Roberts. 'It's a miracle he didn't die outright.' The traffic had stopped again. 'Best if you go on up ahead. You'll be quicker on foot. Don't worry, I'll sort your car out.'

It was starting to rain more heavily now. Wallace ran towards the crime scene, zigzagging between cars and onlookers as he did so. He was tempted to put his hood up but thought better of it. After all, he didn't want to get nicked on his way to his first major crime at Miller

Street. Not all the officers knew who he was, yet. Like this one, who he had seen standing with Bill earlier, and who was now trying to block his way.

'And where do you think you're going?'

'I'm on the job,' Wallace replied. But as he reached inside his hoodie for his warrant card, the officer instinctively stepped back and grabbed the handle of his baton.

'Hey, take it easy. Look.' He held the card up. 'You must have seen me talking to Bill down the road.'

'Yeah. So?' The officer was clearly unconvinced. He examined the warrant card Wallace gave him as if it were a forgery. That really pissed him off.

'Look, I didn't drive sixty miles just to deal with this bullshit. If you don't know who I am, that's not my problem. I'm going in.'

He ducked under the blue-and-white tape. The other officer didn't try to stop him – having now realized who he was.

'Really sorry, sir,' he stammered. 'I . . .' He held the card out to him. Wallace snatched it back and headed grimly onwards. Behind him, he could hear the officer muttering, defensively, 'Well, *I* didn't know . . .' Wallace thought of Miles Davis in the car. Controlled fury. Maybe that's why he liked his music so much. He *knew*.

But the task ahead was more important. Wallace could see four officers in a group near a blood-soaked area on the ground. One of them, a sergeant, met him halfway. 'Hello, boss.' He sounded surprised. The others turned to stare at him, then turned back to the task at hand. 'We knew you'd been informed, but we didn't expect you to turn out. And on a night like this. You were off-duty, weren't you?'

'I was, Sergeant. Not any more.' They all looked at him again, this time with renewed respect. 'What do we have?'

'Young Black lad. Fourteen, fifteen maybe. Dog walker called it in. One shot to the side of the head, close range. Went through the hood of his jacket. Good chunk of his face gone. That's unusual. Could be personal, to get up that close. Or gang related, maybe? Ten to one it's a street weapon. Beretta or Glock 9mm; the guns of choice these days.' He paused. 'Also, I reckon someone familiar with guns, but not used to using them.'

'Why?'

'Because they made a real mess and still didn't manage to kill him outright.'

As they walked over to the others, the sergeant continued, 'You live on the coast, don't you, sir? Brighton?'

'That's right.' Wallace pointed to a blood-spattered object about two feet away. 'What's that?'

'His mobile, we think. Must have smashed when he fell. Definitely not a robbery, then. *I* couldn't afford one like that.' Then he laughed. 'Jesus, you needn't have bothered coming out for this. If these kids think they are hard enough to be in a gang, they can all kill each other, that's what I say.' He handed him a bus pass. 'We found this in his pocket. At least we know what he looked like when he still had a whole face.'

Wallace breathed in sharply and turned away. He'd only seen photos of him in chorister's robes, but he knew who it was. It was all he could do to stop himself retching. Instinctively, he started to raise his hand to his mouth. Only the knowledge that the others were now staring at him made him stop.

'Yeah, it is pretty nasty, sir,' the sergeant said. He tried his best to sound sympathetic, but really, just what kind of people were they promoting nowadays? He was a bloody DCI, for God's sake. Plus, rumour round the station was that he was ex-Army: served in Afghanistan – somewhere like that. He had to have seen worse. 'It's harder when they're young. Still, nothing you haven't seen before, I'm sure.'

'I know him . . . I know his family.'

'You *know* him?' the officer repeated. He might interact with the locals, but he didn't actually know anyone round these parts, and didn't want to. He looked at the boy's bus pass, then back to Wallace. 'Bit young for a CHIS, isn't he?'

'He's not an informant.' Wallace was surprised at how calmly that came out, considering. He paused and tried to collect his thoughts, knowing all eyes were on him, clearly aware something was up. 'Better alert our media people to be on standby. And call the Super. I'll meet you back at the station. I've got something to do first.'

Wallace thought of the hours ahead. This was going to be a long night.

For the first time in nearly two hours, he stood up, straightened up fully, and tried to stretch out the tension which had accumulated in various parts of his body. He looked up at the same struggling moon and wondered why on earth it would want to come out and shine down on such a scene.

5

Driving through the old neighbourhood made Wallace realize just how long it had been since he'd been back. He had shot out of the school gates as soon as he legally could – and he knew the teachers had been just as glad to see the back of him. It had changed, like so many other parts of London; areas that would have been called slums twenty years ago now reframed by eager estate agents as 'edgy' and 'metropolitan', with the price tags to match. The odd derelict building was actually a bonus; it gave enough street cred to be fashionable – as long as there was only one, that is. However, the chi-chi deli, coffee house and organic bakery, all of which he had passed in the fifteen minutes it had taken to drive to his destination, indicated something altogether more aspirational. And why not? He personally had no problem with that. Poor people needed good food too – whether they could afford these prices was another matter.

But as he pulled up outside the Church of God Ministry, it was clear some things hadn't changed. The exterior of the building had always been pristine, even back then. They had to be touching up the whitewash every month to keep it so free from graffiti – unless the Reverend was just as terrifying as he remembered and kept taggers away by the sheer force of his personality.

Still, even from the outside it seemed peaceful, steady – just like the inscription that was wrought into the iron gates. As he opened them, Wallace could see it: *Rock of Ages*. Rusting, but still there. Last time he was here was nearly twenty years ago, and it sounded as if the gates hadn't been oiled since then. At that time, there was only one son in the family. He hoped that wouldn't be the case once again.

He was trying to open the gates as quietly as he could but, as soon as he did so, a light appeared on the first floor. A man's head, heavily flecked with grey, appeared at the window and shouted, 'Who's there?' in a gruff, testy voice.

'Reverend Matthews. It's me, Danny. Danny Wallace. Remember me? Could you let me in? I need to speak to you.'

It was a long time before he got a reply. 'Wait there.'

Wallace waited by the side door of the church building, which also doubled as the family living quarters. The Matthews family had lived above the shop for as long as he could remember, to be on hand whenever needed. 'This church is at the heart of the community,' the Reverend had been fond of saying. 'A community is like family, and when did a member of your family ever have a problem during normal hours?'

He heard what sounded like a million locks being undone before the door was opened. A small man, now wearing glasses, appeared. He was clearly angry at being woken up; the look on his face and the baseball bat in his hand were proof of that. He peered up at Wallace, and then, suddenly, smiled.

'So it *is* you. I wasn't sure. It's been a long time.'

'So I see.' Wallace looked at the baseball bat. 'And I suppose that's a piece of the Cross. You weren't really going to use that as an offensive weapon, were you?'

'This? Oh no, no,' the older man said hastily, leaning it against the side of the door frame. 'But still, you can't be too careful nowadays. Why do you think we have this?' He looked up towards a CCTV camera. 'I didn't recognize you dressed like that. Already had one strange man around here – big, like you – bothering my wife. But don't worry about that.' He stepped aside. 'Come in.'

'Forget it,' Wallace replied as he entered. 'At least it wasn't a knife.'

'I'd take you upstairs, but I don't want to wake Eloise. Come through here.'

Wallace was led along a dark, narrow corridor. One door to the right was cracked open, allowing a little more light to spill out into the darkness. The community kitchen. That brought back unwelcome memories – kicked out of home, sleeping rough or on friends' floors if he was lucky, often looking forward to that one meal a day right here. He could see a dim nightlight up ahead, in the ceiling above a door at the end of the corridor. Reverend Matthews opened it and turned a dimmer switch as soon as they entered. Instantly, low lighting came on and Wallace could see he was actually inside the church, to the side of the altar.

'Come on, sit down. I usually bring people in here if they're in trouble. Like you, when you were a youngster. Remember that time you were caught stealing?'

'Yeah. You, me and my social worker went down the nick. That could have gone either way – a caution or a conviction. It helped that you were there.'

'And now you work at that very same police station. Detective Chief Inspector,' he added, with relish. 'At least you learned your lesson early on. Now Tony . . .' He shook his head and kissed his teeth. 'A lost cause. So, are you in trouble now, Danny?' Wallace watched him taking in his faded grey sweatpants, hoodie and oversized jacket. 'You don't look like you're on duty. Something must have made you drive all this way.'

'I wasn't, but . . . well, something happened.' He took a deep breath. 'This isn't a social visit, Reverend. It's about your son.'

Reverend Matthews sighed heavily. 'What's Tony done this time?' He stood up, his voice agitated. 'I'm fed up with police coming to my door about him! He doesn't even live here, but they always seem to think I know what he's doing. You'd think the last jail sentence would have done it. I want to wash my hands of him, but his mother won't hear of it. I swear, though, if he goes inside again . . .'

Wallace laid his hand gently on the older man's arm. This never got any easier. He was glad they were sitting in semi-darkness. It would help them both. 'It's not Tony. It's Paul.'

6

Tony Matthews, flat on his back, was alternating his gaze from the ceiling to the woman riding him cowgirl on the bed. This one was still wearing her wedding ring. He wondered what excuse she had given her husband. She wasn't bad – he'd definitely had worse – and this was a strictly casual thing as far as he was concerned, so what did he expect – a star performance? She didn't know what he liked, and he couldn't care less what she liked.

He had to give her full marks for enthusiasm, though – and his wasn't matching hers. Luckily, he only had to think of business to get and stay hard. It excited him as much as any woman. And drug dealing was a business. Margins, profit and loss, marketing. That's what people round here didn't recognize. The small-timers knew how to spend it, though – on shit so obvious it was a question of when, not if, the police would show up. Either that or they used the product and then it was game over. Some even wrote things down so catching them was like shooting fish in a barrel. Fucking unbelievable!

First rule of dealing: never use the product. It gets you hooked and cuts into profits.

Second rule: write down as little as possible. It helped that he could do the calculations in his head. If he'd had the chance of an internship at Goldman Sachs, McKinsey or any other City business, he knew he could have taken on all-comers. But getting kicked out of school and being stopped by the police every other week put paid to that.

Tony rolled his eyes at the thought, and as he did so he saw her looking down at him, smiling in triumph. She probably thought he was close to cumming. He sighed; again she seemed to misread that as a positive reflection on her skills. This was what came from dealing with randoms. Just once it would be nice to be with someone who knew what he liked without him having to explain.

His mind drifted back to Fee. Maybe that would help him cum. They had last fucked each other two – or was it three? – days ago. It wasn't important enough to remember. Not like dealing, where he didn't forget anything. Or anyone. Especially if they crossed him. Fee wasn't a regular, but she wasn't a random either. After the first time they had fucked, he had mentally appraised her as he did any-thing else coming into his life. The picture was mixed. She was petite; a little spinner. He liked that. Okay legs. Bony arse. No tits, but nice big nipples. No make-up. Good, because he didn't like women hang-ing around afterwards and ten minutes after they finished (five, if no shower) she'd be out the door; bad, because her naked face was a five, if that. But his women always had one standout feature and hers was her hair. Thick, light-blonde hair in Pre-Raphaelite curls. That, and her mouth and what she could do with it.

He brought his mind back to the present. He really should make an effort here, though. He grabbed what there was of the woman's arse. Truth to tell, that was why he wasn't able to cum. He liked women with a bit more meat on their bones; something softer and more jiggly to hold on to. Fee didn't have much there either but her talent in other areas, and what she would let him do to her, more than made up for it. He could tell by the movement of her body that she was close. Her eyes were closed. The way she was using him like a human dildo, he didn't know whether she was thinking of him, or a fantasy of him, and didn't much care. Fragrant, well-heeled clients like this one would sometimes offer him sex for coke, or just because; would proposition him in the hallway while the husband was in the next room. The posh ones, like her and Fee, loved the idea of BBC – Big Black Cock – especially if it was attached to somebody like him.

Time to move this on. He put his hands on her small breasts and pinched her nipples, hard. He vaguely remembered it had worked with Fee. When he had done that to her she had cum almost immediately and collapsed forward on to his chest, her blonde curls tumbling over his face. He had felt her heart pounding against him, and the sweat on her back from the exertion. It worked now too. He let this one lie there for a few minutes as her breathing returned to normal. The room was dark. He'd put his phones on silent. He couldn't remember the last time he'd done that, but just for once he wanted a tiny sliver of the day for himself. They'd be back on as soon as he kicked her out, and then he'd ring Paulie. He couldn't be bothered to check the time so he had no idea how late it was. He always had the blinds down 24/7. For security, but he also liked it that way. Dark and cool, like a cave. And normally silent; after sharing a jail cell he never wanted to share his space again.

He pushed her hair away from her ear. 'You know I'm not finished,' he whispered.

She raised her head, dazed, and looked at him, her face just inches from his own. God, she was pale.

'You didn't cum? Why not? It was amazing!'

For you, Tony thought. Fee was definitely better. Maybe he was going through a posh-girl phase. When her guard was down, Fee didn't think to hide her accent behind dropped vowels and glottal stops like she usually did. The cut-glass precision of it came through.

There was something he had seen in her face, though, that last time, that he didn't like. He had looked into her eyes and, as they refocused, just for a few seconds, he had seen something else there: a hardness, as if he were being appraised, assessed. Calculating, as if she were one step ahead of him somehow. He didn't like it and didn't want to see it so he had pushed her head back down. He remembered her smiling and licking her lips, never breaking eye contact as she sat back on her haunches on the bed. He had watched as she'd adjusted her position so that she was kneeling in between his open legs. Lowering her head, he had watched her face disappear behind a curtain of curls. He had felt, rather than seen, her take him deep into her mouth and had imagined her tasting herself on him as well. That talented mouth. Skinny ones always gave the best head in his experience but she was exceptional. It was like having the marrow sucked out of a bone. Then he couldn't remember anything after that.

7

The hospital waiting room was the same grey-beige as the corridor leading to it. There must have been a job lot on when this was last painted, which was obviously some time ago. As an overworked NHS surgeon, Malcolm Weir was amazed he still had the mental bandwidth to be able to think about irrelevancies like that now, but he knew that it was the way the mind coped when it was overloaded by stressful situations. Maybe he had performed one operation too many.

Amazingly, for a busy teaching hospital like St Luke's, he hadn't met anyone else along the corridor. Just as well; he didn't want any distractions. He wanted to keep his mind on the job at hand – to focus on the point just after he would have broken the news, when he would have discharged his burden on to someone else's shoulders.

As he opened the door, three faces turned to greet him. Malcolm recognized Hugo Cunningham, the local Tory councillor, at once, particularly as he bore more than a passing resemblance to David Cameron. Although anything was possible in this multiracial borough, somehow he doubted that he was related to the victim. Rather, he had the look of someone who would rather be anywhere else but here. Tense, edgy, wired like an addict. Not so the other two people present. Both were Black. They were dishevelled, badly dressed in mismatched clothing as if they had dressed in a rush, in darkness, to get here. The woman was wearing bedroom slippers. They were both sitting down, but Malcolm could still see the difference in their respective builds. The woman was quite tall but very slight, almost frail. Her hair was haphazardly scraped back, her eyes were red from crying and lack of sleep, and there were deep grooves across her forehead, but it was obvious that twenty or so years ago she would have been considered a great beauty. The man was thickset and seemed shorter than the woman, even sitting down, but projected an air of quiet authority. Although neither was young, he seemed much older than the woman – maybe late sixties – somewhere at the point at which middle and old age meet. But his face was vaguely familiar – a former patient, perhaps. Malcolm noticed he was holding a black book in his hands, rocking back and forth slightly and talking to himself. He wondered whether he was muttering expletives at him, as if he knew he was the bearer of bad news. Or maybe the strain had affected his brain. Then he stopped rocking and Malcolm could see the inscription in gold lettering on the front of the book. The Bible.

Now he knew where he had seen him before.

'Reverend Matthews, isn't it?' he began. 'I didn't recognize you immediately; I'm sorry.'

Desmond Matthews stood up and walked towards the surgeon. 'We met under happier circumstances last time, Mr Weir.' He had a voice you would expect from a man of the cloth – deep and benign and, even with what had happened, self-assured; the voice of some-one who was used to deference. 'We raised a lot of money for the hospital that day.' He squeezed his eyes shut, then opened them again before asking, 'How's my boy?'

'We should wait for Tony.' The woman was still seated, her voice sounding thin and quavery. 'He said he was coming. Whatever it is, I want us to hear it as a family.'

The older man walked over to her and put his hand on her shoulder. It was the first time there had been any physical contact between them.

'My wife is a very patient woman, Mr Weir – far more so than I am, especially at times like this. I know she can wait, but I can't.'

The woman looked up at him, sharply. For an instant, her entire body language seemed to change. 'You know that's not what I meant, Desmond.' Her voice was stronger now, firmer.

'Please, Eloise.' It was a command rather than an entreaty. Her husband's hand tightened imperceptibly on her shoulder, changing from a comforting gesture to a repressive one. She lowered her head; whatever had momentarily flared inside her died just as quickly. When she next spoke, everything about her was trembling, including her voice.

'He's not dead, is he? Please don't tell me my son is dead.'

'No.' It was her husband who answered. 'No, he's not dead. Mr Weir would have already told us – isn't that right?'

Malcolm hesitated, then turned to Hugo Cunningham. 'Mr Cunningham, I'm sure Reverend and Mrs Matthews are grateful for your support, but just for the moment, I'll have to ask you to step outside.'

'Of course,' Hugo replied, a little too eagerly. 'Desmond, Eloise, as your councillor and friend I'm happy to be of any assistance, but the surgeon's right. I'll wait outside.'

Once he had closed the door behind him, Malcolm continued, 'Your son's still alive, but what I have to tell you will be difficult and painful to hear.' He looked at Mrs Matthews, then her husband.

'Go on,' Reverend Matthews said.

'His condition is very serious. He was shot in the side of the head, through the eye. His skull was fractured. As you know, we couldn't operate immediately – we were just concentrating on keeping him alive. We've now relieved some of the pressure on the brain, but –' Weir paused, choosing his words carefully, already knowing the impact they would have – 'it was a long and difficult operation. He's now in a coma.'

'How long will he be like that? Will he come out of it?' The questions were coming fast now, the words spilling over themselves.

'It's really too early to say, Mrs Matthews. We've done everything we could. All we can do now is wait.' *And pray, if you think it might help*, he added silently. He hoped they wouldn't press him further. Anything else he could say would only depress, not enlighten, them. They didn't need to know that he'd spent hours picking bits of skull and bone out of their son's brain before laying it like crazy paving back on the surface. His eyes stayed on Mrs Matthews. She was still trembling, which he found disturbing, annoying and moving all at the same time. He felt like telling her to pull herself together, to be more dignified – a very instinctive, very English reaction from him. This woman was looking anything but dignified – but then why the hell should she be?

Malcolm squatted down beside her chair. He wanted to hold her hand, but as her husband had not, he felt it wasn't his place to do so.

'When can we see him?' she asked, her voice barely above a whisper.

'Not for a while.' Malcolm paused before continuing. 'It wouldn't do you nor him any good, Mrs Matthews. He wouldn't know you anyway.' And probably never would.

'He's only fifteen. Who would want to do this to him?'

'It could have been a mugging – there was no money on him when he was brought in.' The look on Mrs Matthews's face stopped him speculating any further. The other alternatives were even worse: a racist attack or, worst of all, a completely random act of violence for which there was no explanation whatsoever. 'The police are investigating it. Hopefully we should know soon.'

'It's all my fault. I couldn't protect him . . .'

Strange, Malcolm thought. But maybe every mother thought she could protect her children from the evils of the world. It was the random awfulness of some of the things he had witnessed that made him think otherwise.

He stood up. 'There was nothing you could have done, Mrs Matthews.'

'Where did it happen?' her husband asked.

'Not far from the hospital, luckily. He must have been found very soon after he was shot. His clothes weren't as wet as you would have expected, and as you know it's been raining heavily. That almost certainly saved his life. We have his personal effects, but I'm afraid I can't release them to you as yet. The police already have his bus pass and mobile phone. He was wearing a hooded black puffa-style leather jacket with a distinctive design on the back —'

'That's Tony's jacket,' Mrs Matthews said, interrupting him. Her voice was flat and monotone, strangely at odds with her evident distress. 'My other son.'

'What type of gun was it?' Reverend Matthews asked.

Malcolm couldn't believe it. What the hell did it matter? Whatever it was had his son now fighting for his life — if you could dignify his future existence by calling it that. Before he could say anything, the door suddenly banged open behind him and a young Black man ran in. All Malcolm could register was that he had a shaved head and was average height before he was pushed out of the way. 'Mum, I got here as soon as I could.' He squatted by her side where Malcolm had been just a few moments earlier and held her hand. Mrs Matthews touched his cheek, gently.

'You were saying, Mr Weir?' Reverend Matthews was still pressing him for an answer. It was as if no one had come in.

Malcolm glanced quickly at the distressed woman before turning back to her husband. 'I don't think hearing me speculate on what was used on your son is going to help either him or you.'

'Tell me,' Reverend Matthews demanded.

From the look on his face, Reverend Matthews must have known that Malcolm wasn't prepared to be spoken to like that, even by a grief-stricken parent; when he next spoke, the peremptory note in his voice had disappeared. 'Please, Mr Weir. I need to know what kind of . . . savage could have done this to my boy.'

'Yeah. I want to know too.' Tony Matthews rose and moved to stand directly in front of Malcolm. He noticed an old scar on his left cheek, close to the jawline. Not disfiguring, but noticeable. He must have been very young when he got that. Malcolm wondered how he hadn't seen it before, but then this was the first time he had been able to have a good look at him since he entered the room. He was incredibly compact and muscular. Malcolm couldn't imagine him being any respecter of persons; certainly not doctors, from the hard stare he was giving him. Malcolm glanced again at Mrs Matthews. He wasn't going to be bullied into saying anything further to either of these men, particularly as neither of them appeared overly concerned about her feelings. Did they really think she wanted to know, much less cared, what put her son into a coma? If they weren't prepared to consider her feelings, at least he was.

He looked back at the two men. There had been sadness, fear and grief present in the room right from the beginning, and the resulting tension that went with it. Now there was something else too that hadn't been present until now: hostility, mainly from the younger man, but not exclusively. This had to be diffused as soon as possible. Telling them something would help; just not everything.

'I don't know. I'm no expert. But I'm guessing not a very high calibre.' Because it would have blown the back of his head off. He'd seen that before.

'Is that the best you can do?' Tony Matthews sneered. 'I'd better find a proper doctor, then.'

'Do what you like,' Malcolm replied evenly, 'but Paul Matthews is my patient, and no one else can – or will – give you any further information. If you want to know anything else, take it up with the police. Miller Street station is dealing with it, I believe.'

'I want to see him.'

'Well, you can't. He's just come out of surgery and he's in intensive care. No one, apart from me, will be seeing him for the time being.'

Tony Matthews looked Malcolm up and down, clearly getting the measure of the man in front of him. 'You going to try and stop me?'

'Tony, please,' his mother said.

'I wouldn't dream of it, Mr Matthews. But someone will.'

For a long moment the two men simply stared at each other, then the younger man turned abruptly and moved towards the door. Malcolm picked up the internal phone in the corner of the room and was about to dial security when Tony said, 'I know what you're doing. You think any guard would stop me if I wanted to see my brother? I'm going to the police station. Then I'll be back.'

'No!' It was the first time Mrs Matthews had really raised her voice. She half rose from her chair. 'Don't go there. That's the last place you should go, Tony. You know that.'

'Why not?' Reverend Matthews's voice was bitter. He looked at Tony. 'You're the reason he's in here!'

40

His wife gasped. She twisted round to face her husband. 'How could you say that?' She stood up. 'How could you say that?' she repeated, her voice rising with every word. For a moment Malcolm wondered if she was going to hit her husband right in front of him. That was a reaction he would have expected from her son, not her. But, strangely, Tony was saying nothing. He just stood by the door, looking as if his father had physically struck him. All the fight had gone out of him, to be replaced by a look that was angry and hurt, but, above all, guilty.

8

Ricketts Road. When Lee was growing up it had felt like the longest road ever. The lower part was mixed housing and small shops. The houses were two-up, two-down – almost like railwaymen's cottages. Most neatly kept, some not. The shops were the limited selection you would find in an area that had seen better days. A small grocer's; a newsagent's; an old man's pub; a betting shop; a barber's; Blessings, the Caribbean bakery. No chains: all were individually owned except the betting shop – and the manager behaved as if it were.

As the road ran up towards the top of the hill, there were fewer shops and slightly bigger houses. As it climbed still further, the road got quieter and wider. And whiter. Until it opened out at the very top of the hill. It was said to be lovely. It certainly was high enough to have a spectacular view. However, no one Lee's parents knew had ever been there.

And now Lee lived at the top of the hill.

Thinking back to her five-year-old self, Ricketts Road contained her whole life – or all that was important to it. Her school, her home, her playground where her dad used to push her on the swings and stand at the base of the slide in case she came off too fast, and the Caribbean bakery where the three of them – Lee, her mum and her dad – would go religiously once a week. In fact, as her father never went to church, it actually was his religion. At the time Lee couldn't understand why, having worked six days a week, he would want to accompany her mother on his one precious day off. Now, she realized, it was the sights and smells of something long remembered; of home, even though home was thousands of miles and a lifetime ago. Of the home in his heart, which he had never left.

The sight of Ricketts Road today would kill any nostalgia stone dead. The bottom part of the road where she grew up people now referred to as Lower Rick. As she drove down the hill she wondered when that had changed. It might have been when the shops started closing, and crime started getting worse. Boarded-up shop fronts made people not want to live there and so they moved. That is, if they could afford to. If not, they had to stay. First- and second-generation immigrants, like her parents, had lived there for years and raised families there. Now they saw the area where they had felt the most at home – their own little patch of London – becoming a forbidding and sinister place they didn't recognize.

As she pulled up outside a building that was brightly lit from the inside but needed a coat of paint, it crossed her mind that it wasn't the wisest idea to be driving her new Audi in Lower Rick now that it had changed so much. But just as quickly she discounted that idea. She never, ever, wanted to be scared in the place she grew up, of people living here, many of whom looked like her. Besides, the person who ran this place would never let anything happen to her or her car.

As she got out, she noticed something had changed across the street. She frowned, wondering how come she hadn't seen it before, then shook her head as she turned away and rang the buzzer. As she did so she saw a small camera, mounted high on the door frame, move in her direction. That was new too.

Ricketts Road Community Law Centre had been a fixture in the area for years. It wasn't as old as Lee, but close. She had learned what being a lawyer was from this place: working during the school holidays, filing and making tea for the clients. All her teenage self knew was that, more often than not, people would come in there careworn, miserable, worried or all three, and sometimes leave, if not happy, at least with a glimmer of hope. Only sometimes; this was Lower Rick, after all. But just enough to keep you going. That's what had kept Kofi going, after all these years. Not the freshly minted and idealistic young barrister he had been decades ago when he first came to run this place, but the battle-scarred yet compassionate legal fighter he had become. Still passionate, still punching, and treasuring each victory, whether for funding or successful cases won.

It was Kofi who stood at the entrance as the door buzzed open to let Lee in. His big bouncer frame blocking the doorway, he stared at her for a minute, his face impassive at first. Then, slowly, he smiled, like the sun coming out from behind a cloud. He opened his arms wide to give her an all-enveloping hug.

'I didn't expect the boss man himself to greet me at the door.' Lee smiled. 'If you greet everyone like this, the place will be rammed every evening.'

'What do you mean? It's rammed now! People come here for advice we don't even offer.' He shrugged. 'What else is there round here?'

Lee looked at the CCTV camera. 'So this is new. Why the extra security? You never needed it before. Did something happen?'

'Well, I'm here all day and most nights, but not every night. And sometimes people don't like the advice we give them. Or blame us for the results. Gotta protect the staff. And I can't have any more good volunteers like you being run off.'

Lee shook her head. 'They won't run me off. You know that.'

'Oh, I definitely know that, Warrior Queen!' he laughed. 'And I'm glad. We need continuity. And people know and respect you. That you're still here, helping out. Even though you now live on The Hill. We keep getting new volunteers too, which is good. Youngsters, though; keen but less experienced. Anyway, let's go in. Like I said, we're busy. But I need to talk to you about something. Can you stick around after we're done? It shouldn't take long.'

They had been talking in a short narrow passageway, and they had to buzz again to be let in to the main reception and waiting area. Another change. It had only been a month since Lee was last there but even the layout had changed. The room was large, with cheap plastic chairs that had seen better days lining the walls, but the reception desk was now at an angle, reducing the size of the waiting area – leaving enough space, Lee noticed, to allow the person on reception to escape and not be trapped behind the desk if something kicked off. It also had a large Perspex screen now, like a shield. Luckily, the warmth and ebullience of Claudine, the receptionist, could penetrate anything. Lee waved at her.

'Hi, Lee!' At the sound of her voice, everyone in the waiting room looked up. Some regulars recognized Lee and smiled, but most were too wrapped up in their own concerns.

'Hi, Claudine,' Lee replied, walking over quickly in the hope this might make her speak a little more quietly. Outside the courtroom she hated to be the centre of attention. There, her wig and gown acted as armour. Here, without it, she already felt conspicuous enough without the whole room staring at her. 'It's busy tonight,' she continued, looking at the stack of files next to Claudine. 'What do you have for me?'

'Mr Kamara's back again. Same housing matter.'

Lee looked at the elderly Black man sitting in the far corner of the room, quietly reading a newspaper and looking for all the world as if he were settling in for the duration.

'Claudine, you know I can't help him. I don't even do housing law. I did my best last time. I wrote to his local councillor on his behalf. Didn't Hugo Cunningham do anything?'

Kofi took the file and handed it to her, lowering his voice to match hers. 'You think he doesn't know that, Lee? He comes for months and months with the same problem – which isn't even really a problem, compared to what we see here. He's old. And lonely. His son's back in prison again and since his daughter moved to Manchester he's pretty much on his own. It's company he wants, not advice. And,' he added, with a wink, 'he only wanted to speak to you. I think he might have a bit of a crush.'

'Okay, okay.' Lee took the file. 'You know when I come here I'm happy to do whatever. But next time, give me something where I can be a bit more use to you.'

Lee looked over again at Mr Kamara, trying to catch his eye, but he was now engrossed in a dog-eared sudoku puzzle book. As she did so, she scanned the room properly for the first time. The Law Centre was never intended to be only for Black and brown people, but over the years, as the local demographic changed, that was what it had become, and usually the vast majority of those seeking assistance reflected that. But tonight at least a third of those waiting were white, many speaking in a language she didn't recognize. Still, everyone was there because they had the same problems. She thought about the shop across the road that had closed down. She must ask Kofi about that.

Just then Mr Kamara looked up and caught her eye. He seemed so happy to see her that she didn't have the heart to object any more. He got up slowly, a little unsteady on his feet. As he did so, his puzzle book and pen fell to the floor.

Lee was over at his side in a moment. 'Hold on, Mr Kamara.' As she helped him steady himself, a young, slightly built white woman picked up the items he had dropped and held them out, waiting patiently until he was able to take them himself. It was a small gesture, but a sensitive one, knowing that, as old as he was, Mr Kamara would not have wanted to be treated as helpless or an invalid.

'Thanks,' Lee said to her as he took the items.

'Not at all. Happy to help.' She was still in her early twenties, but her voice was low and assured, more than would be expected from someone her age and size, and distinctly posh. Not from round here, then. She was also the only person here, apart from Lee, who was wearing a suit. 'As a matter of fact, I was hoping to meet you, Ms Mitchell –'

'Lee,' she interrupted. 'Anyone who helps Mr K is a friend of mine.'

The young girl blushed. 'Thanks. I'm Sophie – Sophie Cavendish. I'm a pupil at Paper Buildings. I heard you speak at a woman lawyers' event last year. You're a real inspiration to me and my friends.'

'I'm not surprised,' Mr Kamara piped up. 'That's why I only like to see her.'

'Okay, enough, please. This is embarrassing. And there are many other good advisers here too, Mr Kamara, you know that. Like Sophie here. You are a volunteer, right?' It was unlikely that she would need free legal advice.

'Yes. I wanted to do some *pro bono* work. Kofi was looking for someone at the same time, so here I am. And I'm bilingual.' She paused as if deciding whether to continue. 'My mother's Polish; I thought that would be a plus. The Polish community is growing round here.'

'Well, it's great you're here, but there must be somewhere closer to where you live? I know when I was a pupil, all I did was work and sleep. This place was round the corner from me. If anything was too far away – forget it.'

'Oh, it's round the corner for me too. I moved about three months ago.'

If Lee was surprised, she hoped it didn't show. In any event, Mr Kamara was tugging at her sleeve.

'Duty calls. Nice meeting you, Sophie.'

Nine thirty p.m. Everyone had left – some clients satisfied, some not. Kofi had been right about Mr Kamara. He didn't really want or need advice about legal matters – not even for his son, who was in prison for the umpteenth time. Thankfully, he had long stopped blaming himself for his offspring's misdeeds. He was just lonely, and she was happy to chat for as long as he needed. And she was still able to see a couple of other people before closing. Now the building was locked up as tight as Fort Knox, and Lee and Kofi were in Kofi's office.

'So, Sophie?' Lee asked, taking a tentative sip of her coffee, which was still too hot to drink.

'Yes, Sophie,' Kofi laughed. 'You know we've had white volunteers before. None so posh, though.'

'It's not that. She seems nice enough. I liked how she was with Mr K, but I was surprised she's living round here.'

'Yeah. Really round here – less than ten minutes away. I told her not to let people know. I also told her not to wear a suit if she was going to walk home late at night, so at least she drives even though it's no distance. She's good, and she speaks Polish. That helps. The area's changing, Lee.'

'Yes, I can see that. What happened to Blessings Bakery on the corner, near the barber's? I couldn't believe it when I saw it had closed.'

48

Kofi shrugged. 'High business rates, new money coming in. And Syl and Norma wanted to cash out. Forty-five years of getting up early, making bread and patties from dawn to dusk – before dawn, in fact – and keeping that going throughout the day?' He shook his head. 'I couldn't do it. No one ever got rich from a one-shop business. And they're old. They wanted to retire back home. Change that into local currency? They'll live like royalty for the rest of their lives.'

Lee shook her head. 'When I came here last month that bakery was just as busy as ever. I can't believe it. It was like the heart of the community, especially when I was growing up.'

'That's just it, Lee. It's not a community any more – at least, not how I remember it when I opened this place. Back then it was all Black, except for a few Irish, and some white English who'd been here since the year dot – the ones who weren't trying to smash our windows in, that is.'

'You mean the police,' Lee added drily.

'Police, National Front, BNP – same difference as far as we were concerned back then. That's why I learned to box. David still boxing, by the way?'

'When he gets time. Work's busy for him at the moment. Still runs, though.'

'Anyway, now we get more Poles, Eastern Europeans coming in for advice. That's no problem; this place is for everyone. Poor people all have the same issues: housing, employment, immigration, crime. But that's in here. Out there,' he continued, pointing towards the shuttered windows and into the darkness beyond, 'it's changing in a different way. That new money I was talking about? That bakery was on a corner on a good-sized piece of land. It'll either be knocked down completely and turned into "luxury" flats, or it'll become

49

another artisan organic deli type place, with food few people will have heard of and at prices no one round here can afford, except the new people moving in. Like Sophie. She's keen and she means well, but she's also part of the change. I don't like what it's doing to Lower Rick. Anyway,' he drained his cup, 'that's not what I wanted to talk to you about. You've been involved with the Law Centre since you were fourteen. Very keen, like Sophie. Tall skinny girl with thick glasses.'

'Yeah. Thank God for Lasik!'

'From the filing and making the tea to volunteer legal adviser – still doing it even with the kind of heavyweight trials you're getting now.'

'Do you wish you were still doing it? That you hadn't left the Bar, I mean?'

'Sometimes I wonder what might have been, but it was the right choice at the time. I'm fifteen years older than you, Lee. Not a long time, but . . . all the difficulties you had? It was even worse back then. Anyway, you can't threaten to punch a senior member of Chambers and expect to stay at the Bar, even though he made a racist "joke" that half a dozen other people heard. My card was marked. But we make a real difference for people round here, and this place is really respected amongst law centres nationally. That's why we get so many volunteers that we can afford to turn some away. And that's why I don't need you any more as a volunteer, Lee.'

Lee stared at him. She was surprised by how much it hurt.

'Hear me out. I don't want you as a volunteer because I *need* you on the board. I know you can advise on pretty much anything in a general way but your expertise is crime, and we don't get a lot of that here when the duty solicitor picks up the work at the station. What we really need are capable people to help run the place. All this extra security has cost us. I have to keep fighting with the council and I'm pretty tired of doing that myself.'

'If it's money . . .'

'Don't even go there, Lee. You've helped pay for enough over the years on top of volunteering, and you never make a big song and dance about it. I really appreciate what you've done – we all do – but this is a professional organization, not a charity. That's why we need more professionals on the board as well as street activists. Of course, if you're a bit of both, that's even better. You care about this place and you come from here.' Kofi smiled. 'Even if you now live on The Hill.'

'But I like my role here.'

'Listen, if I thought you had the time to do both, I'd jump at that. But truthfully, I'm amazed you've been able to keep this going for so long. I know what it takes to build a busy practice, let alone keep it with those sharks you work with. This is less time commitment too; I run a tight ship with those meetings. Honestly, Lee, you'd be more help to us in this role. And to me.'

It was really getting late now. Lee gathered her things. 'Okay. Can't say I'm not disappointed, but you know how I feel about this place. Let me think about it.'

'Fair enough.' Kofi stood up to walk her to the door. 'And tell your man not to leave it too long until he's back in the ring. You see what happened to Reverend Matthews's boy? Just down the road from here. That's why my son's always training with me. A Black man never knows when he'll have to defend himself.'

9

The bedside clock was the first thing Lee saw when she opened her eyes next morning, Sunday. Eleven a.m. She didn't have to turn over to know that David wasn't there with her. The note under the clock confirmed what she already knew. *'Gone for a run, then at Lily's for a jam session. Come down if you like. D. PS Your mum rang again.'*

Lee stretched and yawned. She wouldn't bother to ring her mother back; she would see her in less than an hour. She thought about the route. She would have to drive past last Friday's crime scene to get there. It was a sobering thought.

The morning was bright and unseasonably warm. The area was still cordoned off. Both pedestrians and cars were being kept away. She saw some teenagers, the boys sombre, the girls crying, trying to get as close as possible to where it happened, some tying bunches of flowers to a nearby lamp post. There were yellow-and-black boards diverting traffic, and blue-and-white boards with the Metropolitan Police insignia and SHOOTING in bold black letters. Lee didn't have a chance to read the wording, but at least it wasn't a fatality – so far.

As she turned into the street where she had grown up, Lee could see her mother standing at the garden gate, looking at her watch then anxiously up the road. The detour had added fifteen or twenty minutes on to her journey, but still, there was no need for her mother to be that worried.

'Sorry I'm late,' she said as her mother got into the car. She was holding a small flowerpot containing a miniature rose bush.

'I was getting worried,' Verna Mitchell replied. 'You know, what with the shooting and all . . .'

'Honestly, Mum, nothing like that's going to happen to me. Statistically, I'm the wrong age, for a start. Besides, it's broad daylight.'

'Statistics mean nothing if it's your child. Reverend Matthews, from my church? It was his youngest boy, Paul.'

'I didn't know you knew who it was. I'm sorry.'

'After the first shock, all I could think about was what I would do if anything like that happened to you. You're all I have, Leanne.'

Lee squeezed her mother's arm. 'You knew I was coming to see you today. Is that why you rang earlier? And before?'

Verna nodded. It was as if she didn't trust herself to speak.

'Look,' Lee said gently, 'we don't have to go today . . .'

'Oh no. You know I can't miss seeing your father.' She patted the plant on her lap.

'Okay, then. Let's take a different route, though.'

It was bitter-sweet, hearing her mother talk about her father as if he were still alive, all these years later. The mound beneath his headstone was already carpeted with flowers. There was even a tiny Guyanese flag nestled in between. It was hard to see where there would be room for anything else, but she knew her mother would find it. She sat on a nearby bench and watched her mother carefully transfer the plant from its pot into the earth. When she was finished, she came and sat next to her daughter.

'I like to see living things here,' she said, surveying her handi-work. 'Cut flowers . . .' She waved her hand dismissively. Turning to her daughter, she asked, 'So, what's happening at work? I keep look-ing to see you on the news.'

'Mum, I told you, not all my cases are like the Omartian case. I've done a lot of others since then. You might never see me on TV again.'

'But if you got this shooting case . . .'

Lee stared at her mum. 'You can't want me to be on TV that badly. You know these people!'

'That's not what I meant. At all. It's just that it'll be a big case. I feel it. And if anyone has to do it, I'd rather it was you. I know you're good enough, baby.' Verna beamed at her daughter.

'Thanks for the vote of confidence, Mum, but I'm not the only barrister around. And I've done gun crime cases. I hate them. Any-way, it's just occurred. A lot can happen before it comes to court – if it even gets to court. They've got to catch someone first.' There was a silence before Lee spoke again. 'David says hello, by the way.'

'Oh yes?' Her mother's disinterest was clear. 'Still strumming some guitar, is he?'

'Don't start. He does more than that and you know it. That soap you like to watch, he co-wrote the score for that. You have to get over the fact that he's not a lawyer, he's living with me, and we're not getting married. Now or ever.'

There was a long silence before Verna said, 'Fine.' The sun had gone behind a cloud. 'It's getting chilly. You'd better take me home.'

Just as well, Lee thought, as she dropped her mother off. Too much death. Time to be with the living. She checked her watch. She could still catch part of David's set.

*

54

The Lily Langtry was a muso's pub, in a very unprepossessing part of South London, on the edge of a council estate. At some point it had seen better days, but that was so long ago no one seemed able to remember. It was certainly well before Lee's time. Even so, it might have retained some sort of faded grandeur had the previous owner, a retired jazz musician, not tried to tart it up by repainting it. And tart it up he had; if the pub were a person it would look like an over-made-up, ageing good-time girl who hadn't realized her good times had already gone.

Ironically, given its location, very few of the residents seemed to drink there, even though it was on their doorstep. Especially the younger ones; not aspirational enough for them. It reminded them of where they were, rather than where they wanted to be.

There were really only two reasons why anyone would be there. One was the music. The previous owner might not have known anything about business, but in the few years before he ran it into the ground financially, he had established it as a place where both aspiring and established musicians would come and hang out on evenings and weekends, play for drinks and for the sheer joy of it after doing the paid gigs – if they had any. The quality was variable, but this just added to its charm.

The other reason was Liliana.

Lee was approaching the pub just as Liliana was fighting her way through the smokers huddled outside the main entrance. Even from a distance she could hear her mumbling under her breath, stacking the glasses with such force that it was only a matter of time before one broke. Lee smiled; she never could do anything quietly. Clearly, she wasn't very happy. Some of the smokers shrank back a little further into the wall. However, when she glanced up and saw Lee she let out a shriek and threw her arms wide, hitting the top of a stack of glasses that wobbled precariously before safely coming to rest.

'My God! Hello, stranger,' she said loudly in European-accented English. She was about half Lee's height, but twice her size, and Lee felt engulfed as she was enveloped in a bear hug and pressed against Liliana's very ample bosom. 'David never said you were coming.'

Lee looked over Liliana's curly red head to the few people still outside, watching the scene bemusedly through a haze of cigarette smoke. 'I hadn't planned to. I just . . . well, I thought it would be nice to come down for a change. Plus, you know, work, been busy . . .'

'Yeah, yeah. You're lucky I'm not one of those women who takes anything personally. Come on in.'

Thankfully, the interior of the pub no longer matched the garishness of the exterior. It still had a comfortable 'old boozer' feel to it, but the seats had been reupholstered in good-quality leather, and the dark wooden furniture looked more solid and substantial than the rickety tables Lee remembered of old. The low lighting made the place feel cocooned from the bleakness outside. It would be possible to spend hours in here and forget if it was day or night. It was, however, depressingly empty for a Sunday afternoon.

Liliana went behind the bar and put the stacked glasses on the counter. Lee leaned against the counter and looked around.

'So, what'll you have?'

'Sorry, what?' Lee replied, absently.

'Oh? So busy looking for your man that you can't stop to have a drink with me?'

'Very funny, Lili. Come on, we live together. It's not like that. He was with me this morning and I know where he'll be tonight.'

'So take a seat, then. After all, I paid enough for these bar stools. You still drink red wine?'

'Bit early in the day for me. Besides, I'm driving. Tonic water, ice and lemon, please.' Lee perched on a bar stool and turned to face her friend. 'Actually, I was thinking I like what you've done with the place, but this area seems smaller than I remember . . .'

'And what can I get you, sir?' Liliana broke off to speak to a tipsy-looking customer who had approached the bar, evidently more interested in their conversation than in his next libation.

'Same again, please, love,' he replied, raising his pint glass and talking to her generous bosom. At the sight of Lee's disapproving stare, he quickly readjusted his gaze upwards. But Liliana didn't seem bothered in the least.

'They still don't know you own this place, do they?' Lee asked as soon as the man was out of earshot. 'You wouldn't have to put up with that if they did.'

Liliana laughed. 'I like being underestimated. There are punters here who actually think I was stupid enough to change my name to match the pub! Come on, Lee. Nothing separates a man from his brain – and his money – like a nice pair: the bigger the better. Doesn't matter if they're covered up, either. You should know, yours are pretty impressive too. Don't tell me the lawyers you work with don't look.'

'Not if I catch them first!'

At that, they both burst out laughing. Liliana raised her glass in a toast. 'Here's to men, then. Can't kill 'em; don't want to.'

'Cheers.' Lee clinked her glass.

'You're right, this area is smaller,' Liliana continued. 'I extended out the back, brought the music area downstairs so I wouldn't have to run an upstairs bar as well, and partitioned it off. Spent a fortune trying to make it as soundproof as possible, but it's been worth it. This part's quieter, for the older punter, but I can also keep an eye on what's going on at the back, which I couldn't before. Look,' she said, beckoning Lee to join her behind the bar, 'see for yourself.'

The back room was now around twice the size of the space they were in. There were about twenty people listening to the music, and Lee could see David and some other assorted musicians on a raised stage area, playing a familiar jazz-influenced number. Some were smiling and joking with the audience; others, like David, were completely engrossed in what they were doing. Lee could see the pianist counting them down to a big finish, and when they all stopped dead on the same note the audience burst into applause. Funny how after so many years together she still got excited watching him play. Or maybe it was simply from watching him.

She was still having warm thoughts about her boyfriend when she saw a young blonde girl in a frayed miniskirt get up and run over to David. She stood in front of him, shifting her weight from one leg to the other, barely able to restrain herself from throwing her arms round his neck. Liliana looked at Lee and followed her gaze. 'Don't worry,' she whispered conspiratorially. 'We can take her, easy.'

'I'm not bothered, Lili.' Lee replied a little more sharply than intended, still staring at the scene playing out in front of her. David wasn't encouraging the girl, but he was certainly enjoying the attention.

'Right,' Liliana said slowly, clearly unconvinced. She held up an opened bottle of Malbec. 'Sure you won't have a glass?'

'Yeah, that would be good,' Lee replied, a little too quickly.

'So,' Liliana said as she poured, 'you heard about the shooting, then? Just round the corner from here too. Maybe that's why the place is so empty, even with the band.' She shook her head. 'Only fifteen. Makes me glad I don't have kids; I'd never have a moment's peace. What is the world coming to? They say he was a good boy – not like his brother. I mean, you know it happens, but a Reverend's son? I'm certainly no churchgoer, but he's a good man. Supported my music licence when some residents round here were objecting. Thought it would encourage noise pollution and drug use. Round here!'

'Anyone been talking about who might have done it?'

Liliana shook her head. 'No. Now if Tony had been shot, no one would have been surprised.' Lee put her hand over her half-empty glass as her friend tried to top it up. 'I did hear he's looking for whoever did it. Whoever it is, they better hope the police find them first.'

Lee glanced back over into the music area. The young blonde was nowhere to be seen. David and the other musicians were now talking amongst themselves, packing up their instruments. He looked up and saw Lee for the first time since she'd arrived. He gave her a brief smile before turning back to the task at hand.

'Anyway,' Liliana continued, 'it would be funny if you ended up being involved in it. Legally, I mean . . .'

'I hope not,' Lee said with feeling. Liliana looked surprised. 'And not just because my mother goes to that church. Cases like that . . . it's nearly always a young person at both ends of the gun. The shooter starts off all hard, and at the end they're crying like babies when they meet the victim's family and realize just what they've done. You don't get any pleasure out of winning those; it's a total waste, all round. Anyway, I'm not the only brief in town, and there are other barristers who would love to get their hands on it.'

At that moment David entered, his guitar case slung across his broad shoulders.

'Hey, babe.' He leaned down and kissed her on the cheek. 'Glad you could make it. Why didn't you come through to the back?'

'I was going to, but Lili and I got talking; you know how it is. Sounded good, though.'

'So how long have you been here?' he asked, leaning against the side of the bar.

'Oh, long enough,' Lili replied, with a wink.

David looked confused for a moment before realization dawned.

'Phoebe? She's down here all the time; you know that, Lili.' Lee stiffened a little but sipped her wine and said nothing. 'Doesn't mean anything as far as I'm concerned.'

'Actually, David, *you* I believe. But if your mates had told me that, well . . .'

'Hey, Lee,' one of the musicians called out to her. 'Remember me? Never thought I'd see you down here again. Fancy you slumming with the likes of us. I thought you were worried you'd bump into one of your clients.'

'Never stopped me going anywhere before, Terry.' She did remember him, and why she disliked him. At sixty, he was the oldest of the group and typified the ageing lothario, using tired pick-up lines and outdated youth slang in a desperate, unsuccessful attempt to hold back the hands of time.

'You haven't got that shooting that happened round here? I heard it was racial . . .'

'I heard a cop did it,' someone else piped up. His voice was slurred.

'Police?' Lee said. 'Well, anything's possible, but I seriously doubt it. Most likely it was to do with gangs.'

'He wasn't the kind of kid to get involved with gangs,' Lili said.

'Unfortunately, they're usually the ones who get shot.'

'The woman's busy.' David put a protective arm round Lee. 'She can't come down here and hang out like the rest of us. Anyway, if it was a police shooting or a racist murder, Lee won't do it. She's got more integrity than that.' He pulled her in closer and smiled down at her. 'Lee Mitchell – nobody's victim.'

Lee looked up at him, and in the warmth of that brief moment it was as if no one else existed but them. She smiled and kissed him lightly on the lips. 'And you're nobody's fool,' she replied. She leaned in closer and whispered in his ear, 'Thank you.'

But Terry was now more interested in something else. 'Hey, David, that chick who keeps coming up to you – can I have her digits? Because if you're not interested, I am.'

David laughed. 'That girl's just past jailbait, Terry. She could be your granddaughter. Besides, if she wanted you to have her number, she'd have given it to you.'

The reference to his age had clearly hit home. 'Don't be selfish. Not all of us are lucky enough to have a rich girlfriend.'

Everyone around them fell silent. Lee drained her glass and was about to say something, but David beat her to the punch. He dropped his arm from Lee's shoulders, straightened up and took a step towards Terry. 'What the fuck do you mean by that?'

Instantly, Terry put his hands up and backed away. 'Nothing, nothing. Jesus! Look, I'm sorry, okay?'

'Don't apologize to me. Apologize to her.'

Lee wondered whether it was her honour David was defending, or his.

'Sorry, Lee. It was a compliment, you know, but I see how it came out wrong.' Lee rolled her eyes. 'Look, can I buy you both a drink?'

'No thanks,' she replied crisply. 'I've got to go.' She looked at David. His face was like thunder.

'See you tonight,' he muttered.

10

'Come in, Wallace. Have a seat.'

'If this is about the Matthews case, sir . . .'

'No,' Superintendent Reid said slowly. 'It's about someone in your team, though. You know, the gay one. Boyce.'

Wallace felt his movements becoming more and more controlled; a kind of watchful wariness honed by his years in the Army but which had begun in childhood, out of necessity. He had become very good at this. He thought about asking his boss why he felt the need to mention Boyce's sexuality but knew that, despite the mandatory diversity training, it would be wasted on him. 'What about him?'

'I'd asked him to go and speak at Fordyce Park as part of our community outreach – though if they think it's going to stop them from joining gangs it's a wasted effort. Rite of passage for most of them; next stop, prison. Anyway, he can't do it and they wanted someone who would be equally keen. So I thought of you,' he concluded with finality.

'If you don't think it works, guv, then why are we doing it? And why did you think I'd be keen?'

Wallace watched as his boss's lips tightened in a straight line. Ignoring the first part of the question, he said, 'You used to go there, didn't you?'

'Yeah.' A lifetime ago, in every sense. 'I was expelled from there too. I don't think they'd want me, of all people . . .'

'Maybe. But you're also the most senior minority officer we have here at Miller Street. And, in this case, Black trumps white queer. I want you to do it.'

'I don't have the time, especially with the Matthews shooting . . .'

'That wasn't a request, DCI Wallace.' Reid leaned forward at his desk and folded his arms. 'Besides, it's only an afternoon, and who knows? You might even pick up some intel. The boy didn't go to that school but the ones you'll be speaking to are all about his age. School rivalry gone bad, maybe? And,' he added, laughing at the sheer incredulity of what he was about to say, 'as an added bonus you might even get one who wants to join us when they leave school.'

'Someone called for you, Ms Mitchell.' Dean, Lee's Junior Clerk, handed her a folded sheet of paper with Chambers' letterhead embossed across the top, his attention already focused on something else even before Lee took it from him.

'Tom's at lunch?' Lee asked, taking the heavy sheet of cream paper.

'Yeah, and he hasn't gone to Greggs neither.' Dean pointed at his own sandwich and coffee from that establishment.

Lee nodded. To be fair to Tom, he rarely left his desk for lunch, but he did have an encyclopaedic knowledge of the fine dining establishments in the City and around the Temple – all from personal patronage 'drumming up work for Chambers'.

'Had to be. You know he'd kill you for using this as notepaper. Who is it, anyway?'

Dean shrugged, his disinterest clear. 'Some school. Not a case.'

There was a scrawled number or name of the caller, but the school was clear. Fordyce Park. Her old school.

Simone? After all this time?

Lee was usually glad to see Mary, the barrister she shared a room with. Their practices, and their lives, were so different that they were a perfect complement to each other. Thankfully, though, at least for now, she had the room to herself.

She was surprisingly nervous as she dialled the number. As she suspected, it went to the main switchboard, but when Lee said who she was the young woman at the other end of the line immediately put her straight through to the Head.

Lee hoped Mrs Cox didn't bear a grudge. She remembered what had happened last time and, whilst she didn't regret it, she had never expected to hear from her again.

'Putting you through.'

A pause, then an unfamiliar voice came on the line. Not Mrs Cox, then.

'Hello. Leanne Mitchell?'

'Yes. Who is this?'

The woman laughed so loudly Lee knew that, whoever it was, they had to be alone.

'Lee? It's Sylvia – Sylvia Thomas. Don't know if you remember me. I was there when you came here to speak, what, two years ago?' She laughed again. 'People still talk about that even now. Hope you don't mind me calling you by your first name? I know you barristers are sticklers for formality.'

'Course not. You know, when I heard the school had called I knew it couldn't be Mrs Cox!' She paused before asking, 'Is Simone back?'

'At the school? No. We kept in touch a little when she first went to West Africa, but you know how it is. After the trial I guess she wanted to put everything behind her – even friends. But that's how it is sometimes.'

Lee wondered whether they would ever be in touch again, and even if they were, whether it would be the same. But she had no time to dwell on that as Sylvia continued, 'Anyway, I'm the new Mrs Cox. The first Black Head here, even though it's the most ethnically diverse school in the borough. Made me jump through hoops to get it too. And that's why I'm calling. I wondered whether you would come back and speak again and do a short Q and A? We'd have you and one, maybe two others so there would be less preparation than if you were carrying it on your own; I know how busy you are.'

'Depending when it is, I'm happy to do it, but you know if anyone asks me what my experiences were when I was a pupil there I'm not going to lie, or say anything different to what I said last time.'

'I'd be disappointed in you if you did, Lee. We needed more "speaking truth to power" back then. Things had started to change but very slowly. After you spoke, it was like a match had been lit under our collective arses. As a school, we're still a work in progress but it's much better now. Besides,' suddenly her tone became more serious, 'Paul Matthews? He was a student here at one time until his parents moved him. Some of the kids you'll be speaking to knew him very well. What with George Floyd and everything that's happened since, everything's on a knife edge –' Sylvia stopped suddenly. 'Shit! Bad choice of words. You know what I mean, Lee. Some think it's gangs but, rightly or wrongly, just as many think it's police. We need to lower the temperature. Something positive and hopeful, even a little aspirational, will help.'

Two days later, as she drove through the school gates, Lee remembered that she had rarely felt positive or aspirational when she attended there, and what hope she had felt was tinged with inadequacy seeded by teachers like Mrs Cox. That was why she liked doing these talks; she had wished someone would have come into the school back then and given a different message.

It was a good thing that Sylvia Thomas met her at the main entrance as she didn't recognize her. However, Sylvia didn't seem to mind. Statuesque and imposing, with a short afro, her no-nonsense demeanour was softened with a ready smile. Her smart but conservative trouser suit was in sharp contrast to her on-trend trainers, something Lee was sure the students both noticed and appreciated.

'It's good to see you again,' she said, shaking Lee's hand and simultaneously looking her up and down. 'You look expensive. They'll like that.'

'Just came from court. Too much?'

'Not for these kids. You know how much stuff like that matters to them. My pet peeve is professional people rocking up here looking like tramps. They wouldn't turn up at Dulwich College looking like that. Luckily, the other person speaking with you looks pretty good too, especially as he was a replacement.' She inclined her head towards the double doors leading away from Reception. 'Let's go through. You're early so I can give you the tour.'

The corridor seemed smaller overall than Lee remembered, but more brightly coloured, with artwork and inspirational messages positioned strategically along its length. 'I didn't get this last time,' Lee commented as she walked beside Sylvia. 'It's different. Definitely an improvement.'

'There's a space for you on these walls – you know, local girl made good and all that.'

'No, no, no,' Lee said quickly. 'Please don't. I'm not here for that.'

Sylvia looked surprised and a little disappointed. She opened her mouth as if to say something but thought better of it. They walked along in silence for a few minutes before Lee asked, 'So where's the other speaker?'

'He was even earlier than you. Nice-looking. Said he went to school here too. He wanted to have a look round on his own so he's around somewhere.'

'On his own?'

'Well, he's a police officer. What's he going to steal? Chalk? Anyway,' she continued as they finally reached the doors of the Assembly Hall and she checked the time on her phone, 'he's supposed to meet us round about –'

'– now.' The voice wasn't loud but it made both women jump.

Danny Wallace stood behind them about six feet away. Sylvia stepped towards him, closing the gap, but Lee instinctively stepped back, increasing the distance between them.

'DCI Wallace –' Sylvia began.

'Danny, remember?' He smiled and looked around. 'I wasn't DCI anything in this place.'

'Danny, thanks for stepping in at the last minute. This is Lee Mitchell.'

'Yeah, I remember Leanne. You look different, though.'

'Lee,' she replied shortly. 'And you look the same.'

Sylvia looked from one to the other. Something was going on but she wasn't sure what.

'Just wait out here a minute. I want to settle them before you both come in.'

'So,' Wallace said as the double doors swung shut, leaving them alone in the corridor, 'how long has it been? Eighteen years?'

'Something like that.' Exactly like that. 'I didn't think anyone from the Met would be down here.'

'No, not a natural recruiting ground. And yet, here I am.'

'You know Paul Matthews has friends here?'

'What's your point, Lee?'

'Are you hoping they'll tell you something you can use if you win them over?'

'Is that why you're here? To get people thinking they can all make it at the Bar like you did, then saddle them with fifty grand in student debt before you swan off to your palace on The Hill?' He was staring at her so hard that Lee knew he could see his comment had hit home. 'Yeah – not nice, is it? These are minors. You know none of that would stand up in court even if they did want to speak to me. You've been doing criminal defence work too long. Not all of us are shits.' Wallace only broke their gaze as Sylvia approached. 'Guess you'll have to wait and see what I'm going to say.'

Lee knew she had been too sharp with him and for the life of her didn't know why, especially when she hadn't seen him in nearly twenty years. She should apologize. Maybe.

As it was, she didn't have to wait long to hear him speak. There was a low murmur as they both entered the hall, followed by silence when Wallace stood up to address them, the complete absence of sound like a wall of pent-up resentment and rage.

'Now, everyone,' Sylvia warned, 'I told you how this would work. After you've heard from both DCI Wallace and Ms Mitchell you can ask questions, but not about Paul Matthews. I know some of you here knew him, but Mr Wallace can't talk about an ongoing investigation.'

'I don't mind what they ask me.' Wallace's words surprised both the Head and Lee. 'I mean,' addressing the audience directly, 'you can ask me anything, but sometimes I won't be able to give you an answer.'

Sylvia looked at Wallace as if he had lost his mind. 'You sure?'

He nodded. She shook her head and shrugged as she sat down. 'Okay.'

'First, let me tell you a bit about me because I know someone else was supposed to be doing this. I used to go to this school. The last place I ever thought I'd find myself was back here, speaking to kids about the same age as I was when I was kicked out. Well, transferred to a Pupil Referral Unit; same difference to me at the time. I also got nicked quite a few times, including by police from Miller Street. Sometimes for stupid petty shit – sorry, Ms Thomas,' he said, smiling. 'Sometimes for being Black and walking home late. Or for hanging around outside the chicken shop or in the park during school hours.' He laughed a little and shook his head, as if replaying it in his mind. Lee wondered how he could find any humour in this, but something about that laugh eased the tension and antipathy in the room, just enough.

'Anyway, I was in juvenile court for something stupid but this time it could have gone really badly. Someone spoke up for me, and that just about persuaded the Magistrates not to send me down. I'll never forget that,' he added quietly.

'So, what do you do if you're a young lad who's into fitness with a lot of energy and anger to burn off? You join the Army. I did my time, then decided to leave. Then joined the police as a constable. I would always volunteer for the tough ones no one wanted to put themselves forward for, just like in the Army. And here I am. Back at Miller Street, but this time going through a different door.'

Lee watched as Wallace took off his jacket and hung it over his chair before turning back to his audience, folding his arms. It was both an authoritative and defensive stance. He always used to stand like that.

'So, ask away.'

The questions came like rapid machine-gun fire, the hands shooting up in the air, the students almost daring him not to answer, to see if one of them would ask the question he would be too embarrassed to answer.

The first one was easy. 'How many tattoos you got?'

'How you know I got any?'

'All squaddies have tattoos. My brother's got seven.'

Wallace laughed. 'I haven't got seven but I've got a few.'

'You have any medals?'

'Yes.' He sounded almost bashful.

'For what?'

'I'm not talking about that.'

Not so the next question.

'You ever shoot anyone?'

'Anton!' The rebuke from Sylvia was both swift and sharp.

'Yes.' Wallace's reply was just as quick. Sylvia stared at him.

'More than once?'

'Yes.'

'Dead?'

'That's enough!' Sylvia interrupted.

Wallace locked eyes with the young man. He was the same at that age – truculent, angry, bordering on violent. And yet there was something else in his eyes: a vulnerability that he was deliberately trying to suppress, and almost succeeding.

'Yes. As a soldier. And that's completely different to two gangs shooting each other on the streets.' Wallace continued to stare at him. 'We don't talk about that with civilians. I only answered because I'm here and you didn't think I would. But if you meet another soldier, don't ask that question. Ever.'

Anton was the first to look away. The room was silent again until a young girl with a ponytail tentatively raised her hand.

'When you was getting in trouble, what did your mum do? Or

your dad if he was around?' She faltered. 'Maybe it's different for boys . . .'

'They weren't really around when this was happening.' Wallace's tone was softer now, trying to put her at her ease, but also sad. 'I was in Clairview. I'm sure some children's homes are good but that wasn't, not for me. A lot of things can happen to "looked after" kids.'

'So who was the person who spoke up for you? You know, at court?'

Wallace wondered whether he should say. He wondered whether anyone at the station knew. Emotionally and in every other way it felt too exposing. But he sensed the students had warmed to him, appreciating his candour; someone being straight with them.

'It was Pastor Matthews, Paul's dad.' There was an audible gasp. 'My social worker too, but mainly him. I never thought in a million years I'd be investigating this shooting and I'm sorry I have to, because I really wish it hadn't happened. But I'm happy to be leading the team to catch whoever did it.' He held up his hand. 'I know some of you know Paul but don't ask me any more about this. Besides,' he smiled as more hands continued to go up, 'you still have to hear from Ms Mitchell.'

Follow that, Lee thought as she moved forward to stand in the spot Wallace had vacated. For the first time in forever she felt like the after-thought, the support act, not the main event. Some of the students weren't even pretending to listen; they were still looking at Wallace, now sitting behind her to her left. Then, about ten minutes in, just as she had managed to engage their attention, she could feel it wandering again. She glanced over; his chair was empty. Wallace had left as quietly as he had appeared when he had surprised her and Sylvia in the corridor. Sylvia passed her a note. '*He had to get back to the station. Something came up.*' And she still hadn't had the chance to apologize.

After the fourth ring, Jack Lambert stretched out and felt for his alarm clock. Without raising his face from the pillow, he threw it at the wall, where it smashed into five uneven pieces. It was only then he realized that wasn't it. He shook his head gingerly. It was painful, but although he had the hangover to match, that wasn't it either. It was some minutes before he realized it was the doorbell, and some minutes more before it became clear whoever it was wasn't going to go away. He didn't even know what time it was, and now he'd broken the clock he'd be none the wiser, but from the angle of sunlight it wasn't yet afternoon. Too early for him to be getting up. The very few visitors he had knew never to call on him before midday.

Slowly, he got out of bed. The beam of sunlight caught and held the whorls of dust in the room. His trousers were still where he had thrown them, in their usual place draped over the mirror. As he walked over to retrieve them, every step he took was on something other than the carpet. He kicked an empty lager can out of the way before putting them on. As he did so, he tried, and failed, to avoid looking at himself in the mirror. Time this vest went into the wash. Four days on the trot was long enough. He stood sideways and sucked his stomach in. No difference. He went towards the front door, kicking his jacket out of the way.

'Shit!' He had stubbed his toe on something hard and solid. He looked at the crowded bedside table, but his mobile was in its usual spot. He was about to pick up the jacket and check what was in the pocket when the doorbell rang yet again. 'Fucking hell! All right, all right! I'm coming!' he shouted.

He squinted and shielded his eyes against the bright sunlight as he opened the door to the man standing there. Now he remembered what he had in his jacket. Nothing like people from your own nick turning up on your doorstep to jog one's memory. He'd have to hand it in or get rid of it, but for the moment, it was safe; the last place anyone would look for an illegal firearm was in a copper's home.

'Christ, Jack, whatever you were doing last night, I hope it was worth it. You look dog rough.'

'What the fuck are you doing here, Bill? I'm due on later today. What's so important that you're waking me up this early?'

'It's half ten. I've knocked off and I'm on my way home, so I thought I'd stop by.'

'Piss off. You don't live anywhere near here. And if this is a social visit, that would be a first.' He and Bill Roberts were friendly enough, but Lambert didn't encourage visitors, not even when he'd worked with them for years. He stiffened suddenly as he noticed a younger man ten feet or so behind his colleague in the middle of the unkempt front garden. He must be more hung-over than he thought not to have clocked him immediately. He jerked his head towards him.

'He with you?'

Bill looked uncomfortable but didn't say anything. He'd been surprised when Wallace agreed that he could accompany him; the younger ones treated him like a placeholder with one foot out the door. No respect. But not this one. Even he was floored, though, when Wallace had asked him, the more junior officer, to take the lead. *'You two have worked together for years. You're about the same age. He*

73

won't give you any trouble.' That was the official reason. But everyone knew DCIs didn't step back without very good reason, and they both knew that wasn't it. Bill knew his boss wanted to really assess not only the man they were taking in but everything about him: where he lived; potential escape routes; nosy neighbours he could come back and question. He wished he could shake the feeling that he was being assessed too.

'What the fuck's going on, Bill?'

'You're right. It's not a social call. You've got to come in, Jack.'

'If they want me to do an earlier shift, I —'

'Now, Jack. They wanted to come down mob-handed, but I said I would do it.' Bill paused. 'It's nothing to do with your shift.'

An unobtrusive black Ford saloon car turned off the busy main road into a quiet South London side street, then turned again to enter an even quieter police station yard. Slumped in the back seat directly behind the driver, Lambert gingerly raised his head and looked out of the rear car window. It had been nearly an hour since Roberts had come to fetch him. He had cleaned himself up and had drunk two cups of coffee so strong it looked and tasted like sludge, but it still felt as if someone was tap-dancing on his head with stilettos. Even so, he could recognize the back of Miller Street police station. He'd done this journey every day for more years than he cared to remember. Usually, he'd be the one sitting up front, with someone handcuffed in the back seat.

He wasn't in the driver's seat today, that was for sure.

Bill Roberts switched off the ignition then turned round to face the man seated directly behind him. He hated uncomfortable silences. No one had spoken throughout the journey. He had attempted to make small talk with his colleague, but he was as unforthcoming as their passenger. Now he tried to smile at Lambert encouragingly, a smile that soon disappeared when he saw the look on the other man's face.

'Still going to tell me you don't know what this is about, Bill?'

'I already told you, Jack, I don't know.'

'Bollocks!'

The expletive, spat out as it was, split the silence in the car. At this, the man in the front passenger seat turned his head. He looked at Lambert impassively before returning to stare fixedly out of the windscreen.

'Look,' Roberts continued, his composed voice a total contrast to Lambert's belligerent tone, 'all I know is that they wanted to bring you in, and I thought it would be better if I did it.'

'And you brought laughing boy here to back you up, I suppose. Couldn't hack it on your own.' Suddenly Lambert leaned forward, his face now so close that Roberts could smell the pungent odour of coffee and stale alcohol on his breath. It was all he could do not to recoil, but he knew Lambert would see that as yet more proof of his weakness.

Lambert stared at him, searching his face for long seconds as if looking for clues before he spoke again.

'You know, I almost believe you. You never did keep your ear to the ground, Bill. Always thought yourself above all that, didn't you? Fat lot of good it did you.'

Roberts's expression of goodwill faded. Abruptly he turned away and got out of the car, closing the driver's door and simultaneously opening the passenger door behind him.

'Get out of the car, Sergeant.'

Lambert almost stumbled as he got out. The sun had gone behind a cloud now, but as far as he was concerned it was still too bright.

As he walked round the back of the car, he came face to face with the other, younger, officer. He was taller than expected, with a boxer's build. Close as they were, Lambert had to look up slightly in order to look him in the eye. That, to his mind, put him at a disadvantage. He didn't like that one bit, especially where this type was concerned.

'Makes a change, one of you lot bringing me in. It's usually the other way round with me.'

'Knock it off, Jack,' Roberts warned.

'What, can't he speak for himself?' Again he addressed the younger man directly. 'What's your name, anyway? Dwayne? Leroy?'

'DCI Wallace, *Mr* Lambert.'

The reply was like a slap in the face and intended to be so. Lambert could almost taste the bile rising in his throat. 'Yeah, and I bet you didn't have to wait fifteen fucking years, neither. That's how long it took me just to make sergeant. Was it the funny handshake that did it or did they have to fill their quota for local colour, what with all this diversity bullshit?'

He saw someone look out of one of the windows overlooking the yard and knew he must have raised his voice. Suddenly he felt as if he were going to throw up. The ground seemed to shift beneath his feet. He felt someone grab his arm as if to steady him. On realizing it was Wallace, he immediately shook him off. 'Don't touch me. I don't need *your* help.'

'Come on, Jack,' Roberts said. 'Everyone's watching.' He jerked his head towards the rear door. 'Come in the back way.'

'What? Like some fucking crim? Every time I've come to my station I've always gone in the front. I'm not going in any other way when I've done fuck all.'

*

No one looked at Lambert as he walked into the station. That was when he knew something was seriously wrong. Wallace took him straight to Superintendent Reid's office. Reid stood up and smiled at Lambert as he was brought into the room. Lambert wondered where he had seen a smile like that recently, before remembering it was on the face of the tiger painted on the door of his local Chinese takeaway.

'Glad you could come in, Sergeant,' Reid said as he gestured for him to sit.

Lambert looked at Wallace as he took his chair. 'Didn't think I had much of a choice.' As his words hung in the air, Reid looked at him expectantly, his eyes suddenly hard. Lambert remembered. 'Sir,' he added, almost as an afterthought. 'So, why am I here?'

'We just wanted to talk to you about something – something that maybe you could help us on.'

Lambert looked slowly round the office. He'd lost count of the times he'd said that himself. He was always asking the questions, never answering them. He never answered to anyone.

'We?'

'You know. Those Who Must Be Obeyed.' Lambert wondered why the Super was being so deliberately vague. Reid paused before continuing. 'Ever had dealings with a Black lad named Paul Matthews?'

Lambert thought before replying. 'Can't say that I have – but then most of the people I arrest are Black. Or whatever they're calling themselves these days.'

Reid sighed. He didn't even bother to glance over at DCI Wallace, now quietly leaning against the door. He had to be prepared to expect this kind of thing when he was on the job. In any case, his expression indicated that he'd heard much worse. 'I didn't ask whether you had arrested him. I asked whether you had had any kind of dealings with him. Or anyone else in his family. His father's Reverend Matthews.'

'I'm not likely to know anyone like that, other than professionally, sir.'

'Tony Matthews is Paul's brother.'

Reid watched as realization dawned on Lambert's face. His expression grew very still. 'Well, I certainly know him. You know that.'

'Yes. I do.' Reid shifted his position in his chair. To anyone outside the room, it would have appeared as if he were dropping his guard, but his eyes never left Lambert's face.

'Paul was shot in the face ten days ago. "Life-altering", they say. At the very least, he'll lose an eye. He was found not far from where he lived. Some Good Samaritan called it in straight away. Saved his life. For what it's worth, that is; he's in a coma and on life support. The best the doctors are hoping for is that he wakes up; he's not expected to make a full recovery.'

Any hopes that Lambert would be moved by this died a swift death. He merely shrugged his shoulders. 'Did he live with his parents?'

'Yes. Why do you ask?'

'Well, if they're living over the shop, as it were, then it's off our patch, sir. What's it got to do with this station? Or me?'

'It's only just off our patch. Someone said you were there. Didn't think you were a churchgoer, Jack.'

'Who said that?'

'Were you there?'

'I want to know who's accusing me first. Am I under arrest?'

Reid looked at Wallace. 'Would you give us a minute, please?' He waited until they were alone before he spoke again. 'Look, Jack, we all know you didn't like Tony Matthews. Plus, from your attitude, we know you're not too keen on Blacks, BME, BAME – whatever. Nor women, though God knows there are few enough round here.'

'I don't have to like them to work with them, sir. There's a poof – excuse me, "homosexual" –'

'Gay officer,' Reid corrected.

'– whatever – in the station too. Is he complaining about me as well?'

Reid sighed. 'I would send you on Diversity Training – yet again – if I thought it would do any good.'

'Half the people in this station think like I do,' Lambert said. 'They just don't say it.'

'That's the trouble with you, Jack. Can't keep your foot out of your bloody mouth. As far as I'm concerned, you're missing the point about the training. I don't care if you learn to love the station queer or not, I just don't want you to insult him or anyone else. Makes the station look bad. How many more complaints to the IOPC can you take?'

'Yes, I'm really concerned about those, sir,' Lambert said sarcastically.

'And that attitude is precisely why you're here. This is how it looks, Jack. Whoever shot that kid was planning to kill him, no question. There's nothing on him – no convictions, cautions, nothing, not even an arrest. Maybe it was racist; maybe he was mistaken for his brother. He was wearing his jacket. Everyone knows how you feel about Tony, plus we have a sighting of you at that church within an hour of the 999 call.'

Lambert sat bolt upright in his chair for the first time. Before, he had been scanning Reid's face for some indication of why he was here. Now, he no longer had to.

'So, this isn't just a friendly chat, is it, sir.' It was a statement of fact rather than a question. He glanced over his shoulder to the door behind him and, as he turned, saw that Wallace had re-entered the room and was again standing, arms folded, in his former position by the door. For a big man, Lambert noted, he was very light on his feet. He hadn't heard him come in. Turning back to his senior officer, Lambert asked, 'Am I going to be allowed to walk out of this room?'

'Come on, Jack, you're not under arrest. This isn't an interview room, and as you can see, me and DCI Wallace aren't taping this. I'd be breaching all your PACE and human rights if I did otherwise, and I'm certainly not going to try that on a fellow copper. Besides, I'd also have to ask if you want a solicitor or your Federation representative present.'

'Do I need one?' Lambert interrupted. 'A solicitor, that is?'

Reid shrugged. 'I thought you'd want to help out on a very serious offence – what could still turn out to be a murder. You know, answer a few questions, clear up a few things, get us one step closer to catching who did this.'

'You mean "help the police with their enquiries"?'

'Something like that,' Reid said. 'So, what were you doing at the church that night?'

Lambert paused before replying, measuring each word.

'You know, sir, I do want to help, but I think I'd better get a solicitor before I say anything else.'

'If that's really how you want to play it, Jack.'

'Nothing playful about this situation from where I sit, sir.'

'Your choice, then, Sergeant.' Reid's matey tone had completely disappeared. He looked past Lambert at the Black officer behind him. 'DCI Wallace?'

Wallace came over to stand facing Lambert. As he was now the only one standing, he physically dominated Reid's office. He crossed his arms and stared down at Lambert, who glared back at him. In the silence, the room was thick with tension. Finally, Wallace spoke.

'You're free to go, Sergeant.'

Lambert stood up slowly until the two men were just headbutting distance from each other.

'Bet you wish I wasn't, though,' he sneered.

Their dislike for each other was palpable. Even though Wallace looked like he wanted to punch Lambert, he was still the more outwardly controlled of the two. His body was rigid, but his face remained impassive. He wasn't going to say or do anything that could make the case fall apart should there be a trial down the road: that this was a vendetta by a Black officer with a chip on his shoulder hounding a suspect just because he didn't like his views.

'Absence of evidence is not evidence of absence, Sergeant. You ought to know that.'

'Oh, very clever. Well, since there is no evidence, I'll see myself out. After all, this is still a free country and this is still my station. How long've you been here? A week?' Lambert turned and nodded to the Superintendent. 'Is that all, sir?'

'For the moment, Jack. You can go.'

Back outside in the station yard, Lambert squinted into the bright light. He knew a stitch-up when he saw it; he'd done it himself often enough. No way was he going to hand the gun in right now. He'd have to hide it. But first . . . he looked at his mobile. He might just be able to make a couple of calls before the battery died.

'Hello? Who is this?' an official-sounding voice answered.

'It's Jack Lambert – you know, one of your regulars.'

Pause. 'Thought I told you last time to call someone else. There's more than one Fed rep, you know.'

'Yeah, but you're mine.'

'Nice try, Jack. I know why you're calling. How long did you expect that to stay quiet? Someone tipped us off as soon as you were pulled in. Miller Street is like a fucking sieve. I bet your Super's on to Professional Standards right now. Ten to one they'll contact the IOPC – and you know how much I fucking hate dealing with those bastards!'

Lambert shrugged. He couldn't care less about the Independent Office for Police Conduct. 'So what? They've got no evidence.'

'No evidence. Remember Nelson Samuels, Jack? He's dead now, you know that.'

Lambert paused. That was a name he hadn't heard in years and thought of even less. 'Why are you bringing that up? He was resisting arrest. Besides, I didn't kill him. Like I said, no evidence.'

'*Resisting arrest*. Yeah, funny that. Shame it took him years to die after the beating you gave him. Punching a disabled pensioner to the ground . . . do you think that's what did it, or was it the kick to the head? He was Black as well, wasn't he?'

'You should know. You were my Fed rep then too, so don't come all high and mighty with me.'

'Yes, I was. Not any more. Before that, the petty shit? We could turn a blind eye; it could be any one of us. But that? You're getting worse, Jack. Now it's guns? Do yourself a favour, Jack. Next time you want to use excessive force, stick to batons and kickings. We've got you off those before. Secondly, pick on some gang vermin that no one could give two shits about. Do you have any idea who Paul Matthews is?'

'I know his brother is drug-dealing scum. Don't tell me he wasn't running for him.'

'His father is Reverend Matthews. You know, the one who stopped

Flowerfields Estate from going up in flames last year? The one who runs "Guns Off Our Streets" from his church, and gets weapons we would never have a hope of tracing? The one who has the ear of the Borough Commander and the local councillor? And the top people at the Yard? *That* Reverend Matthews. But I'm sure you knew that; after all, you were the one hanging around outside his church the very night this happened. It's only a matter of time before they pull you back in again, and then the IOPC would be the least of your worries. Call Slater and Gordon, Jack.'

'Those shyster lawyers? No chance. I'm just a walking pound sign to them. Just how hard do you think they'll work for me when they'll get their big fat Federation retainer whatever happens?'

'Do what you want, then. Consider yourself advised. Don't call me again.'

'You can't turn me down . . .' But the disengaged tone at the other end signalled that he was talking into thin air. Fuck them, then. He could do without the Police Federation. He wasn't going to call Slaters, either. He needed someone desperate – desperate enough to fight even for the likes of him.

He punched in some numbers on his phone, still squinting against the wintry sun as he did so. As soon as the person answered, he spoke.

'I know you know who this is,' he said without preamble. 'I need to speak to you . . . no, not on the phone . . . do you think I'd be ringing you if it wasn't fucking urgent? This afternoon, four o'clock, usual place . . . well, there's something in it for both of us. You make the time.'

12

Brendan Donnelly loved the law, but he hated lawyers, even though he was one. His boss, Jason Abrams, was precisely the reason why. He knew Lee Mitchell would have appreciated the difference. She was also one of the few lawyers who would have agreed with him. Absently, he reached for the telephone as if to call her, but just as quickly changed his mind. He had tried so many times before: there was only so much rejection a man could take – even him.

Jason Abrams stuck his head round the door of Brendan's office without knocking. Brendan had managed to avoid him all last week – surprisingly successfully, considering how small the law firm Abrams Donnelly was. He couldn't get used to that name; his old clients still called it Donnelly & Co.

Evidently today his luck had run out.

'Oi, Brendan, you finished your billing yet?'

Brendan sighed. What a start to the week. Without looking up from the brief he was working on, he replied, 'No, Jason, I haven't.'

'What do you mean, you haven't?'

'Because I'm preparing additional papers for Counsel for this afternoon's conference. You know, real work.'

Jason had come right into his office now. 'Real work in a publicly funded firm includes billing. You ought to know that. Oh, I forgot – you don't. I saw your books before I took over this firm. Complete shite. Just like this office,' he added, his disgust clear as he slowly took in the overflowing desk, full-to-bursting cabinets and the apparent absence of any filing system. 'There's no point in doing the work if we don't get paid for it. None of this *pro bono* bollocks.'

Finally, Brendan looked up. 'Make yourself at home, why don't you.'

'This might be your office, but it's not your firm now, remember?'

'Well, it's not really your firm either, is it? Your dad put up the money for it, so don't come that with me.'

Jason flushed, the same way he used to when he was a fresh-faced trainee all those years ago, and Brendan was his supervisor. How times had changed.

'Whichever way you cut it, I'm still your boss. Your name's only on the door because people recognize the brand. Don't fool yourself into thinking you're still running things round here.'

Brendan leaned back in his chair and stared at him. Arrogant little prick. He never used to be such a shit. Amazing what a bit of power could do. 'When I was training you,' he subtly emphasized the words, 'you didn't believe being a lawyer was all about making money.'

'God!' Jason burst out laughing. 'You actually believed me? I must have been good!' He was still laughing as he got up to leave. As he reached the door, he paused, turned back and added, 'Okay, seeing as you're going to the Temple, I have two other briefs you can take down for me. You can finish the billing tomorrow.'

Brendan angrily jabbed his finger on the pile of papers in front of him. 'I'm going for a conference on *this* brief. I might be working for you now in the firm I used to own, but I'm not your bloody errand boy!'

'Did I say that?' Jason asked with a look of mock innocence. 'It's just more cost-effective. Don't be so touchy. Still, don't forget to pick them up on your way out.'

Brendan's flash of anger died down as soon as Jason had left his office. He couldn't afford to get too high-handed with his boss or piss him off unduly. He was lucky he still had a job in the profession at all, considering what he had done. If he got himself sacked, it would be virtually impossible to find another, and even if he did it would be in the same basic junior solicitor role. Worse even, a paralegal – certainly not as a partner. And, as hard as it was working here now, at least some of his old clients still thought he was in charge, and when Jason wasn't around he could successfully keep up that fiction.

He looked at the clock. Three thirty. He'd better get going. He had no idea why Lambert had rung, or why he wanted to meet him – the defence solicitor who had fallen so far from grace – but if he was calling him, it had to be serious. And he had to be out of options.

Brendan wouldn't normally be caught dead in the Flag. However, he knew it would be virtually empty at four o'clock on a Monday after-noon. The pub was sandwiched between a dismal housing estate and a run-down row of terraced houses beyond the gentrification of even the most ardent estate agent. The few people that had jobs were out working; the rest – the vast majority – would have already spent their benefit money in here, and other places, over the weekend.

He was nursing a half when Lambert arrived. He watched him buy a pint, and then come over.

'Top of the morning to you,' Lambert greeted him in a mock Irish accent.

Brendan stared at him as he sat down directly facing him. 'Don't do that,' he said finally.

'What's the matter? Can't take a joke? Thought you people had a sense of humour.'

'Look, I've had all the crap I'm prepared to take today. I didn't come down to this shithole to take any more from you.' Brendan looked around the menacing, unfriendly pub. 'What is it with you and this place, anyway?'

'It was my local when I lived round the corner. Remember Ray Willis? Used to work the door here sometimes, specially to pull in the ladies. Course, they don't need him now his face is all chewed up. Bad for business. Called the English Flag back then, before the PC police made them change it. Same way they changed the Met from a Force to a Service.' Lambert said the last as if it left a bad taste in his mouth. He took a sip of his pint. 'Liked both better back then.'

'Yeah; thought it had a "no Blacks, no Irish" feel to it. Look, I've got a conference in Chambers at five thirty, so I've now got –' he looked at his watch – 'fifteen minutes, tops, to spend with you. What's so important that you had to see me now?'

'Read the news today?'

Brendan shrugged. 'Waiting to get the free *Standard* when I go up town.'

'Tight bastard. Christ, I knew things were bad when you got done, but not that bad. Well, even you would have heard about this. Front page.' He threw his copy of the *Sun* down on the table between them.

Brendan glanced down. 'The Choirboy case? Sure, who hasn't? His father's the local saint.'

'Yeah, yeah, so everyone keeps telling me. Did you know he was related to Tony Matthews?'

'Yeah, but what's Tony got to do with . . .' Realization slowly dawned on Brendan. 'My God! It was you, wasn't it? They said they'd pulled someone in.' He chuckled. 'Who'd have thought the person "helping the police with their enquiries" actually *was* a policeman?' He leaned back in his chair and looked at Lambert.

'Well, you haven't been formally arrested or else you wouldn't be here; not on something as serious as this. So, why are you talking to me?'

Lambert gulped his pint. 'I think,' he said slowly, 'I might need a lawyer.'

'You think you *might* need one? And why would that be, Jack?'

'Because they need a scapegoat. They won't look for anyone else; they want it to be me. They know my views on all this political correctness diversity training bollocks. They know I've been after this boy's brother for years. The father's got a lot of pull, and people seem to think he can walk on water . . .'

'Who's "they"?'

'Everyone, including the Fed.' Lambert's voice sounded bitter. 'Even my Super thinks I did it. Comes to something when your own won't stand by you.'

'So go to one of the big police firms.'

'They won't fight for me,' Lambert said dismissively. 'It'll make no fucking difference to them whether I get done or not.'

'And what makes you think it'll matter to me?'

Lambert put both arms on the table and leaned forward until his face was just inches from Brendan's. 'Like being the tea boy in your own office, Brendan? Like working for someone you trained? You did "the right thing" by turning yourself in to the Law Society, but where did it get you? You lost your firm. Fifteen years ago you started off working for someone else; now you're back once again working for someone else. It must be a lot harder second time round. And your wife – how much longer do you think she'll stick around? Women don't do too good with failure.'

'Leave my fucking wife out of this!' Brendan hissed. 'You must be thinking about yours.'

'I am. That's how I know. Oh, she said it was the drinking, but I know she would have stayed if I'd been promoted. You know I'm right about all of it. Look, if – when – I get charged, you take this case on and it'll put you back on the map, even if I get convicted.' Lambert leaned back in his chair. 'Let them prove it, though. I've got faith in our wonderful criminal justice system; it lets all sorts of guilty people off. Far as you're concerned, it could even be "Donnelly & Co" again. But –' Lambert took another swig of his pint, then wiped his mouth with the back of his hand – 'that Black barrister you briefed on Omartian; I want her too.'

'Forget it. She won't do it. And what do you mean "too"? I haven't said I'll take it.'

'Oh, you'll take it, Brendan. But, thinking down the line, I want her as my trial brief; the two of you as a package, or it's no deal.'

'Then it's no deal. I could see how a Black barrister would help you, but I haven't spoken to her in a year.' Brendan stood up abruptly. 'I've got to go.'

'Running errands for your boss?'

Brendan looked down at the top of Lambert's bulbous head, his scalp gleaming under the thinning hair. He always did go for the jugular. He turned and left.

Brendan barely made it to the conference on time. Thankfully, the client, who only lived walking distance from the Temple, was late. They were now well behind schedule, but for once he was grateful. He looked at the two additional sets of papers he was supposed to deliver for his boss. His mobile, switched to silent, was showing two missed calls that he was sure were from Chambers, both awaiting their respective sets of papers. One of them was Maple Court, Lee's Chambers. If he had to go there, the later the better as far as he was concerned. That way, he was less likely to bump into either Tom Mannion, the Senior Clerk, who now treated him like dirt, or Lee Mitchell. The only woman in his life he'd genuinely liked and hadn't tried to sleep with, he thought wryly. A friend.

It was nearly 7 p.m. when he finally climbed the steps up to the entrance of Maple Court. All the barristers' names were listed on the outside, in order of seniority. He noticed Lee's name had moved up a couple of places, with the addition of some junior tenants at the bottom of the list. Some modern Chambers listed their barristers alphabetically, but most, like Maple Court, went by year of Call. This was how barristers measured out time – moving up the ladder in slow increments until you became a KC, Head of Chambers – or dropped off the perch and died. Ironic, though, that as soon as a barrister was appointed a judge you went to the bottom of the list.

He had hoped that, at this time of evening, the only people in Chambers would be the hapless barrister waiting for the brief, or perhaps Dean, the Junior Clerk. The last person he had expected, or wanted, to see was Tom. As Senior Clerk, he acted like the CEO for Chambers – which in many respects he was.

'Finally.' Tom leaned back in his high-backed leather chair as Brendan entered. 'The late Brendan Donnelly,' he added, pointedly looking at his watch that was worth more than Brendan's current annual salary. 'Suppose that now applies to your career too, doesn't it?'

Brendan knew the best way to deal with Tom's remarks was to ignore them. But, Christ, he seemed to be fair game for everyone at the moment.

'Sorry about that, Tom,' Brendan replied, more supinely than he would have liked. 'Conference overran. You know how it is.' He put the slim bundle of papers, folded and neatly tied with red ribbon, on

Tom's desk like an offering, and forced an apologetic smile. 'So, who's got the brief? He's one of Jason's recommendations, not mine. I've never used him before.' He looked round the Clerks' Room. 'Suppose I should meet him –'

'Well, you can't,' Tom interrupted. 'Mr Smith-Jones has left for the day.'

'What? Without the papers for tomorrow?'

Tom shrugged. 'Return came in. Multi-handed robbery at Southwark; one of the barristers got sick. So as from tomorrow, that's where Mr Smith-Jones will be. Got a pupil lined up to do . . . this.' He picked the brief up disdainfully with his thumb and index finger before letting it plop back on to his desk. 'Judging from the size, this looks just about his level.'

If a good return – a last-minute trial that for some reason suddenly became available – came into Chambers, it was generally understood that it would take precedence over a less important hearing. But it was also understood that clerks like Tom would try to replace the barrister with someone of similar age and experience; not give a pupil, or trainee, barrister a case originally intended for someone with at least some expertise. Brendan felt his face flush red with anger. First Jason, then Lambert, now this. 'Well, you could have fucking let me know!'

'I didn't have to fucking tell you anything. I rang your boss.' Tom emphasized the last two words. 'Let's just say he was . . . surprised and disappointed that you weren't here yet. I expect he'll be discussing that with you.' He jabbed at the brief Brendan had given him with a thick fountain pen. 'Anyway, this is hardly the crime of the century.'

'That's not the point.'

'Really? What is, then?'

Silence. The two men stared at each other before Tom said, 'Well, if that isn't good enough for you, Mr Donnelly, feel free to instruct another set of Chambers. Good luck trying to do that at this hour.' He could not have sounded less concerned if he'd tried. He switched off his computer screen and started to pack his things away.

Brendan knew Tom had him over a barrel; worse, he knew that Tom knew.

'You think you can piss all over me just because things are different now.'

'You're right. Things are different. You're not the boss any more, and as Senior Clerk they're the only ones I deal with, the only ones who have anything I could possibly want. So, what are you going to do with your little case?' When Brendan didn't reply, Tom added, 'Thought so. I'll tell the pupil to come down.' He turned away. 'I think that's all, Mr Donnelly.'

'I've got something you'd love to get your hands on.'

'Sorry, I'm straight,' Tom replied, without looking up.

'The Choirboy case.'

'No, you don't. I've had my spies out to find out who's been briefed on that since it happened.'

'Well, I've just been instructed today. Two hours ago.' He paused. 'Even Jason doesn't know yet.' He hoped and prayed the police would charge Lambert. If nothing came of this, Tom would think him even more of a loser than he already did.

Tom turned back to face Brendan, clearly interested now. 'So, who did it, then?'

'Fucking unbelievable. Two minutes ago, you were treating me like something nasty you'd stepped in. And since when did you start taking me for a complete fool? Unless I send the brief here you don't need to know that. Anyway, the client wants Lee Mitchell.'

'You send that brief here, and that won't be a problem.'

'I'd need a bit more fucking respect from you before I do that! Besides, I'm keeping the case, and she won't work with me – not after Omartian.'

'Make no mistake, no barrister wanted to work with you after you fucked her over in that trial. It could have been any of them. But it's in the past. For this case, Bin Laden could have done it and you'd have them lining up to defend him.'

'Not Lee. She can't have changed that much. And I'd want a guarantee.'

'I didn't say it would be easy. But anything's obtainable. I want that brief in these Chambers, and if you want Lee Mitchell as your barrister, Maple Court is the only way you'll get her.'

13

Fee Smith slammed the door of her council flat behind her, with the usual two attempts necessary before it clicked in. On any other street, or in any other block, making such a loud noise every time she entered and left would have raised a complaint from her neighbours by now; or even caused a fight, depending on the person, the day, the mood. Especially now, after the Paul Matthews shooting and all the racially charged tension in the air. But pretty much everyone was in the same boat as her – neglected doors on old flats making it a battle even before you left home.

Now for the security. She locked the heavy iron grille across her front door. Not every flat on the estate had them, but every one on her floor did, looking like rows of prison cells – which in a way they were: cells holding entire families. At least with her flat she was the only occupant.

From the outside the flats might all look the same but inside hers was very different. Some charity shop and cheap IKEA stuff, yes, but also a couple of genuine antiques she had filched from home. It all looked old, though, so if she were broken into no local burglar would know the difference or consider it worth taking.

Fee knew deep down that she was better than her neighbours. As long as she didn't show it she didn't see what the problem was. If her neighbours and the community group she was involved in knew she

94

felt that way they would definitely call her entitled – and probably worse. But so what? It was true. Better bred, better educated. A cushion to fall back on; connections that could parachute her out if the worst came to the worst – like crossing Tony. That was what made her so fearless and uncompromising when protesting, or challenging authority, rather than any innate courage. That was also why she liked to lead. She knew what was best.

Tony's flat didn't have a security grille and she didn't expect him to. No one would dare break in there, not if they valued their life. Or their kids'.

She grabbed her hair, the most recognizable thing about her, twisted it and pushed it up haphazardly under an old Army green beanie hat, shoving the last stray blonde curls up under the fraying woollen edge with her fingers. Picking up her rucksack, she slung it on her back and strode as purposefully as she could towards the stairs.

It was five floors down but despite the weight of her rucksack she couldn't risk taking the lift. People had been stuck in there before. She felt claustrophobic at the best of times, let alone there. She even felt that way in her tiny flat – a flat that could not be more different from where she had grown up: a country estate, not a housing estate. But she preferred it here. At least on Flowerfields the problems were in your face, not swept away into fragrant corners.

The stairs going down were anything but fragrant – equal parts bleach and piss, one trying to mask the other, both failing. Thankfully, the users preferred to hang out there at night, only the detritus on the steps a sobering reminder of what had transpired there less than twelve hours before. When she had first moved here, she had been astonished to see such obvious signs of drug use. Now it barely registered, and wouldn't have done so today if it hadn't been for a familiar, scrawny figure loitering one flight down at the bottom of the stairs.

Fee saw JT before he saw her. Amazingly, from his lack of reaction to her clumpy boots on the stone steps, it seemed that he hadn't even heard her. That was why he was such a rubbish lookout that none of the crims round here would use him for even small burglary jobs. Instinctively, she stopped when she saw him, stepping back into the shadows. She didn't want to deal with him today. Besides, five flights down was no easy feat, especially when the rucksack was almost the same weight as she was. It would be a relief to take it off for a bit. She watched him trying to appear relaxed and nonchalant, but in such a studied way it made him look anything but. He seemed agitated and on edge – but then, he always did.

Fee knew JT, both through Tony and 'around'. JT was always 'around'. He seemed to have no backstory, no family – except for a local hard man who came round occasionally; a shadowy figure with obvious facial scarring, who people on the estate seemed to respect. Depending on who you spoke to, JT was either a helpless dupe, always at the mercy of someone bigger and stronger, or a low-level street dealer who, when he was on his own, no one was particularly afraid of. There had even been a rumour that he was a police informant, which round here was worse than any drug dealer. Luckily for him, people also thought he was a little simple. If he was halfway competent or streetwise that rumour would have stuck and become a literal noose around his neck.

Fee just thought he was a loser – one she had no time for. She noticed for the first time that he was as pale as she was – except hers was the pallor of generations of careful selective breeding to produce an unpolluted blue-veined bloodline. His was the result of poverty. Poor nutrition and food banks. Of falling through society's cracks. Of drug use laced with fear.

She checked the time on her mobile. Shit! If she didn't get going there was no way she would be able to get on the bus with all the kids spilling out of school and taking up every available space, especially with what she was carrying. She stood up and struggled to put the backpack on again, only it seemed even heavier now. As she did so she saw JT moving out of the shadows towards the open area that most of the younger kids used as a playground. Fee didn't expect to see anyone in it at this time of day but as she got to the bottom of the stairs she saw a woman walking quickly towards JT, dragging behind her a little girl who looked about five or six years old. It was too early for children to be let out of school, even as young as this girl was. As JT and the woman met each other they were about a hundred yards away from Fee. The woman was wearing cheap shiny leggings so thin they were almost see-through, but with expensive trainers. Her face was so aged and hardened by life that the only clue to her youth was the flat smooth skin on her stomach exposed by her crop top and belly chain. She stared straight in Fee's direction and scowled. Fee wasn't sure if she had actually seen her or not, but it looked as if she was moving towards her until JT grabbed her arm, muttered something in her ear and pulled her roughly back. Both adults then turned away, their backs towards her.

But the little girl kept looking in her direction.

Fee was not sentimental or emotional by nature – a helpful characteristic when your fuck *de jour* was Tony Matthews, the local drug kingpin – but there was something about this little girl . . . perhaps it was her hair, long curly blonde ringlets just like her own. Perhaps it was her large brown eyes, full of natural childhood curiosity but, even at this distance, tinged with sadness, just like hers had been at that age. She had a rucksack as well, much smaller, and pink to match her trainers. Strange how little girls all over the world liked pink. She had liked pink too – loved it, in fact. She never wore it

97

now and hadn't done in years. She thought back to her father's friends who also liked to see little girls in pink . . .

JT and the woman seemed to be arguing now – more from the gestures and body language than any words she could hear. The woman was clearly getting the better of JT, who was cowering away from her as she pointed her finger in his face. The little girl looked up and touched her mum's arm as if to ask her a question but her mother shrugged it off and turned her daughter around so that she was once again facing Fee's direction. What at first appeared to be a maternal gesture to protect her daughter from what was going on now turned out to have another purpose. The woman was rummaging around in her daughter's little pink rucksack. The girl kept trying to look over her shoulder to see what was going on, her mother repeatedly turning her head to face front. Finally, the woman seemed to find what she wanted and handed something to JT.

Fee couldn't see what it was, but she didn't have to. She watched as he hesitated for a moment, staring at the woman's outstretched hand, disgust and shame on his face. Then he silently took it, put it in his pocket and lightly patted the little girl on the head. She smiled up at him and waved, then looked hurt and confused as he abruptly turned away.

It all happened so quickly: an everyday encounter between two young adults and a little girl in an open play area on a weekday afternoon. Hiding in plain sight. Fee watched as the mother grabbed the girl by the hand and pulled her away – the youngest drug mule on the estate, her little pink rucksack now empty, sliding down her narrow back.

14

Wallace woke up with a start, blinking his eyes to get adjusted to the sunlight streaming through the window straight into his face. He leapt out of bed, his heart racing, scrambling for his phone before he realized this was his day off. He dropped the phone on the bed and walked to the window. He really had to get some blinds, curtains – something. True, his bedroom wasn't overlooked. The room was small with dark wood furniture and dominated by a king-sized bed, so needed all the light it could get, but there was no point triple-locking the doors to the flat when he was so exposed here. Especially for a DCI. Standing in front of the window, he yawned and stretched. Naked. Good job no one could see him now.

It was a good day for a run. Bright but cold outside. Perfect. From his place down towards the Marina and along the seafront would be a good five miles. He'd save the longer runs for another time.

It wasn't that early, but it was Sunday so it was still quiet. In this party town, most people would be sleeping it off, or wondering who they had woken up next to. He hadn't done that in a while and at the moment didn't miss it. Nothing like knowing a brain-dead teenager's family to kill your libido. That, and the driving to and from London every day.

After his warm-up, Wallace selected his running playlist. He never wore headphones when running if there were a lot of people about, and never when running in London, period. As a police officer you had to be hyper alert. As a Black man too, come to that: for people too close behind or next to you; for cars driving alongside, too slowly. But here there was no one around. That would change when he got into Brighton proper, but for now . . .

He put his playlist on shuffle. He'd been compiling this for so long he'd forgotten some of the early ones he'd put on there, so every tune was a pleasant surprise. He always felt the most free when listening to music, putting together completely different genres like a melodic mosaic, with no judgement, even of himself. There was Des'ree with her low, strong voice. Whatever happened to her? Stormzy. Soca, salsa, reggaeton – anything with a beat. Then, as a lovely surprise, some classical music by Sheku. And of course, always, Miles.

His head was still bobbing to the music as he got into the city itself. He knew just when he would meet more people on the street – running, walking, driving. Some were even brave enough to sit outside for the first coffee and cigarette of the day; sunglasses for the hangover, the glare or both, wrapped up in winter coats and sitting under big outdoor heaters trying to fool themselves it was already summer. He paused the song playing mid-flow and took the headphones off. It was then he realized he'd stopped outside his old gym. Force of habit? He missed gym work, doing weights. Too much running made you less muscular, too lean for the job. He wasn't at that point yet, but he should find another. This one had been too much of a pick-up scene for him. Oiled up and preening – and that was just the men. He didn't like being hit on when he was working out.

Running definitely had its advantages, though. You were out in the open air, and you could be in your own head. But the music had been a distraction. Without it, details of the Matthews case came flooding back into his mind. He never usually had this trouble; after all, even before he joined the police, when he was still a soldier, he had seen more gruesome things, with younger victims. Apart from when he had had to tell Reverend Matthews the terrible news about Paul, the last time Wallace had seen him was before he'd left to join the Army. He could always ask to be reassigned . . .

He had hit the seafront now. Both the cold and the sunlight were magnified by the water, the sun bouncing brightly off its surface while the cold wind was whipping up and blowing across his path. His T-shirt was plastered with sweat against his torso. He had to squint, but still kept up his pace. He could see the end in sight.

When he reached it, he was surprised, and disappointed, that he was more out of breath than he'd expected. He went to a nearby kiosk selling water and asked for the coldest one he had.

'Got any big ones?' he asked as the vendor gave him a small 500ml size.

'Come on, mate. It's a kiosk, not Tesco.'

'Okay, give me another one, then.'

Wallace sat on the nearest bench and peeled off his T-shirt. At least both bottles were ice cold. He drank half of the first in one continuous gulp, then closed his eyes, leaned forward and poured the rest over his head. He could feel the rivulets running between his shoulder blades and some on the front of his chest, right over his old Army tattoos. Eyes still closed, he raised his head and leaned back, allowing himself just a moment to enjoy the feel of the sun on his face and the sound of the waves.

Then he wiped the water out of his eyes and looked up. There, about a hundred yards to his left, sat a young couple, drinking coffee and staring at him openly. As their eyes met, the girl giggled and looked away, but the young man continued to stare.

'You're not usually that winded. Longer run today?'

Wallace looked at them, scanning their faces for some form of recognition. Both were in their early to mid-twenties. Neither was dressed for the beach nor for exercise, though they were both wearing trainers more fashionable, and more expensive, than his own. The man was white, with a pallor that went with his reddish-blond hair. Not very tall, but muscular. The woman was mixed race. She had a jacket wrapped around her that was almost the length of her dress, which she was trying, but failing, to pull further down her thighs.

'Do I know you?'

'Don't think so.' The young man looked him up and down. 'Unless you're a clubber and you don't look like that's your thing. Not any more.'

'We haven't been home yet,' said the girl, raising her takeaway cup. 'That's why we need these.' She smiled at him. A really lovely smile, Wallace noticed. 'But we've seen you out here before. Best part of our morning. I'm Tash, this is Colin.'

'Danny.' Wallace took a long swig from his remaining bottle. 'I'd have thought a young couple like you would have better things to do to each other than sit out in the cold watching runners.'

Tash looked at Colin and they both burst out laughing.

'Us, a couple? No, he's my brother. Same mum, different dads, before you ask. Besides, Colin's still deciding. It's boys this week, I think.'

Colin blushed and elbowed his sister sharply in the ribs. 'You being biphobic?'

Still laughing, Tash hugged her brother. 'Nah. You know I love you. But fancy anyone thinking you and I are together!' They were both laughing now. There was clearly a genuine bond between them, Wallace noticed. He would have loved that, growing up.

'Anyway, enough chat.' He pulled his T-shirt on. 'I'll definitely be fitter next time you see me.'

He started slowly running back the route he'd come, warming up before fully getting into his stride. He hadn't gone more than a hundred yards when he heard footsteps running quickly behind him. He turned round to see Tash looking up at him.

'When's that gonna be?' she asked. She sounded breathless, whether from exertion or embarrassment, Wallace couldn't tell. 'Colin said he'd buy me breakfast if I asked for your number, but I . . . I thought I'd give you mine.' She paused, bravado faltering. 'Same difference, right?'

He smiled down at her. Out of the corner of his eye he could see her brother, still by the bench but standing now, craning his neck to see what was going on.

'Well, you make sure he buys you a proper one, not just some roll from Greggs.' He gave her his phone and watched as she tapped in her number. He'd been living like a monk for far too long. Maybe this would take his mind off the case. And why choose? 'Bring him too, if you want.'

15

It was a rare day when Lee didn't have to work, either preparing for trial or actually in court, and she was determined to enjoy it. A lie-in was definitely in order. She could get her nails done, perhaps even a massage. Of course there was the 7 p.m. board meeting at the Law Centre – her first – but beyond the short minutes of the previous meeting there was nothing to read. In the minutes, Kofi had mentioned there would be two new members joining, so he must have been very sure she would say yes. She wondered who the other person was.

Even though the centre was closed to the public, Claudine was her usual cheery self when Lee arrived.

'I'm glad you're early. You know how Kofi is about timekeeping, especially for these meetings.'

'Lucky for me I didn't have to work today, then.'

'So I see. I can't remember the last time I saw you in jeans. They look more Bond Street than high street, though.'

Lee laughed. She looked into Kofi's office. From the changed layout it was clear that it also doubled as a small boardroom. Some of the old plastic chairs had been brought in from the waiting area to provide additional seating. 'How big is this board anyway?'

Claudine shrugged. 'Six people, apart from Kofi? There've been some changes so it might end up bigger or smaller. I just take the minutes. Kofi's good at a lot of things but he's a more hands-on person – advising, running this place. Also, Imran's one of the people who's stepping down; he's the Treasurer, and you know this place definitely needs one of those. We have to make every penny count. We've had so many run-ins with the council they're just looking for a reason to withdraw our funding, especially if our books are not in order – which would shut us down.'

'Treasurer? That's not me, I hope?'

'No, with you I think he just wants someone sensible and savvy, who cares about this place. No – the other one is someone called Hunter. They'd better get here soon, though.'

Kofi's views on poor timekeeping were legendary. Not even the King himself would have delayed the start of the meeting – especially if he hadn't called.

'Right,' he said, as the minute hand hit 7 p.m. 'Let's get started.'

'Can't we wait just a few minutes, Kofi? I'm sure she'll be here soon. London traffic: you know how it is. And she's never been here before. Besides, Leon's not here; is he even coming tonight?'

'No, he's not. And that's a separate conversation I'll be having with him, but at least he called. Look, Imran – what do they say when minorities run things? We're always late! I'm sorry you're stepping down as you're a great Treasurer, and if you've nominated this woman, I'm sure she's good at her job –'

'She's in one of the Big Four accountancy firms. We're lucky to get her . . .'

'But she's late! And evidently doesn't know how to use a phone. I know she's giving up her time, but we all are, and we deserve some respect. We're not some piece-of-shit organization just because we're not a paying client. Lee's the other new member, and she's here. We're quorate. Let's start.'

Just then the buzzer rang. Imran looked relieved. The ringing became ever more frantic as Claudine made her way to the door. Moments later, an elegant and distinctly flustered white woman entered the room.

'Hello, everyone. I'm terribly sorry I'm late,' she said in confident, cut-glass tones. 'Client meeting overran.'

'At least you're here, Marianne. Marianne Hunter, everyone.' Imran was trying to put her at ease, but the woman was too busy unwinding her scarf from around her neck and simultaneously looking for a place to put her many bags, one of which, Lee noticed, was the same handbag as hers.

Kofi glared at Imran.

'We normally start these meetings at six thirty, Marianne. I pushed it back by thirty minutes on this occasion to accommodate you. We know you don't have to do this, but you volunteered, and we take what we do here very seriously. If you were going to be late you should have at least called.'

As she finally sat down, Marianne gave Kofi a smile so dazzling that Lee was sure it would disarm most people, especially men. She watched it slowly fade when it failed to have the desired effect. Marianne evidently wasn't used to that reaction, and it showed.

'You're quite right of course, Kofi. I'm sorry.' She looked at Lee as if she were about to say something, but then poured herself a glass of water. 'It won't happen again.'

'Okay.' Kofi looked at the six people around the table. 'I don't know what you'd call this; an Extraordinary Board Meeting crossed with an interview, maybe. We've already got one vacancy, and Imran is stepping down as Treasurer. Imran, I want to extend my personal

thanks to you, as well as the thanks of the board, for all you've done.'
Everyone murmured their assent.

'It's not easy with a day job, I know, and we don't have much money, but you're an expert at keeping our books straight and doing more with less. We've never failed an audit yet and, unlike other places, our books are available for inspection anytime, anyplace.' Kofi applauded and everyone joined in.

'You all know Lee,' Kofi continued. 'She's been with us for the best part of twenty years, mostly as a volunteer. She's kept the lights on more than once . . .'

Some people looked surprised. Lee held up her hand, embarrassed. 'Come on, Kofi.'

'No, it has to be said. But enough of that. You, Marianne – all we know is that you're an accountant. Imran speaks highly of you, so that's a big plus, but tell us a bit more about yourself.'

'Well, I don't live too far from here . . .'

'You do?' Kofi sounded surprised.

'Yes. On Hillcrest.'

'Oh. On The Hill.'

Lee glanced at him. She knew what he meant. That wasn't really 'round here'. That was a place of huge houses, big gardens and expensive flat conversions like hers. Even the air smelled different. She knew Kofi was conflicted about the fact that she, too, lived there. He admired her self-made success; that she would always be connected to the area and hadn't forgotten where she came from. But she was still the girl who made it out of Lower Rick and was now living among people who, in his mind, literally looked down on him and the people he served.

Marianne might have been late but she didn't deserve to be judged on where she lived. And Lee was no hypocrite. No apologist either. 'I live there too.'

To her surprise, Marianne replied, 'Yes, I know. I thought I recognized you.'

'Have we met?'

'No, but sometimes I see you in the cafe on the square. With your partner? Very handsome, I must say. And Suzette's only had two of those bags. I wondered who bought the other one.'

'I suppose I'm easy to spot. I'm the only woman who looks like me living on Hillcrest.'

Marianne's face reddened.

Kofi tapped his pen on the table. 'Focus, people. And why us? Why do you want to be our Treasurer?'

'Well, I've been an accountant for about twelve years now and I want to give something back to the community.'

'But why here?'

'So, Imran and I have kept in touch on and off since university. He told me he was stepping down. Our firm also has an outreach programme where we try to encourage social mobility by helping underserved communities. So,' she clapped her hands together, 'I thought it was a perfect fit.' Again, that dazzling smile.

'Can you give the necessary time commitment to be our Treasurer? We only meet once a month, but there's other work to be done in between, especially in that role.'

'Look, I know I was late this evening but that won't be a problem in the future. There might be an occasional meeting I can't make if I have to fly out to one of our major overseas clients, but the firm is very good about allowing time for this sort of thing. In fact, demonstrating social commitment is expected if you're serious about making partner.'

'So, that's the reason,' Kofi said slowly. 'Making partner? And anything you do for us is to help facilitate that?'

'Well no, not really, not just that. And anyway,' her voice suddenly sharper, more defensive, 'does it really matter? I thought you needed a Treasurer. I can be a very good one for you. So we both benefit.'

Lee heard Kofi mutter under his breath, '*Lady Bountiful.*' This could get out of hand very quickly. She touched his arm.

'How about a break, Kofi? I could certainly use one.'

Kofi looked as if he were about to say something, then thought better of it.

'Okay, let's resume in twenty minutes.' He looked at the clock. 'Sharp.'

For a number of reasons, not least the tension in the room which had abated but not disappeared, everyone wanted to leave early and so they whizzed through the agenda in record time. It was just the two of them left now. Lee had offered to stay to help Kofi clear up the glasses and coffee cups. It was usually Claudine's job, but she was grateful to push off as soon as the meeting was over.

'Well, I'm glad you're onboard, Lee. But that Marianne?' Kofi kissed his teeth and shook his head. 'I don't know about her.'

'You didn't vote against her, though.'

'It wouldn't have made a difference. Everyone voted in favour. Even you.'

'That's because we need a Treasurer. Right now. No one else on the board could take on that role and you know it. How long was it going to take to find someone else willing to do it, and with her experience? Besides, you trust Imran's judgement, right?'

'Yes, I do, but . . .' Kofi was clearly frustrated, moving the furniture back into place more noisily than needed.

'Look, whatever it is, just say it. Don't take it out on the chairs.' When he didn't reply, Lee continued, 'You care about this place,

Kofi, but you're also very strategic. It's not like you to let emotions cloud your judgement.'

Kofi stopped, and turned to face her. 'You heard her, Lee. She sweeps in here – late – and within ten minutes it becomes clear that she wants to make partner by helping "social mobility and underserved communities".'

'So what? This is the real world, Kofi. Everyone's got an agenda. You just have to make sure hers matches yours.'

'I can just see her at a dinner party talking to the people on The Hill about how much she's doing for the underprivileged in Lower Rick!'

Lee leaned against the door frame and crossed her arms. 'People like me, you mean.'

'Come on. You know I don't mean you.'

'Yes, you do.' Lee put her thumb and forefinger together. 'Just a little bit. But that's your issue, not mine. And as for Marianne – none of us have to hang out together. If she forgets herself, you can put her in her place. You only have to see her once a month and at least you'll have a Treasurer for the next two years. And now,' she took her car keys out of her bag for easy access as soon as she stepped out of the door into the night, 'I might pop round my mum's to see if she's still up. Before,' she added pointedly, 'I head up to The Hill.'

16

Every Black man knows you go to the barber's for a shave, a trim, a fade or whatever, but you stay for the chat. For some it's a way to catch up with your mates; talk about things you wouldn't in the company of women; watch football if it's on. For others, it almost takes the place of a free counselling session – for men who can't, or won't, seek that kind of early mental health intervention but who in fact need it the most. And Headz was just such a place.

David had been coming here for years, ever since he and Lee started living together. The Hill was a lovely place to live; working with music and musicians all day, he particularly appreciated the quiet. But, frankly, it was too white for him. If Lee wasn't there, he would never have moved there by choice. However, he completely understood her position. Even though the areas were so very different, she had grown up in Lower Rick and had a strong connection to this place, so she didn't want to be too far away. And her mum was here, fiercely independent but getting older. He loved that about Verna Mitchell, even though he knew she was still hoping her daughter would find another barrister to replace him. He laughed at that thought. If only she knew how unlikely that was.

Leroy, the owner, looked at him.

'Always glad when people leave my place happy. Good for business.'

David fished out his wallet, trying but failing to find anything smaller than a fifty-pound note. Leroy held up his hands.

'Seriously, D? You ain't got nothing smaller?'

'Sorry, Leroy. Just got back from tour last night and this is the first place I came to this morning; you try finding someone who *really* knows how to cut Black hair in Hungary. Plus, I know this is a strictly cash establishment.'

Leroy took the note. 'And this is why, anyone but you, I'd have told them where to stick it. Least I know it ain't fake, coming from you. But,' he opened the till, 'I'm low on change. If I give you what I got that's me clean out.'

'Keep it. You know I'm gonna be back. Take my next cut out of that.'

'Sure? Well, it's good you got it like that, fam.'

'For now. You know how things go in the music business. But I'm hungry, man. That place just down from you where Blessings Bakery used to be – what's it like?'

'Don't know. Some deli. Not my kind of place. They don't sell proper food in there. And a name like that? For food?' Leroy shook his head. 'They wouldn't know hard dough bread, Guinness punch or a real pattie – not a pasty – if it bit them in the arse. You see how busy we are? They could have had a lot of business from us. But then, maybe that's the whole idea.'

'Everything's not for everybody, Leroy.'

'Then they shouldn't be around here if they're not catering to local people!'

'Hey – don't put all Black people in a box. Some of us might like what they're selling.'

'You really telling me, David, that you wouldn't prefer a pattie and a Supermalt right now?'

David had to laugh. 'You're not wrong.'

'And you won't find it in there, I guarantee you.' Leroy folded his arms as if there were nothing more to be said.

'Well, I'm going to check it out. I'll tell you what it's like next time I see you.'

As David headed for the door, Terry came in. They hadn't seen each other since the argument in the pub. On seeing David, he stopped dead in his tracks.

'Y'alright, D? We cool?' He held out his hand, nervous and agitated.

David looked at his outstretched hand but didn't take it. He'd never noticed how small his hands were before. 'Yeah, we cool. See you, Leroy.'

DSD – Dirty South Deli – was actually scrupulously clean. That was the only thing it had in common with the Caribbean bakery it had replaced. In every other way they were as different as it was possible to be. With the passage of time the bakery had become shabby chic – the mark of a place that had been worked in and much loved, aged by time and use. This brand-new establishment had been aged as a style point.

The walls and floors had been stripped back to exposed brick and faded painted wood, the kind you would see at a beach hut on the English Riviera. The food counter was at the far end directly opposite the door. There was artwork along the length of one wall, some by local artists, others from promising students from the well-known art college nearby. On the opposite side there was less wall space as half of it had been replaced with floor-to-ceiling windows, forming an L-shaped area of light. There were five wooden tables with deliberately mismatched chairs, two of which were occupied. In the far corner nearest the door there was a small rack of vintage clothes and some costume jewellery on display.

The whole effect was both calming and unsettling at the same time, as if created by an artist who occasionally remembered they had to eat. David thought back to his conversation with Leroy; if he could see this, he would feel completely vindicated about the customers they were trying to attract – and to keep out.

He walked up to the counter. A young girl with pink hair and a septum ring smiled at him. 'Can I help you?'

'I don't know yet. Let me see what you got.'

'That's okay. Take your time.'

The produce was beautifully laid out behind the counter but there was nothing Leroy would have described as 'real food'. There were black, green and Kalamata olives; chorizo, Parma ham and other cold cuts of meat; different types of cheeses and a variety of salads. There was also a short list of the different types of bread available, and a variety of cupcakes. In other words, nothing that the guys in the barbershop would like.

'Don't you have anything hot to eat?'

'Sorry, just hot drinks at the moment. We've only just opened,' she added by way of explanation.

'Okay. I'll have a little bit of everything, then. And a black coffee. And some water.'

'Take a seat. I'll bring it over.'

David went to the table nearest the window and chucked his jacket on a chair. He wandered around the open space, looking at the artwork. Some pieces were really very good, including a painting by a local man whose name he recognized. The jewellery was eclectic. One piece was particularly beautiful – a necklace with a jagged, rough-cut stone pendant about three inches long, set in copper, with varying shades of blue and green, lighter at the edges and getting darker towards the centre, like diving into the Caribbean Sea and swimming down into the depths.

The waitress came up behind him. 'I've put your food on the table.' She pointed at the pendant he was holding. 'Do you like it?'

'It's the best piece here.'

'I think so too, but I'm biased. It's one of mine.'

'For real?'

She nodded, blushing. 'Mind you,' she continued, lowering her voice, 'I couldn't afford to buy it myself retail, not with what Jonny pays me for part-time hours.'

'Art student?'

She nodded.

David turned the piece over. Inscribed on the back in tiny cursive script was one word, *Clem.*

'It must be a sign.' He pointed at the name. 'That was my grandmother's name. Clementine.'

'Really?' She smiled brightly. 'Mine too. Well, almost. Clemency.'

'I'll take this. My girl will love it.'

'Great.' Her smile, still friendly, became fractionally less bright. 'I'll wrap it and keep it at the counter. Think I've got a nice presentation box too, seeing as it's a gift.' She looked over at his table. 'If your coffee's too cold, I'll get you a fresh one. On the house.'

The selection on his plate wouldn't have been his first choice, but for what it was it was okay. He liked his coffee extra hot and it was a touch too lukewarm for him. He could only manage a few sips before deciding to wait for the next one – which, thankfully, Clem brought almost immediately.

'Here you go.'

'Thanks. So, why the clothes? The artwork I understand, even the jewellery. But clothes? I don't get it.'

'Jonny's idea. He wants a whole hippy chic, "inherited my mum's clothes" vibe.'

'Feels like I'm eating in someone's bedroom.'

Again, she lowered her voice. 'That's the real reason why we don't have hot food. He thinks it'll make the clothes smell.'

David shook his head. 'It's the wrong vibe for round here.'

'You think? The area's transitioning.'

'So? "Transitioning" doesn't mean you give up everything that makes an area unique! The place before you in this spot? It was iconic. Everyone knew Blessings Bakery, and it welcomed *everyone*. You seem like a cool person, but this place? It feels like it's designed to exclude, not include.'

David was still working on his coffee but had finished eating. Clem silently cleared his empty plate and left. He thought about what he had just said. His tone was perhaps a little too sharp but he meant every word. He loved Lower Rick. There were good, hardworking people here, and it deserved to be respected for what it was.

Just behind him he could hear whispers: '*We don't give out free coffees!*' '*But he bought the necklace. The most expensive one too.*' '*Your piece? Then you pay for his coffee.*' Time to go. He walked up to the counter. Jonny was there, and as they looked at each other, the wary suspicion in his eyes was immediately replaced with a fawning politeness. 'Was everything okay?'

'Some hot food would have been nice.' He saw Clem bite her lip as if trying not to laugh. 'The coffee's good, though. I heard what you said. Don't take it out of her wages. I'll pay for it.'

'Oh, there's no need . . .'

'No, I insist. I always like to pay my way.' David looked at Clem. 'The necklace too?'

She nodded. 'Here it is.' It was beautifully wrapped in a small presentation box, tied with blue-green ribbon the same colour as the stone.

'One of our more expensive pieces. You have great taste,' Jonny commented.

'How come they're not in a display case, or protected in some way?'

'Oh, we don't worry about people round here stealing it. Not blingy enough for the locals.'

The silence that followed that statement was deafening. Clem turned bright red and looked as if she wished the floor would open and swallow her up. From the icy stare David was giving him, Jonny realized too late what he had said.

'I mean –' he began.

'They're positioned by the window in direct sunlight. That will cause them to fade. A display case would protect them. That's what *I* meant. But don't worry; no one was coming in here anyway to eat in a place with "Dirty" anything above the door, especially once I tell people what you really think about them. See the barber's next door? The owner's lived here for decades. He knows everyone. He also owns a lot of property round here and could buy and sell you ten times over. Have some fucking respect!' He picked up the gift and looked at Clem. 'I'm only buying this because you made it. But I'd look for another job if I were you because, trust me, this place won't be here long.'

17

Flowerfields Estate. It was as unlike its name as it was possible to imagine. The town planners must have been on crack when they named it. No doubt it was intended to be inspiring, but in fact it was a sick joke on the beleaguered residents living there.

But there were children playing outside today. That was unusual, even in broad daylight during half-term, as very few parents thought it safe enough to let them out. But it struck a nice, normal note – kids playing hide and seek, laughing and yelling and giggling as children should.

It was hard to pinpoint exactly when in the game childish yells turned into anguished screams, but when their mothers rushed over the cause was clear. Jimmy Thomas, slumped under a stairwell hardly anyone used, blond hair plastered to the side of his face, matted with dried blood. His skull had been pierced by a single bullethole to the temple, his mouth stuffed full of wraps of crack cocaine. And by someone who knew no one would dare touch those drugs, clearly left to send a message, even round here.

It was the perfect hiding place for a child. Or for a body.

Canteen coffee. Shit as ever. Lambert had been determined to report for duty as usual, but as he sat and stared at the others on their mid-afternoon break it seemed the only person at Miller Street who wasn't shocked to see him there was himself. He knew by now everyone would have heard about last Monday, so he wasn't surprised that people were treating him like a leper. It might have been his imagination, of course. He hadn't been Mr Popularity for a long time. The few he knew and liked had moved on, or up, or out, and he had no time for the bunch of snowflakes coming out of Hendon now, making the station look all 'culturally sensitive' and 'woke'.

Just then, the tannoy crackled into life. '*Would Sergeant Lambert please go to the Super's office at once.*'

Lambert's head jerked up to see all eyes on him. He scraped his chair noisily back along the floor and heaved himself to his feet. As he did so, his gut popped a button on his shirt, exposing four inches of hairy, pallid belly. Great.

He grabbed his uniform jacket and buttoned it up on the way to Superintendent Reid's office.

'Nice to see you back, Sergeant,' Reid said as he entered his office, in a voice which indicated anything but. 'Take a seat.'

'Just reporting for work as usual, sir. After all, no reason not to.'

'You know a Jimmy Thomas – street name JT.' It was a statement rather than a question.

Lambert paused before replying. 'He's one of my informants, sir. I'm sure you know that. Not that he's given me much useful lately, though.'

'And he won't be now. News just came in. He's dead.'

Lambert's face was impassive. 'How?'

Reid leaned back in his chair and stared at him.

'Nothing gets to you, does it, Jack? Always the hard bastard. You had the same attitude last week when I told you about Paul Matthews. Funny, JT was shot in the head too. You wouldn't happen to know anything about that, of course?'

'No, I wouldn't, sir. And as for who would want him dead – pick a number. Peckham's a dangerous place for a small-time drug dealer, especially a weedy runt who ran drugs for Tony Matthews and who hardly ever carried a street weapon.'

'Have a bit of respect, Sergeant! He might have been a little shit, but he's not yet cold and here you are mouthing off when he probably got shot because of his connection with you.'

'These things happen in his line of work, sir. He knew the risks – or should have done. Anyway, I've got little time for anyone connected with Tony Matthews – even if they have been useful to me in the past.'

Reid leaned forward and rested both elbows on his desk. His eyes searched Lambert's face. 'Seeing as the common denominator between Paul Matthews and JT is Tony Matthews, what do you think the chances are of ballistics proving both bullets came from the same gun?'

'I wouldn't know, sir.' Lambert thought about where he'd hidden the gun he had taken from JT. He wasn't out of the woods on Paul Matthews yet.

'Well, we'll soon know. I've asked them to put a rush on the Matthews one, at any rate. By the way, seeing as you're so concerned,' he added sarcastically, 'boy's on life support. No brain-stem function. Doctors want to switch it off, but according to Family Liaison, the parents won't have it. They and their whole bloody church turn up every day, singing, praying for a miracle, and generally making a complete nuisance of themselves. They've had to move him to a private room just to keep the noise down for the other patients. Superstitious mumbo jumbo,' he concluded with disgust. 'Anyway, that'll be all, Sergeant.'

Lambert checked his watch as he left Reid's office. He knew

someone who would know what happened to JT, and why. If he left now, it would look suspicious. Four more hours until he could knock off and go looking for him.

The match was on. After a year of using this pub, Ray Willis was getting used to it. He didn't think he could ever love it, or even like it, but he was getting used to it.

He looked around from the shabby corner that had become his usual spot. If ever there was such a thing as a Mockney pub, this was it. It was dark, posh and faux down-at-heel. It was the kind of place that would pride itself on its diversity, even though it clearly wasn't. Still, he supposed he counted now.

It was less than a mile away from what used to be his local, but the two places were so different that they could be on opposite sides of London. His old boozer used to smell of hand-rolled cigarettes and draught beer; had a motherly barmaid who knew how to pull a pint of real Guinness and a pop star wannabe who didn't. He'd been going there ever since he could drink legally, which was two years after he'd started drinking at all.

He missed his old place; heard on the grapevine that people were still asking after him, even after all this time. He was sure that some of them thought he'd be back – just walk in, like nothing had changed. But that wasn't going to happen, as too much else had. He couldn't stand to see the pitying looks of friends, or the frightened ones of children, on top of the curious stares from people who didn't know what had happened to him. He didn't have that history with the people here – in fact, he had chosen this place for just that reason. In spite of their relative proximity, no one in his old place would ever be caught dead here. Besides, he liked it that they were a bit afraid of him in his new boozer. That meant they left him alone, for starters.

He suspected that he added just the right amount of gritty working-class authenticity for them – so long as he stayed in the corner, at a distance, in the dark. So they both benefitted.

He was rolling a cigarette when he heard a beer bottle plonked down on the long wooden table right in front of him.

'Piss off,' he said, not looking up.

'So it *is* you, then.'

Ray looked up so quickly, he forgot to angle his head as he usually would.

'Ray Willis. In a place like this,' Lambert said, sitting down and shaking his head in disbelief. 'Never trust a place where they don't serve beer on tap; only this bottled shite.' He looked over at Ray's pint. 'Or Guinness, and I hate that.'

'Who asked you to sit down? I said piss off. What are you still doing here?'

'Well, I thought I'd come to join you and all your friends,' Lambert sneered, looking down the long trestle table at which they both sat, empty except for the two of them. 'It's busy here tonight – can't think why – but no one's coming anywhere near you. Why is that, Ray?' Lambert took a swig of his beer, then grimaced with disgust. 'Bet they love having you here. You look like a proper South London villain, especially with a face like that.'

Ray felt himself flinching.

'Oh, don't mind me – I've seen worse. But not much.' Seeing Ray's right arm twitch, Lambert added, in the same conversational tone, 'And don't bother trying to punch me out. I thought you were avoiding attention these days.'

Ray glanced over Lambert's shoulder and saw about half a dozen people pretending not to look at them, the two men who were already so clearly out of place.

'So let's go outside so I can knock you spark out for speaking to me like that.'

'Oh, you're not going to do that, Ray. For the first time in a long while, I can't nick you for anything. But I could for that. You're going straight at the moment, I hear. Working for Trojan Security, doing clubs. That's how I managed to track you down. Took some effort, though. You know how people don't want to talk to the Old Bill – especially me.'

'Yeah,' Ray said. 'I heard you got pulled in for that shooting. Anyone else would have been nicked already.'

Lambert didn't even bother to ask how he knew. 'Don't worry, I'm sure that's coming. And if I end up on remand, I'll probably be dead. You know how many people on remand would be waiting to stick it to me?' Lambert made a stabbing gesture with his hand. 'Stick it to me the other way too, if enough of them caught me in the showers. Anyway, the boy's not dead – yet. And I didn't do it.'

'So, what do you want with me, then?'

'You heard about JT.' It was a statement of fact rather than a question. Ray Willis hadn't been going straight that long. Even this early, he would know.

'Yeah.' Ray looked away. 'He was always the runt of the litter. Thought he was hard, but petty thieving was his level. He wasn't cut out for drugs.' His face hardened. 'Or to be a grass. You're probably the reason he's dead. Anyway, you know I know him. So?'

'So you two used to be tight. You two were virtually the only white boys in Peckham. Until you became Mr Wigga, hanging out with all these Blacks, liking your women that way too. Better watch out it doesn't rub off. Dick first.'

Ray's temper was legendary and he had the criminal record to prove it. But apparently something else had changed as well as his face. If Lambert thought he was going to get a rise out of him, he was mistaken. 'Even though half my face is chewed up, I still get more pussy than you. When was the last time you fucked anything other than your hand?' As Lambert's face flushed, Ray continued, 'That long. So, let's stick to talking about JT. No – I don't know who killed him, and you'd be the last person I'd tell if I did.' He drained his pint. 'Tell you what, though, the police better find who did it before I do.'

'Why are you so bothered?'

'Because he didn't deserve to be shot and left to die in his own piss. Not even him. Anything else?'

'Well, after spending all this time tracking you down, I just thought I'd drop by and tell you your girlfriend is going to be my new brief.' At Ray's puzzled look, Lambert added, 'You know, the Black one, always acted for you. Did that Eurotrash rich Jew boy, Omartian.'

'I know who you mean,' Ray interrupted. 'Do I look like I give a shit either way? Anyway, never gonna happen.'

'I've got her mate, that Mick solicitor. He'll talk her round.'

'You'd better check your sources. They're not friends any more, not since their bust-up after that case.'

'Well, it's either that or she gets disbarred. I do know a bit about the law, you know.'

'Yeah, enough so you can shoot that kid, or have him shot, and no one would know it was you. I know you nicked his brother plenty of times. Isn't that what they call a motive, seeing as you know so much about the law?'

Ray knew from the expression in Lambert's eyes that what he'd said had hit home. Although Lambert didn't raise his voice when he replied, his tone was menacing.

'What's the matter? Oh, I know – you probably have her picture on your wall. Or wanking off to it in your lap. You defending her honour? Her "integrity"?' He spoke the last as if it were a dirty word. 'You think she's too good to represent me, is that it? I've never met a barrister yet who wouldn't flog their own mother, literally, for a good case. You know, I always thought you fancied her. Think she'd ever look at you? Especially now?' Lambert leaned forward, his voice softer. 'You better have a whole face before you speak to me like that again, sonny.'

Ray leapt out of his seat and pulled his right arm back, his hand balled into a fist. Lambert ducked. It was only the sound of Lambert's bottle and Ray's glass smashing on the stone floor that brought Ray back to his senses. He stopped and saw that everyone was looking at the tableau he and Lambert made in the corner.

Lambert straightened up, grinned, patted Ray on the shoulder and spoke to the onlookers. 'Very passionate about his football, my mate.' He turned back to Ray and continued, his voice lower this time.

'Nah, we shouldn't be fighting, Ray. We white English? Got to stick together. Looks like you might have to find yourself another boozer, though – just when you were making yourself so at home here.' Lambert grinned broadly, as if they were best mates. 'Be seeing you.'

Lambert thought about the conversation on his way home. He had deliberately tried to get a rise out of Ray but hadn't succeeded. Not until he mentioned Lee Mitchell. He was still thinking about that when he got back to his house.

As soon as he stepped inside, he knew something was wrong. He didn't know how someone had managed to get past the triple-locked door. That alone told him it was a professional. Whoever had been here was so keen to cover their tracks that it was actually tidier than when he left it ten hours ago.

He'd lived here for years and no one had ever burgled him before. This wasn't about money.

Lambert charged straight into the bedroom. Sure enough, it too was neater than when he'd left it. His heart was pounding in his ears as he flung the pillows behind him and pulled the fetid sheets away from the mattress. He stopped to wipe the sweat pouring down his face. He knew he should have moved it earlier. It was too obvious, even for a temporary hiding place, and it had already been far too long. He grabbed hold of the mattress and tugged it away from the divan base, knowing what he would find. Or not.

The imprint of the gun on the base was all that remained.

18

Hugo Cunningham was conducting his regular ward surgery. He was only a local councillor, not an MP, but he could no longer stand pitching up to the library to carry out his business, so he paid privately to rent a small office. After all, he could afford it. It was a simple shop-front premises, efficient, but not ostentatious. There were two rooms: the shop area was now the waiting room, where Norma, his secretary-cum-receptionist, sat and tried to keep order as much as possible, and the back room served as his office.

It was there that he was hearing the umpteenth version of the same problem he usually heard. Bad housing. Rogue landlord – often the local council. Disrepair. Rent arrears. Could he help? It was only because it was Mrs Appleby, his oldest regular whom he suspected just came for the company, that he had even taken this much time. It was at the end of a long day and he was on automatic pilot, reaching for the appropriate forms he had asked Norma to keep in ready-made packs, blaming his jitters on too much caffeine whilst surreptitiously checking his mobile for missed calls and texts. Still nothing. All this, he thought, and a family funeral looming.

Suddenly he could hear raised voices in the waiting room – first Norma's, then the deeper tones of a man. The man's voice in particular was becoming more and more insistent, until finally he heard, in rough Jamaican patois, 'I want to see him. Now!'

This wasn't the first time an angry member of the public had made such a demand, and Norma had been employed precisely because she was a formidable match for any difficult customer, both in size and in attitude. But when she came in, she looked genuinely frightened. She closed the office door and leaned back against it.

'Can you hear that, Mr C? He's scared off everyone else who was waiting. Should we call the police?'

'You know I don't like to do that unless I absolutely have to, Norma. Has he got a weapon?'

'I don't know; he might do. I'm not going to ask him!'

'A weapon?' Mrs Appleby repeated. She quickly gathered up her things. 'I'll come back tomorrow.'

Just then there was banging on the door so hard that they all jumped. Hugo slid his hand to the panic button under the desk. Because of his involvement in the Paul Matthews case, he knew he wasn't flavour of the month with some officers at Miller Street police station. But even so, if he needed them, he knew the police would be there in minutes.

'It's all right, Norma – let him in.'

No sooner had Norma moved aside than the man burst in. His eyes surveyed the room, staring at Norma, then Mrs Appleby, before coming to rest on Hugo.

'It's all right, Norma,' Hugo repeated. 'Take Mrs Appleby out. I'll see what this gentleman wants.'

Norma looked doubtful. 'If you're sure . . .'

'Yes – go on.'

When the door closed, Hugo said, 'I didn't recognize your voice. I've never heard you speak like that before.'

'Because I don't, normally.' Tony Matthews made himself comfortable in the chair Mrs Appleby had just vacated. Tilting back, he put both his feet up on Hugo's desk. 'I only put on my accent when I want to frighten people. I didn't want to have to deal with too many questions. I'm sure you wouldn't have wanted that either.'

'How's Paul?'

'I'm not discussing my brother with you.'

'I haven't heard from you in nearly three weeks.'

'I know – and it seems longer when you want a fix. Anyway, I've been busy. As you know; you were at the hospital with my dad.' Tony said the last word as if it left a bad taste in his mouth. 'Getting desperate, were you? For this?' Tony fished out a small envelope from his pocket and shook it. 'Hope there's no cameras in here.'

'There are!' Hugo hurriedly put the envelope in his inside breast pocket.

'Got something else for you too.' He slid a small solid object, double-wrapped in a Sainsbury's carrier bag, across Hugo's desk, its metallic sound scraping the surface.

'You can look,' Tony ordered, 'but don't bother taking it out, seeing as we're on *Candid Camera* and all.' But Hugo had already guessed what it was. He shuddered.

'Come on, I know you've been given guns before to hand in to the police. Besides, I thought you posh country estate types grew up with guns.'

'Not street handguns, no. How did you get it?'

Tony's face hardened. 'You know better than to ask me that. You just tell them down at Miller Street that it might be connected to JT's shooting. Maybe others too. You know the deal, Hugo. You help me out, I'll help you out.' Suddenly he stood up. 'You can get the old lady back in. I'm not stopping.'

*

Hugo thought of the incongruity of cycling to a police station in a suit with a gun in his briefcase. Good thing he wasn't casually dressed. Or Black.

He had to fight his way past a small group of protesters to get to the main entrance. Their presence was almost a fixture at Miller Street nowadays. There were two officers on the steps leading to the entrance, looking tense and watchful. The station increasingly had the air of a building under siege.

Inside was the usual disheartening mix of local residents, coming to report a crime but having next to no expectations that anything would actually be done about it. As he walked up to the main counter, he could feel the eyes of several people boring into his back.

'Oi!' he heard from behind him. 'What do you think this is? We're all waiting, you know!'

Before he could reply, a female officer came to his rescue. 'Hello, Mr Cunningham. The Super's waiting for you. Let me buzz you through.'

Miller Street, like all other police stations, existed in two distinct parts, out of necessity. There was the part the public saw. The front counter that Hugo had just been ushered past. The cells, if you were unlucky and came in the back way. Perhaps a boardroom somewhere if you were Someone Important who needed to be humoured, wooed, co-opted, or all three; a local councillor like himself, or a community leader like Reverend Matthews. But there was always a part that the public didn't see. Miller Street was an old building, an anachronism in the area; maybe that was why the corridors felt narrower, darker and more maze-like the further in he was taken, like an impenetrable core.

Up one flight of stairs, then another, then a long walk across. As Hugo followed her, the female police officer must have known what he was thinking. 'Nearly there,' she said encouragingly. She pointed at her Fitbit. 'Ten thousand steps a day, easily, just walking round here.' She pointed to some stairs in the distance. 'Up those to the top, then we're there.'

As they approached the final flight of stairs, a large, looming presence unexpectedly stepped out of a side room on to the corridor. The police officer stopped so quickly Hugo bumped into her.

'What are you doing here?' she snapped. 'You're not supposed to be on this floor!'

'Nice to see you too,' Lambert replied with a barely disguised leer. The woman looked at him in disgust.

'None of us can leave, you know that? All because of you. We're all trying to act like everything's normal while that mob out there – it's you they want! I've got kids to get back to!' There was a note of real fear in her voice. 'Oh, I forgot – you don't have a life.'

The complete lack of interest, or response, from Lambert to her outburst was worse than anything he could have said to her. Instead, he stared at Hugo.

'I read about your grandfather. Good man.' They had never met, but clearly Lambert knew who he was. Hugo looked at the older, paunchy man. He would never have taken him for someone who read obituaries in broadsheet newspapers. Instantly, Hugo chided himself for that thought. He had always considered himself above such stereotypes.

'Thank you.' Hugo's words hung in the air. He hated awkward silences, so he continued, 'He had been a recluse for several years. Dementia. I'm surprised both *The Times* and the *Telegraph* covered it; probably because he was a lifelong Conservative.'

'Oh, I didn't read it there. Papers leave out the most important things. Online, chatrooms – that's where you get the interesting stuff. Things the papers sometimes won't publish. He wasn't always a Tory, was he? He was more . . . patriotic than that when he was much younger. Links with Mosley's UM, so I heard. Wanted to preserve the British way of life. No, not British. English. English values. English culture. Like I said, good man.'

'My grandfather was no fascist!'

The police officer tapped his arm. 'Ignore him. Come on. The Super's waiting.'

Superintendent Reid's office overlooked the front of the station. From there he could see everything. His door was ajar, but the room was in semi-darkness. Reid was in uniform, standing next to the window with a tall, casually dressed Black man. As Hugo entered, the Black man turned to leave. One thing as a local councillor you remembered was a face, even if you couldn't remember names. This was the first person since he'd arrived that he knew he had met somewhere before. He was equal parts happy and uncomfortable to see him, especially here.

'Hello. Nice to see you again,' he said, extending his hand, trying not to sound too delighted.

'Have you two met?' Superintendent Reid asked.

'No, we haven't. DCI Wallace.' His voice was friendly enough, but his grip was firmer than necessary on the handshake.

'Hugo. Cunningham,' he added, as an afterthought. 'Yes, I'm sure we have.'

Wallace's grip tightened imperceptibly. 'No, we haven't. Unless I've arrested you for something . . .' Wallace laughed, but it was without warmth, and with his free hand quickly wiped under his nose. It was so swift, Reid would not have seen it in the half-darkness, but it was enough of a warning to Hugo, and Wallace knew it.

'Sorry, my mistake,' Hugo muttered, withdrawing his hand.

'That's okay, Mr Cunningham. I know you meet a lot of people in your line of work. It's easy to get confused. Must have one of those faces.'

Oh no you don't, Hugo thought as he watched his retreating back. Then he remembered where he was. Reid, still by the window, was looking at him now, world-weary resignation etched on his face.

'I think I just saw Jack Lambert downstairs. He's who they want, isn't he?'

'Yes. We couldn't get him out quickly enough, so now we're all trapped here. For now. Here, have a look at this.' Reid beckoned him to come over. Hugo leaned the briefcase carefully by the side of the desk. 'All for Paul Matthews, of course. You'd think we don't have any other crimes to deal with. Here, so they won't see you.' There were more people now. Reid opened the window, just slightly. Instantly, the jeers and protests drifted up the three floors to where they were standing.

'What are they saying?'

'Oh, the usual. *Black Lives Matter* – as if white ones don't. Police racism, incompetence, inaction, cover-up: take your pick. And there's the chief culprit.' Reid jerked his head downwards. 'You can always expect to find Fee Smith in a ruck like this. No doubt she's turned up at your surgery with a list of demands about something or other. Always prolier-than-thou, these posh types. No offence,' he added, sounding as if he didn't care whether he gave offence or not.

'None taken.' Hugo felt a lurch of recognition even before he looked down. He could see a small, blonde, curly-haired woman, the distance making her even paler and more fragile than she clearly already was. 'Anyway, I understand Ms Smith doesn't believe in cooperating with any organ of the state – even a lowly councillor.'

'Well,' Reid said, 'at least there aren't any reporters tonight.' He shut the window, instantly killing the noise below, closed the blinds and switched on the lights. 'We'll have to do something soon, though. Don't want my officers to be the next gun-crime victims. Or have the station petrol-bombed. So, what was it that was so urgent you had to see me straight away? I'm sure DCI Wallace could have dealt with whatever it is.'

'I didn't want to see him,' Hugo said quickly. He picked up his briefcase and opened it. 'Someone dropped this off at my office. Thought this was the best place for it.' He shuddered. 'I hate guns.'

'Me too.' It was a rare moment of candour from Reid, which quickly passed. Taking a linen handkerchief from his trouser pocket, he gingerly lifted the weapon from its plastic bag and held it up to the light. 'I'm sure this has been doing the rounds. Don't suppose you know who brought this to you – sorry, "dropped it off", I think you said? Or that you'd tell me if you did?'

'That's the first time you've tried to get a name out of me, Superintendent. Whatever happened to "don't ask, don't tell"?'

'Mr Cunningham, I've had two shootings in less than three weeks on my patch. One dead, the other might as well be. You then bring me a common street weapon, and you think I'm not going to ask? If it turns out that this was used in either shooting, I'll have to do more than just ask. Much more.'

'Well, as I said, it was dropped off. Don't know who by.'

It was the second time Hugo had lied that night. He hoped he was as good at it as politicians were reputed to be. From the look on Reid's face, he wasn't. 'I see,' Reid said, slowly. 'DCI Wallace is briefing the team tomorrow. I'll make sure he gets this so he can send it to ballistics. Well, home for me.' He stood up and as he did so glanced out of the window again. 'Seems I spoke too soon about reporters. If you don't want your face all over Sky News, you'd better follow me out the back way.'

19

Wallace looked at his team in the briefing room. They could at least try to look awake. None of them had had to drive up from Brighton, for Christ's sake. He wondered whether they were lacklustre because of the early start on a cold February morning, or because they knew Lambert was liked for this, even though he wasn't officially a suspect. Wallace had vetted them himself, but he couldn't rule out that last possibility. He'd have to break up the team and start again if it was still like this next week.

He'd asked everyone to report where they were with their respective tasks. It was exactly three weeks since Paul Matthews had been shot. There wasn't a lot of new information; no juicy stuff to get their teeth into. It was a young team mostly, and clearly boring grunt work wasn't part of their idea of working on a sexy major investigation, but nevertheless it was necessary. Everyone knew you had to gather as much information as possible in the early days of any investigation. Trails went cold very quickly.

The gun was an interesting possibility, though. True, at the moment there was no direct link to the Paul Matthews shooting, but Hugo Cunningham's ward covered both that crime scene and Flowerfields Estate where JT was found. Ten to one there was a link to one or the other. His, he hoped.

Now he'd have to brief the Super.

*

Wallace could hear his boss having a heated conversation on the phone. He knocked on the door and waited. Eventually, he heard him replace the handset. 'Come in.'

Reid looked up at Wallace as he was shown in by a young female officer. She was one of the best-looking women at the station and was gazing at Wallace with such a potent mix of admiration and naked lust that Reid could feel himself getting hard. But, to his amazement, Wallace's reaction was a mixture of discomfort and disinterest.

'I hope you're going to tell me something I want to hear,' Reid said as soon as they were left alone. 'I've just had the Yard giving me earache about the Matthews case. Wants to know where we are with it, and whether we are really equipped to deal with this on our own.'

'These things take time, sir. You know that. Especially when nobody's talking.'

'So this will only get worse. And he's not even dead yet. I do not want to have another conversation like that!' He almost spat the words out. 'So, what do we have?'

'So far? We know Paul was shot sometime around midnight. And we know Lambert was at the Church of God Ministry that night. We've got external CCTV footage of him talking to Mrs Matthews at the door for about two minutes before he goes inside, but she can't remember what it was about. Too traumatized.'

'Can't? Or won't?' Reid asked. When Wallace said nothing, he continued, 'What about the gun?'

'We know Paul was shot by a 9mm, but we don't know whether it was that one. Should do soon, though. I've asked them to put a rush on it for ballistics and fingerprints.'

But Reid was still looking at him expectantly. 'Is that it?'

'Well, a woman came forward anonymously, with something on a man matching Lambert's description –'

'About the Matthews shooting?' Reid interrupted.

'No. She saw him following JT just before she got on a bus.'

'I don't give a shit about some bloody drug dealer! They can wipe each other out for all I care! I'm not going to lose my job if we don't solve that, but we'll all be in deep shit if we don't find who shot that boy. I for one don't plan on retiring as just a Superintendent!'

Wallace looked at his boss. For a man who must have nearly twenty years' service under his belt, he was easily rattled. Far too easily.

'Well, JT was Lambert's informant. Lambert has arrested the victim's brother several times in the past; no love lost there. Lambert was with JT and at the church on the same night, if what the woman says checks out. When Paul was found, he was wearing his brother's jacket and had his mobile. We're still interrogating the phone. All this happened close to the Matthews crime scene. But it's all circumstantial; nothing solid.'

'People have been convicted on circumstantial evidence before.'

Clearly his boss had been a desk jockey for far too long. 'Not a police officer. It has to be airtight. If it was Tony Matthews, it might have been more plausible, but even then, we don't have any solid evidence. Or a motive.'

'The jacket – how about that for a motive? Mistaken identity. Lambert could have shot him by mistake.'

'Sir, I've been running this team from the beginning. I've already considered every possible motive. Do you know what the Federation would say, let alone Slater and Gordon, if we started accusing a police officer who's not MO19, not firearms trained, of shooting the son of one of our most prominent local citizens in the head? Without hard evidence? Let's leave Lambert aside for a moment; yes, mistaken ID is a motive, but Tony Matthews is a drug dealer – much bigger than JT. Any number of people could have it in for him – or anyone else in the Matthews family. It's also possible that Paul could have been in a gang himself. Unlikely, I think, but it can't be ruled out. Maybe he didn't want to join a gang and paid the ultimate price for refusing. It might be a racist shooting . . .'

'It might be another type of hate crime. Maybe his father is some kind of zealot about gays. Condemning them with fire and brimstone sermons, trying to scare them straight. Someone getting revenge on him that way?'

For a moment Wallace wondered whether Reid had heard the rumours too. It made him reply more sharply than he had intended.

'And exactly how do you know this, sir? Not every Black man hates gays!'

'Take that tone out of your voice when you're talking to me, DCI Wallace! I'm sorry if you think that's racist, but there we are.'

No, he hadn't heard. He felt some of the tension leave his body.

'Look, I'm sorry, sir. The parents, these local activists, the Yard – I know everyone wants a quick arrest. I want to make the right one. Your suggestion – of course I've considered it, but I think we're just clutching at straws. We're floundering around in the dark until we get some hard evidence. Let's hope something comes up with the gun, either way.'

Suddenly Reid leaned forward and stared at Wallace. 'Why are you so keen to row Lambert out of this? I'd have thought you of all people would be dying to kick in his door and nick him. You saw how he was last Monday. Everyone knows how he feels about Blacks and other minorities.'

'Really? So why wasn't he sacked before now, sir? Or at least suspended?' Wallace watched the flush rise up Reid's neck from his collar to the roots of his greying hair. 'All my years in the Army, then on the job – think I haven't come across types like Lambert before? They love jobs like these to abuse the little power they have. I don't worry about them; they're easy to spot. It's the ones who know how to hide it with PC words: they're really dangerous.'

It was the ping of Wallace's mobile that broke the awkward silence that followed. He looked at it. 'Got to go, sir. Ballistics – they've got something.'

As he drove deeper into the Home Counties, leaving London further and further behind, Hugo now found himself looking forward to this funeral. He wasn't glad his grandfather was dead, of course; it was just that with every passing mile he felt he was returning to something reassuringly familiar. Where everyone looked and sounded the same as he did. Where it wasn't a crime to be privileged. Where the smell of poverty, and the disappointment and low expectations on the faces of the people he was charged to help but couldn't, didn't haunt him constantly.

St Stephen's was a quintessentially English church, now too large for the tiny Buckinghamshire village it served – an indication of how much of the rural community had died off in the three hundred years or so since it had been erected. The two oldest buildings in the village were the church and the house in which generations of his family had always lived, the line becoming more illustrious and aristocratic the further back it went. He was the last of the line, and the first not to have a title.

As his car crunched on to the gravel outside the church, he was struck by how well-dressed everyone was. All in black, of course – not the cheap market-stall black worn by the people he saw every day, but the deep rich black of Savile Row. Some were genuinely sad, but others looked anything but mournful. They were smiling condescendingly at local villagers as they walked up the path to the church, glossy and sleek as ravens, clutching their invitations smugly as if they had been invited to a society wedding instead of a funeral.

As he got out of the car, he heard someone call out, 'Young Mr C!' There was only one person alive who would still call him that. He walked over to the stone wall, which stood like a barrier between the locals and those attending the funeral.

'Hello, Joe.' Hugo looked at him. The elderly man was not dressed in black and Hugo knew that, stickler for formality as he was, this meant he had not been invited. He jerked his head in the direction of the church. 'Why aren't you coming? You and grandfather always got on very well together.'

'Well, it's been a while since I was head gardener. Don't think there was room for the likes of me. I'm not complaining, mind. I mean, I would have liked to have paid my respects, but when you've lived as long as your grandfather and I have, you know a lot of people – especially him, what with his Regiment mates, people up from London and the like. But there's going to be a memorial service later in the year; most of the folk round here will be going to that.'

Hugo didn't have to ask whose idea that was. He was embarrassed, but the old man in front of him genuinely didn't seem to mind, which somehow made it worse. He put his hand on his frail shoulder and squeezed it, then went into the church, slipping into the front pew next to his mother just before the service began.

'Hello, darling.' Margaret Cunningham gave him a kiss on the cheek that somehow managed to be completely without warmth.

'Late as always. I thought you were going to arrive much earlier.' She pursed her lips. 'You're only just in time.'

'I've just seen Joe,' Hugo hissed. 'Why wasn't he invited?'

'Joe?' For a moment, his mother looked nonplussed. 'Oh! Well, there were a lot of people, and we couldn't invite everyone. Not ex-staff.'

'Not even when they've known the deceased for fifty years?'

'I daresay some people here have known him almost that long. And,' she lowered her voice conspiratorially, 'there were some other people that I thought you should meet. No one gets into the House without help.'

'Really? A grandfather with connections to an organization Oswald Mosley set up is no recommendation nowadays. The optics are bad. And I'm tired of apologizing. Do you think I want any part of that?'

'This is not the time or place, Hugo.' And with that, his mother ended their discussion in the way she had done so many times over the years.

The number of people who actually bothered to attend the grave-side was a great deal smaller than those attending the funeral, which seemed to Hugo to be missing the whole point. Still, there were quite a number. Mostly extended family.

One of whom he hadn't expected to see. At all.

He was about to walk over to her when he was collared by Oliver Fisher, a cousin so distant he couldn't remember which side of the family he was from. Strangely, he seemed happy, though whether it was to see him or because of the newborn baby he was holding, he couldn't tell. His wife, Mary, was with him.

'Hugo! Why don't you come and see us, you old bastard? We live in London too remember; North London's not a foreign country.

Why should the family only meet at these kind of events? I mean, I know there are millions of us, but still.'

'It's good to see you too, Oliver.' Hugo touched the child's head. 'What's his name?'

'Still deciding. I think Edward.'

'And I think not!' Mary said.

Hugo laughed and kissed Mary on the cheek. 'Hello, Mary. How's life in Chambers?'

'Okay, when I was last there. I want to lose the baby weight before I go back, but I've literally just had this one; my first outing since the birth and it's at a funeral. I hope I drop the weight quick; I need to get back into my suits and I don't know what my Senior Clerk is doing to my practice. Out of sight, out of mind there.' She paused. 'That near-murder in your area . . .'

'Which one?' he quipped.

'Come on, Hugo, that's a bit sick. The one that was in all the papers, with the church connection. Apparently, they want someone in my Chambers to do it. Still all very hush-hush, so you didn't hear it from me.'

'Prosecuting?'

'Defending. I don't think she'll do it, though. She's a friend, but I haven't told her about you, or that we're related – by marriage anyway.'

'Enough of work. When are you going to get one of these, then?' Oliver asked, patting his son's head.

'I thought only women asked that question.'

'If you want to be an MP, you'd better get it sorted. I don't care how trendy the Tories think they are nowadays, these things matter.'

'Have you ever thought, Ollie, that this might be the reason I don't come and visit?' Out of the corner of his eye, Hugo saw the woman he had recognized earlier walking away. 'Anyway, good to see you both again. Excuse me.'

He walked towards the retreating figure as quickly as he could without drawing attention to himself. When he got close enough, he called out, 'Fiona. Fiona, wait!'

He wasn't sure she would stop, but she did.

'I didn't see you in the church,' he continued, slightly out of breath. 'I'm glad you've come. I must say, though, I'm surprised to see you.'

'Why? He was my grandfather too.'

'Because you cut us all off. You didn't have to, especially not me.' He paused, before continuing, 'I saw you, outside Miller Street . . .'

Fee Smith scowled at him, her contempt obvious. 'Inside, right? Shows what side you're on. Look, this doesn't change things.' She waved her hand dismissively at the assembled mourners. 'None of this is part of my life any more.'

'You can't get rid of the trappings of our class that easily, or what people might know about Grandfather. God knows, I've tried.'

'Not hard enough. Tory councillor? Would-be MP?' She almost spat the words out with disgust.

'And your comrades in London, you think they don't know about you?' Hugo was angry now too. 'At least I'm not a hypocrite!'

'Aren't you?' Fee lowered her voice and leaned towards him. 'Planning on a big political career, Hugo? Still got that little problem? I'm surprised you've got this far without anyone finding out.'

Hugo leapt back as if he had been scalded.

'What?' She laughed derisively. 'Thought I didn't know?'

He didn't even try to stop her as she walked away. He felt as if he had been punched in the stomach. If she knew, how many others did?

He went back into the church. It was completely empty. He sat in the darkest, quietest, most secluded corner. There was only one thing that would help him now, and it wasn't prayer.

He fished the envelope Tony Matthews had given him out of his inside breast pocket and stared at it before taking out its contents. He opened the little sachet of white powder, poured it on the wooden pew and expertly cut it into lines.

20

Lee picked up a copy of *The Times* on the way into Chambers. A quick glance at the headline, echoed in various forms by the front pages of all the folded and stacked newspapers, told her the story of the hour: SHOCK ARREST IN CHOIRBOY CASE. The words were different, but the main story was the same. Reading on, she didn't know what was more surprising: the fact that it was a police officer who had been arrested, or the fact that there had been such an early arrest at all.

She had only met Jack Lambert once, when she was representing Clive Omartian. She would have been hard pushed to describe him physically on the basis of that meeting, but the photograph brought back memories of that ugly encounter. It seemed to be the same one all the papers were using. He had put on weight and had lost more hair, but it was definitely him. It wasn't clear whether he was handcuffed or not, but he was flanked by grim-faced uniformed officers and the expression on his face made him look like a caged animal.

When she arrived at Maple Court, Dean, Tom's junior, was alone in the Clerks' Room. He was sitting staring open-mouthed at the large flat-screen television mounted high on the opposite wall. On seeing Lee, he hurriedly tried to busy himself with work.

'Don't mind me, Dean. I wasn't supposed to be in today, anyway. Where's Tom?'

'In with Mr Townsend, then he said he had to go somewhere. Whatever's going on, he's not telling me. That means it's big.' Dean shrugged. 'Funny, he said something about wanting to talk to you urgently. Is that why you've come in?'

'No.' Now Lee was watching the screen too. A television in a Clerks' Room, as well as online news sources, far from being a distraction, was often very profitable for Chambers. As soon as there was any news of a serious offence having been committed – and often before – Tom would be working the phones, using all of his many and varied contacts to ferret out information and get the brief into Chambers. Now, Sky News was streaming news of Lambert's arrest in the early hours of the morning. The sound was off, as usual, but the subtitles were on and the collage of images alone more than told the story. There was a photograph of a smiling Paul Matthews in his chorister's robes, now depressingly familiar; of his tearful parents arriving at the hospital as they did every day; and of Lambert himself being led into the station, with irate protesters waving placards in the background. Oddly, there was something like resignation in his eyes, which the newspaper picture hadn't caught, as if he had expected this all along.

'Any idea why he wants to see me?' Lee continued, not taking her eyes from the screen. A small, thin, angry-looking woman she had never seen before was speaking a mile a minute to camera. FEE SMITH, COMMUNITY ACTIVIST flashed up at the bottom of the screen. Suddenly, she found herself squinting. The camera had turned to DCI Wallace, unusually in full uniform. It was the first time she'd seen him since Speech Day at Fordyce Park three weeks ago.

'Never thought I'd see Danny Wallace in a police uniform.'

'You know him?' Dean asked.

'I went to school with him.' It was a bit more than that, but she wasn't about to discuss her private life with her Junior Clerk. 'Honestly, he's the last person I ever thought would join the force. He was always getting nicked, for one thing.'

'Really?' From Dean's twenty-something perspective, Wallace was suddenly interesting. He nodded in approval. 'We need more police like that. You know, not too squeaky clean.'

Lee thought of Lambert. 'Not too dirty though, either. Well, tell Tom I'm in my room if he wants to speak to me.'

As she walked out of the Clerks' Room, Lee looked to her left, down the long corridor towards Giles's room, and wondered what the two most influential people in Chambers could possibly be discussing.

'What's happening to my practice, Tom?' Giles Townsend KC asked without preamble as he picked up the solitary brief on his desk and let it fall, distastefully, from his fingers. It landed with a soft plop on the leather-topped surface. He leaned back in his chair and looked up expectantly at his Senior Clerk.

Tom had not been invited to sit down and did not expect to be. He knew, from previous experience, that Giles Townsend liked to leave him in no doubt as to who was boss, particularly since taking Silk. Ever the tactician, Tom weighed up the best approach to take.

First, reassurance.

'Well, it's early days yet, sir. Your appointment is still fairly recent. It takes time to build up a Silk's practice.' Particularly if it wasn't much good before.

Townsend's voice was icy. 'Forgive me, Tom, for observing that comment is total bollocks. Taking Silk must make a difference, otherwise so many people wouldn't apply for it every year.'

Tom looked at the Head of Chambers. Evidently, he did not

appreciate the distinction between making a difference and working miracles.

Next, stroking the ego.

'It's not that work isn't coming in, sir, but I think, frankly, it's beneath you. After all, what if your peers – not to mention solicitors – saw you doing work like that?'

Evidently, this was the better tactic. Giles looked slightly mollified, but only slightly.

'You may have a point there, but what are you doing to improve matters? Lee Mitchell's shelf is groaning under the weight of work and *this*,' he said, jabbing at the brief with his fountain pen, 'is all I've had today. First new instructions in months! This can't go on, Tom.' Suddenly, Giles leaned forward. 'What about this case in the papers? The Black kid in a coma?'

'What about it, sir?'

'Don't give me that. Everyone knows that they've arrested a police officer. Now, you're one of the most well-connected clerks in the Temple. That's why we employ you. You must know more than I do.' When Tom didn't reply, Giles added, slowly, 'I would hate to think Chambers was mistaken as to your abilities in this regard, Tom. For your sake.' He leaned back in his chair.

'At least I won't have to worry about Lee Mitchell nabbing the case; after all, I prosecute, and I've acted for the Police Federation. That should cover all the bases. Somehow, I don't think she's on the Police Commissioner's Christmas card list. That will be all, Tom, thank you. Oh, just a minute,' Giles added as his Senior Clerk reached the door. As Tom turned to face him, he asked with some concern, 'Just how badly injured is this boy?'

'Still on life support, the papers say. He's not out of the woods yet.'

'So there's a possibility . . . well, you always need a Silk in a murder case.'

Even Tom, no sentimentalist himself, didn't expect that. Christ, what a cold bastard. As he looked at his Head of Chambers, he hoped it didn't show. 'I'll see what I can find out.'

'You do that. Shut the door on the way out, will you?'

Back in the corridor, Tom leaned his back on the closed door. Arrogant prick. He breathed out the tension that had been collecting in his lungs, knowing that the heavy polished wooden door was so thick it would muffle the sound. Then he straightened up, fixed his tie and headed for Lee's room.

Lee had just finished reading the article about Lambert when Tom knocked on her open door. 'Come in.'

One look at his agitated face as he entered told her that Dean was right. Something was up. Something big. He closed the door behind him.

'Glad you're in, Ms Mitchell. I'll get straight to the point. The defence brief on the Choirboy case has come in. It's a real coup for Chambers, as you can imagine.'

'We've got that? Already?' What with the article in the paper and Tom's news, it was slightly surreal – like receiving information in stereo. She was glad she'd never made the mistake of underestimating Tom. Like everyone else in Chambers, she knew he was personally untrustworthy, devious and Machiavellian, but professionally there was no doubting he was good at his job – perhaps even because of his personal shortcomings.

'God, you must have been working on getting that since the story first broke. That's major, even for you. How did you do it?'

'Don't worry about that. The point is, Chambers hasn't got it – *you* have. Both the solicitor and lay client want you to do it.'

'Lambert? From Miller Street? No way. I've only met him once but I would have thought I'd be the last person he would want.'

'He specifically asked for you. Won't accept anyone else – not even Mr Townsend, and believe me, he'd be very keen to do it.'

'I see,' Lee said, slowly. 'I've never acted for him before, and out of everyone in the Temple, he wants me? Even turning down the Head of Chambers? Seems to me this is just about having a Black barrister. If so, he can find someone else.'

'You're not the only Black barrister around, Ms Mitchell. Everyone knows you're a fighter, even on hopeless cases. Maybe that's what he's counting on.'

'He'd better not count on that too much with me. I still know people who live near where it happened.'

'No, Ms Mitchell. I know you. If you took this on, your professional pride wouldn't let you screw it up. Nothing like someone with a point to prove. Believe me, I should know.'

'Anyway, there's no sense in us having this discussion because I'm not doing it. Whatever his reasons. I'm sure he won't have any problem getting adequate representation elsewhere. Besides, you know I don't need the work that badly. I've got back-to-back fixtures and trials lined up for months ahead.' She took a sip of her coffee. 'Who's the solicitor anyway?'

Silence. 'Brendan Donnelly.'

'What? Are you seriously asking me to accept instructions from him after all that happened?'

'And are *you* seriously going to reject instructions from a solicitor on a major case because of something that happened over a year ago?'

'What do you think? I can't work with someone I can't trust, Tom.'

'Why not? You work with me. And don't bother trying to deny you don't trust me. I don't care either way.'

'I wasn't going to. But that's different, Tom. You know it.'

Tom crossed his arms over his chest. 'Let me speak frankly, Ms Mitchell. The problem with you barristers is that you think you run Chambers. You don't; I do. You also think you're bigger than Chambers, but Maple Court is more important than all of you. I've been here man and boy, when it was just me and Mr Townsend and he didn't have a pot to piss in, in spite of all the airs and graces he has nowadays. My primary loyalty –'

'– is to yourself,' Lee interrupted.

'No, it's to these Chambers, which I helped to build, over any individual barrister. Luck had fuck all to do with getting this brief. I worked hard to get it here, and you were part of that deal. This kid's likely to croak too, so it might even be a murder trial. Jack Lambert, potentially on trial for murdering a Black teenager? It's Stephen Lawrence with cops. Do you really think I'm going to let you turn this down?'

'You're not going to "let" me do anything. I just won't allow myself to be used. End of.' Lee paused, before continuing, 'If you're speaking to me like this, you must already think I've got one foot out the door. If so, I could walk out of here and into another Chambers tomorrow. You know Devereux want me to join them.'

'And just how long do you think that offer will be on the table if you're reported to the Bar Council for breaking the cab rank rule? Refusing instructions that you are competent to accept? Think they'll want you then? Or anywhere else?'

Lee stared at him. This was getting dirty. 'And how are the Bar Council going to know? Are you going to tell them?'

There was a long pause before Tom replied. 'I'm sure that, between them, Lambert and Donnelly are more than capable of working that out.'

'With a little help from you, you mean. Well, I'll take my chances.'

'Will you, Lee? Really? After the last time? You know, once before the Bar Council – that's unfortunate. Twice? That's a pattern. One that can seriously derail a career.'

Lee blinked. She didn't think even Tom would stoop this low. 'You bastard! You know the reasons for that.'

'I wouldn't want the whole of the Bar to know I'd had a nervous breakdown either. Not when my career was well and truly on the rise. And you know what the Bar's like. More leaks than a sieve. Anything to get an advantage over the competition. A criminal brief who can't hack it, who cracks under pressure . . . how much high-profile work do you think you'll get then?'

But Lee wasn't going down without a fight. 'I'll take it to Chambers Committee, then. You think they'll keep on a clerk, even a Senior Clerk, who's trying to blackmail a member of Chambers?'

'Who do you think they'll choose, Ms Mitchell? You, or the person who makes sure they're in court every day? You'll never get enough support for that. You're not senior enough to have that kind of clout on your own – not yet. Plus, you've been so busy being independent, ploughing your own furrow, that you don't have a network of support. You've got one good friend here, and she's on maternity leave. The law's a blood sport. People on the outside think it's so genteel just because barristers walk round in fancy dress and have posh voices, but they don't know the half of it. Queensberry Rules, my arse. They'll be dying to get a crack at your work. We both know that.'

The silence echoed round the room. When Lee next spoke, she

hated that uncertain, tentative voice which she barely recognized as her own.

'My episode – that was three years ago, Tom. Are you going to hold this over my head forever?' As she looked at him, something like a conscience flickered across his face, but was gone just as quickly. She shook her head. 'I should never have said anything to you . . .'

'You think I hadn't guessed? You were spending more time here than at home, round the clock, seven days a week; trying to prove you weren't some token . . . the fact that you let it slip to me, of all people, meant you couldn't tell anyone else. I bet your family still don't know, do they?'

Lee got up from her desk and walked towards the window. The lovely view across Temple Gardens was all but obscured by a grey and overcast sky, a light drizzle completing a miserable day. As a woman, especially a Black one, the stakes were higher, the pressure greater – and it was further to fall. All it took was one mistake, one sign of weakness . . .

Tom said what she was thinking. 'It's a long way down, Ms Mitchell.'

When she next spoke, her voice was calmer and more composed.

'A clerk reporting one of his own barristers to the Bar Council. Blackmail, pure and simple,' she said, without turning round.

'Desperate times, desperate measures, Ms Mitchell. A brief like this would boost the reputation of Chambers, that's all I'm concerned about. Nothing personal, you understand. In fact, I have more respect for you than most of them here, including Giles Townsend – though I would deny it if it ever left this room. You're a grafter. You haven't had anything handed to you on a plate. Neither have I. That's why I hope you won't do anything that could lead to you getting disbarred. The choice is yours.'

Finally, she turned round to face her clerk. 'If I take this, I want your word –'

'You have it.'

'Shut up and listen. I want your word that it ends here. I won't have you holding this over my head any more, do you understand me? Everyone's got secrets. I'm sure you've got a shedload and I'll make it my business to find out. I can fight dirty too.'

'I've no doubt. But you won't have to. You have my word as your Senior Clerk and fellow professional.'

'Then we don't have anything more to discuss.'

Tom nodded. 'I'll bring the brief up myself.'

'No. I don't want you back up here. Give it to Dean.'

Tom opened his mouth as if to say something, then changed his mind. He nodded curtly, then left the room.

21

Wallace was waiting to cross the road to get to St Luke's. The hospital was big, sprawling and ugly. Clearly, it had been built with no thought of aesthetics. The original structure was well over a hundred years old, and you could tell from the mishmash of architecture the different decades when extensions were added to the main structure, concluding in brutal 1960s concrete. He normally preferred to be unobtrusive, but as he went through the main entrance and looked at the signs to the different wards and departments, he realized he had neither the time nor inclination to look for Intensive Care himself. He went up to Reception. The middle-aged woman on the counter smiled at him as he approached.

'Intensive Care, please?' He flashed his warrant card. The woman's smile became even broader. 'Paul Matthews.'

'ICU? Fourth floor, Douglas Wing,' she said. 'Just follow the noise when you get there.'

Wallace was surprised at how small the ICU was. It was reassuring to see the high ratio of medical staff to patients. It was clear that Paul Matthews was getting the best care. However, not even that could change what he and everyone else knew: that there was no hope. The only people who didn't want to acknowledge that were his parents.

It wasn't a noise so much as a low hum drifting out into the open-plan area of the ward. As Wallace looked around, trying to work out exactly where it was coming from, he saw a doctor about his own age, maybe a little older, looking at him quizzically.

'Can I help you?' His voice was authoritative but harassed.

'DCI Wallace, here to see Paul Matthews.' He went to show him his warrant card, but the man stopped him.

'No need for that, officer. The PC guarding Paul gave a good description of you. Reverend Matthews too. He said you might come. The family are very careful about who they actually let into their son's room – with good reason. I don't think anyone should be there, really.' He glanced towards a closed door to his left. 'I'm Malcolm Weir. I operated on Paul.'

'Any change?'

'In his condition? There isn't, and there won't be. He was shot in the head. There's no brain activity at all, and that's been the case since he was first brought in. I've told his parents this over and over. I think the father is beginning to accept it, but the mother? She may believe in miracles, but I don't. Plus, she's starting to worry me. She may be on the brink of a nervous breakdown.' He looked at Wallace hopefully. 'Maybe if they heard it from you . . .'

Wallace shook his head. 'It's not my place. You know that.'

Malcolm Weir looked embarrassed. 'Sorry. It's just that . . . well, you can see how small we are. He's not even the only gunshot victim in here. There are others we could actually help . . .' His voice trailed away. 'Sounds cold to you, I know.'

'No, I appreciate your position. But if you want me to tell Reverend Matthews to switch off his son's life support so that you can have the bed, you're out of luck.' He pointed to where the surgeon had glanced. 'Over there?'

Wallace wasn't surprised Paul Matthews had a private room. But the door he opened led not directly into his room, but on to a short corridor, at the end of which he recognized the young, uniformed PC he had posted to stand guard. Nearby was a small group of middle-aged and elderly women clustered in a huddle, murmuring in prayer, some kneeling, some sitting. Wallace suppressed a smile at the bewildered look on the young officer's face. Obviously, he had never been at a prayer vigil before. For Wallace it was vaguely familiar, bringing back memories, reminding him of why he had left all that behind.

The women were so intent on what they were doing he thought he could get past without them noticing. No such luck. He felt a tug on his arm. 'Daniel Wallace? Is it you?'

Wallace looked round, then down, at the petite woman standing next to him. 'Mrs Mitchell, isn't it? Leanne's mum?'

'She hates being called that now. You and me, we must be the only two people left who still know her by her full name. Good to see you, son. You've done well for yourself. Though it's a shame to meet you again like this. I was . . . surprised to hear you'd joined the police. Detective Chief Inspector too!'

'I think "shocked" is the word you're looking for, Mrs Mitchell, the path I was on. Don't worry – so was everyone else.'

'You know, I always believed you had good in you.' She smiled. 'Somewhere.'

'Yeah, somewhere is right. Deep, deep down!' Wallace would have laughed if the mood wasn't so sombre. 'What made you believe in me, though?'

'Well, Desmond Matthews didn't give up on you and other youngsters. Some it worked with, others not – including in his own family. But also –' she paused for a few seconds before continuing – 'did you know my son was called Daniel? The baby who died? He would have been Leanne's big brother had he lived. Did she ever tell you about him?'

'No.'

'Well, we don't talk about him much . . .' Her voice trailed away. Then she squeezed his arm. 'I like the name.'

Out of the corner of his eye, Wallace noticed some of the other women now seemed rather less concerned with their prayers and more with him. He put his hand on her shoulder. 'Good seeing you again, Mrs Mitchell. But,' he said gently, his hand on the doorknob, 'I'd better go in. Are both his parents here?'

'Round the clock. They're always here.'

It was hard to get over the impact of seeing such a young person wired up to so many machines. Paul was almost the same height as his brother, Tony, but much skinnier. Lying there, dwarfed by the equipment, he seemed very small. At fifteen, he hadn't yet filled out to manhood. The depression of his face and skull where the bullet had entered was visible even beneath the heavy bandages. There was some grime music turned down low, from an artist Wallace didn't recognize, coming out of a small speaker next to a phone on top of the bedside cabinet.

Reverend and Mrs Matthews were on either side of the bed. Mrs Matthews was to the left, holding her son's hand, stroking his arm. Standing by the door, Wallace could see that, whilst Reverend Matthews made no attempt to touch his son, unlike his wife, as he turned to face him grief and helplessness were etched on his face. Slowly, he got up and went to the far corner of the room, signalling for Wallace to join him.

'Where's the FLO?' Wallace asked, keeping his voice down so Mrs Matthews wouldn't hear.

'Family Liaison? I sent her home. I don't have a problem with her, but not at my son's hospital bed. What can she do here?'

'Look, maybe we should talk outside,' Wallace whispered.

'Eloise? She's so wrapped up in Paulie, she wouldn't hear us. Besides, I'd have to face all the church sisters if we go out there. I know they mean well, but . . .' His voice trailed off.

'What?' Wallace asked, gently.

'They have faith. Even I'm starting to doubt, and I'm their preacher. All my life I've been a faithful man of God, and He lets this happen? To Paul?' He shook his head. When he next spoke, his voice was heavy with resignation. 'The son I had is not coming back. Mr Weir's shown me the scans. He'll be blind in one eye and brain-damaged. That's the very best we can hope for – if he ever wakes up, I mean.' He looked back at the bed.

'You know what it's like seeing my son lying there and not be able to help him?' He was almost choking on the words. Wallace watched him try to compose himself before he spoke again. 'Anyway, you're on official business, I assume?'

Wallace looked at Paul. 'I was hoping to ask him some questions, but . . .'

'You can ask him whatever you want, but don't expect an answer. We keep saying to him "blink", "squeeze my hand" . . . we even brought his music in today; we thought him hearing his favourite tunes would help. All the stuff I used to say he couldn't play at home; it was too ungodly.' He started to cry now. 'But nothing.'

'How's Tony taking it? I've been hearing things. I hope he's not going to try and do anything stupid.'

'He's no son of mine!' The venom was a shock, in total contrast to his grief. 'I don't care what he does or what happens to him! Paul was wearing his jacket when he got shot. They were probably looking for him. Eloise keeps saying it's her fault – no, it's his. His fault!'

Just then Wallace heard raised voices outside the door. His officer was speaking to someone – a man, possibly in his fifties, but the voice was unfamiliar. He went to investigate.

'Keep it down. What's going on?' he asked, closing the door behind him. Thankfully, the Greek chorus of churchwomen had disappeared. They were alone, at least for the moment.

'This man says he wants to speak to the victim, sir. Says it's all been arranged, but I don't know anything about it.'

'Oh yes?' Wallace looked at the older man. 'Who with? This is my investigation, and no one said anything to me.'

'I contacted the DPS; they arranged it with Superintendent Reid. Not trying to step on your toes.' The man extended his hand. 'Mike Collier –'

'– from the IOPC,' the PC concluded, barely managing to keep the disgust out of his voice.

Wallace frowned. No need to be impolite; the Independent Office for Police Conduct had a job to do, after all, even if that job was to investigate police officers. This PC was too young in service to have had a run-in with the police watchdog already, so he was just going on what he had heard. What all officers heard about the IOPC. None of it good. His suspicion was understandable.

'Who sees Paul Matthews is up to me. Lambert's been arrested for attempted murder, so this case is now *sub judice*. You have no right to speak to the victim.'

'If you'd arrested him when you said you would, DCI Wallace, instead of bringing it forward and doing it in the middle of the night, it wouldn't be *sub judice* and I'd be entitled to speak to him.'

'Criminal trials take precedence over IOPC misconduct investigations.'

'I know. I used to be on the job too. Look, I know you know we've been keeping tabs on Lambert for years.'

'I won't let you jeopardize this investigation. Your best result would be to get him dismissed. If we get a conviction, he'll do a long stretch – maybe even life.'

'Not much evidence against him at the moment, though, as far as I know. You really think you can prove this to a jury with what you have right now? Beyond reasonable doubt? We would only have to prove it's likely he could have done it. True, he wouldn't get any jail time, but at least he'd be out of the force where he couldn't do this again.'

'Yes, he could. If he's capable of it, he'll do it as a civilian. What's to stop him?'

'We do what we can. We both do. So, are you going to let me see the boy?'

Reverend Matthews came out to join them. 'What's the matter?' he asked.

Before Wallace could say anything, Collier stepped forward and offered his hand. 'Reverend Matthews? Mike Collier from the IOPC. I wrote to you, and we spoke on the phone.'

'I've met your boss, Clare Johnson, on other business.' Reverend Matthews shook his head, sadly. 'Never thought I'd be involved with the IOPC like this.'

'He wants to speak to Paul,' Wallace said. 'You don't have to agree.'

'No, you don't,' Mike Collier agreed. 'But on behalf of the IOPC, I'd very much appreciate it. After all, as I was saying to DCI Wallace, we're all on the same side.'

The PC standing guard made a snorting noise. Wallace gave him a warning look. 'It's up to you, Reverend.'

Reverend Matthews sighed. 'Well, you won't get anything out of my son. But I'm willing to let you try – for a few minutes at least.'

Eloise Matthews looked up at the three men who now entered the room and crowded round her son's bed.

'Eloise,' her husband said, 'this is Mr Collier from the IOPC.' She looked puzzled. 'Independent Office for Police Conduct. He . . . he wants to ask Paul some questions.'

'Why?' It was the first time Wallace had heard her say anything since he'd arrived.

'Anything he says, or shows us, might get us one step closer to who did this, Mrs Matthews,' Mike Collier said gently. 'Any kind of response at all.'

'Says? He hasn't said anything to me, his father, the doctors, the police . . .' Her voice was rising with every word, with a thin edge of hysteria. 'What makes you think *you* –'

'Please, Eloise.' Her husband was firm. 'Let him do his job.'

Whatever had flared up was quickly extinguished. 'If you think it's best, Desmond,' she said, dully.

Collier stepped forward. Wallace was surprised to see real compassion in his face as he looked down at Paul.

'Paul.' He touched his arm. 'Hello, son . . .'

His mother's shriek split the room. She leapt out of her seat and flew at Collier. 'Don't you dare touch him! He's not your son! He's not your son!'

Instantly, Collier stepped back.

'That's enough. Let's go.' As Wallace took Collier's arm, he could see Reverend Matthews grappling with his wife, looking at her as if he'd never seen her before.

'Bet you're happy that I had to leave,' Collier said as they stepped outside.

'So you wouldn't compromise my investigation? You're right; I'm not unhappy. I know you and Lambert were mates . . .'

162

'*Were*. Long past tense. I've never hidden that. The amount of times he's been reported to the IOPC, think I like having that always flung in my face? Anyway, I didn't do anything wrong in there.' Collier was defensive and it showed.

'Not saying you did. But you had your chance. You won't get another.'

22

Lee had been in court every day since her showdown with Tom, which was a blessing. She had only seen him once since then, and he had smiled at her benignly, as well he might – like the cat that got the cream. It was too much to stomach. She might be experienced and wily in the criminal courts, but she hadn't counted on being so completely outfoxed by her own Senior Clerk. Now she was boxed into a corner, and no mistake. But she had given her word. She would have to take Lambert's case. As strange as it was to think her integrity would be measured on the basis of whether she would be prepared to defend someone like him, she wouldn't back out now.

Dealing with other trials, it was easy to try, at least, to put her present predicament out of her mind. But there were some things that couldn't be put off.

It was the end of the day. Late, even for Chambers. The only people still there apart from herself were Tom, who knew how important the next hour or so would be; and the person who was now knocking on her door.

'Come in.'

'Hello, Lee. It's been a while.'

Over a year, in fact – since the Omartian case, and what she had found out about Brendan during that trial. His voice, South London with Irish overtones, still sounded the same. Although she missed him, since that trial she had felt she hadn't known him at all. That was the last time they had worked together. He was still wearing the same scruffy, shabby raincoat he had owned for as long as she had known him, but underneath was an expensive suit for someone who had fallen so far from grace.

'Yes.' This had been so long in coming it was hard now to know where to begin. 'If we're going to be working together, we need to clear the air.'

'Yeah, Tom said as much. He even suggested we do it over drinks. You know, like the old days.' Brendan's smile faded as he saw the expression on Lee's face.

'I only drink with friends, Brendan.'

'Okay, I'll let you have that one. How many more of these zingers am I going to have to put up with?'

'I don't know. You wanted me to take this brief, remember?'

'Not with some sarcasm on the side. It's in the past, Lee. You had good reason to be fucking pissed off at me because of Omartian, but you know what happened to me after that. I turned myself into the Law Society, remember? I lost my firm. Fifteen years ago I started off working for someone else; now I'm back once again working for someone else and, I'll tell you, it's a lot harder second time round. Why my wife stayed with me through this I'll never know.'

Lee glanced at the beautifully cut suit. 'You don't look like you're doing too badly.'

'This?' Brendan picked at the lapel. 'It's my only one! A monkey in classy *schmutter* is still a monkey, and I'm getting paid peanuts to prove it.' He paused. 'Can I sit down, at least?'

Lee nodded. Whilst the request was polite, the kind of friendship they used to have didn't need such formalities. It was another sign of how estranged they had become.

'So, why me?' she asked as he settled into the chair.

'Do you mean why did I brief you on Lambert, or why did I fuck you over in the Omartian case? That *is* what you think, isn't it?'

'Both. I'm dying to hear your reason for Omartian. After all, you've had a long time to think one up.' She stared at him, a sense of betrayal rising in her chest. 'We used to be friends, Brendan. Good friends, for this profession.'

He looked away. 'There's no fancy reason. I was desperate and greedy, running a Legal Aid firm on a shoestring. Throw in a pregnant wife and there you have it. A perfect recipe for temptation.' Lee saw his face flush. 'I know. Pathetic and self-serving, but there it is. Now with Lambert . . . this is my second chance, Lee. And he wouldn't let me keep the brief unless I could get you on board.'

'Believe me, if I could get out of this, I would. If I did, Lambert would drop you like a stone. Then what would you have? Nothing. Except a taste of what it feels like to be done over by someone you thought you could trust.' Lee leaned forward now, memory making her angry. Anger making her words tumble out one over the other. 'Omartian stalked me, did you know that? He made an implied threat about David, he had Ray's face chewed up for trying to warn me . . . And now Lambert. You know the kind of man he is. Even you can't have changed that much. Are things so bad that you've been reduced to this?'

'Yes, things *are* that bad, Lee. High-earning briefs like you can afford morals. When I had my own firm, I could too. Now I've got my family in some poxy rented flat, and I'm working as second flunky for some kid I trained, morals are too expensive for me. When I get back on my feet I'll be able to afford them again. You've acted for any number of low-lifes. They haven't all been the victims of some massive state conspiracy, and you know it.'

'At least I know who I'm dealing with. I never expect them to be anything else. I'll take a good honest criminal any day over a disloyal solicitor and a man who's a disgrace to his uniform.'

'All right! All right! Look, I worked it out about Ray. I didn't know about you or your fella. I didn't think I could feel any worse after what happened, but I do. Satisfied?'

'Not even close. You know your way out, Brendan. From now on, unless it's about the case, I don't want to have anything to do with you.'

Driving home, Lee saw the road stretching ahead of her, disappearing into the evening darkness. But also, in the back of her mind, she was starting to remember. Something she had spent so long trying to bury now jumped into her mind, unbidden. She should have moved Chambers after it happened – a fresh start somewhere else – but she never thought that even Tom, the keeper of so many Chambers secrets, would throw hers back in her face. She should never have forgotten who she was dealing with and that, if necessary, he would use it. The fact that it had happened so long ago – before she met David, before her life was one hard-earned success after another – had made her complacent.

Appearing before the Bar Standards Board, whilst not ideal, wasn't career-ending for most barristers, and it hadn't been for her. She had been reprimanded and paid a small fine and that was the end of it. But people remembered. Lee hated to think of herself as weak but images of that time now flooded through her mind, like a dam that had burst. As she drove, the road turned misty before her and she realized her eyes were welling up with tears. She hardly ever cried but now she was crying for the woman she had been on that weekend: wrapped in a duvet on an unseasonably hot day, rocking back and forth, legal papers strewn around her, unable to function, much less go to court. 'Late withdrawal' was the complaint by the furious solicitor who felt she had dumped his Legal Aid client for a more lucrative option. Burnout was the plain and simple truth of it, but the truth was rarely plain and never simple. Far better that people believed she was just another unscrupulous money-hungry brief dumping a client for a better option rather than endure the shame and ridicule she knew would follow if people thought she was cracking up.

She thought about her meeting with Brendan. One down, two to go. Now she was committed to this course of action, she would have to tell both her mother and David about taking Lambert's brief. It was too big a deal to be just another case, and the trial would be in the papers anyway. Shit! Shit! Shit!

She was less than half a mile from her flat when suddenly she turned her car towards her mother's house. The route she chose took her past rows of houses that became more and more shabby the further she drove. Some of it was barely recognizable to her, even though she had grown up there. It wasn't the way she normally came any more but it used to seem more familiar than this. She turned a corner and there at the end of the road was her mother's church, where Paul's father preached. Thanks to Verna Mitchell's boasts, she was sure the whole congregation knew who she was and their relationship to each other. As she drove past, she wondered how much longer her mother would be able to attend once the trial really got under way.

Verna Mitchell still lived in the first house she and her husband had bought when they moved to England. Though modest, they had saved years to get it; now it was hers outright. This house had seen the birth of their first child, a boy; his death, aged six months; Lee's birth years later – a happy surprise when Verna thought she was too old to have any more children; and her husband's death. All her memories were here; even the bad ones were comfortingly familiar. She would never leave.

Lee let herself in with the key her mother insisted she keep. Some cosmetic things had been changed. The hallway had long been painted a subtle cream colour in place of the flock wallpaper she had grown up with and which had embarrassed her so much throughout her teens. The living room was warm and inviting, and now in constant use – not the chilly mausoleum she remembered only being used for special occasions, with the store-perfect furniture still in its plastic. But the smells were the same: a combination of clean laundry and Caribbean spices which she found soothing, especially now.

Verna Mitchell, wiping her hands on a tea towel, came from the kitchen towards the hallway. She smiled broadly up at Lee. 'Oh good, I see you still have the key.' She paused, then added, 'You haven't given me one to your flat yet, you know.'

'I know,' Lee replied. The thought of her mother turning up unannounced at the home she shared with David during an intimate moment was too much to bear.

Verna looked at her daughter. 'When was the last time you had some proper home-cooking?'

Lee was hungry, but she knew this was more about her mother, who, out of force of habit and to stave off loneliness, still cooked enough to feed a family, rather than just herself.

'I haven't felt much like eating these past couple days . . .'

'Then whatever you need to tell me can wait. Sit yourself down.'

Lee watched her mother bending down to move the footstool in the kitchen and knew she was trying to reach something on the top shelf. She walked to the kitchen and opened the door wide.

'Let me get that,' she said.

'I can manage,' Verna said.

'No you can't. I can barely reach it, and you're half my height.' Lee stretched up and pulled down two plates. 'Why do you keep plates up so high anyway? Every time you reach for them you could pull them down on your head.'

'I don't use this every day.' Verna paused. 'This is the special china.'

There was an awkward silence, then Lee put her arm round her mother's shoulders. She could feel her body resisting, before she leaned against her daughter. Lee kissed the top of her grey head. No further words were necessary.

Her mother pulled away first, embarrassed. 'So, what's happening at work? I keep looking to see you on the news.'

Lee took a deep breath. 'Well, you might do – very soon. That's what I came round to talk to you about. Let's sit down, Mum.' She would kill for a cigarette right now. She reached for her bag, then remembered her mum's no-smoking house rule.

'What's happened, Leanne?'

It was a while before Lee spoke again. Sitting in her mother's small, neat dining room, the consequences of what she had agreed to, for her and those closest to her, loomed large. 'I don't want you to worry. I haven't even told David yet.' Lee chose to ignore her mother's pleased smile at that last comment. 'You know Reverend Matthews's son?'

'Tony or Paul? The one where they caught the policeman who did it?'

'That one. And that's the point. The policeman . . . he wants me to defend him, and I've agreed. It's complicated. I couldn't refuse; trust me, I would if I could.'

Verna sat back in her chair. 'You! I mean, I know you're a good barrister but why you?'

Lee shrugged. 'He knows me from before. Anyway, I was going to be reported to the Bar Council if I didn't take it. I could deal with being suspended, but . . . I could get disbarred.'

Her mother stared down at the china dinner plates she was now holding in her lap. She was frowning. Then, suddenly, she looked up at her daughter.

'But you're going to take it, of course, so that won't happen,' she said with finality.

Lee stared at her.

'You don't have to look so shocked,' Verna continued. 'Trust me, I hate, *hate* even the thought of you defending the man who shot my pastor's son. But I know what this is about. I didn't raise no fool for a daughter, and you don't have an idiot for a mother either. I've lived in this country nearly fifty years. There's not one thing you can teach me about racism. And you don't have to tell me a Black barrister defending him couldn't help him get off. If I were white, and on a jury, it might sway me. But the alternative? You getting disbarred? I won't let the likes of him make you give up all that you worked so hard to achieve.'

'Mum, I'm really glad for the support, but I can't believe you're saying this. It could get difficult for you too. You've been attending that church since you came to this country. How could you look them in the face if I took this case?'

'I'd rather look at them be vexed with me than watch you make a decision I know you're going to regret. You're my family, Leanne. My only family, now.'

'Thanks.' Lee could barely get the word out past the lump in her throat. She didn't trust herself to say anything more.

Her mother leaned over and squeezed her hand. 'I know, baby, I know. Now,' she got up and went into the kitchen, 'let's eat.'

David had been working in Manchester for the last few days. Lee wasn't sure whether he would be home. When she opened her front door and saw him there, she didn't know whether to be glad or sorry, particularly as he seemed so happy to see her. He pulled her close and smiled down at her – a warm, teasing smile she hadn't seen for a while. She hugged him back. He smelled good – he always did, to her.

'I've not seen my girl for nearly a week.' He was rubbing her back in a way that was both comforting and, increasingly, sexual. He kissed the back of her neck. 'I missed you.'

'You missed me? Or "it"?'

'Mmm. Both.'

'I need to talk to you first.'

He kissed her again. 'Not first.'

Two hours later, as they were lying in bed, David kissed her yet again and said, 'Now tell me you didn't miss me.'

It was nice lying here in the dark. Without thinking, she ran her fingers up his right bicep, tracing the elaborate cobra tattoo all the way to its head and fangs splayed across the right side of his chest. Silent, swift, waiting to strike, but deadly when it does. She had never seen that side of his character in all the years they had been together. She always felt warm, solid and safe with him. She felt his chest muscle twitching beneath her fingers.

'Sorry. I forgot you were ticklish.'

'No you didn't.' He leaned over and kissed her.

She had missed all this. It could almost make her forget about everything else.

'What's up?'

'Nothing,' she replied automatically. He must have felt her muscles tensing up. 'No, there is something . . .' Her voice trailed off.

'Is that what you wanted to talk about before? It's not your mum, is it?'

She was touched that he was concerned for her mother, even though they were barely on speaking terms.

'No, nothing like that.' God, this was going to be hard. She wanted to savour these moments – she didn't know how much what she was about to say would change things.

David sat up in bed and pulled her back so that she was leaning against him. 'Is it about work?'

She took a deep breath. 'I know we agreed not to talk about work in bed, but . . .'

'Don't worry about that. Come on.'

'You know the Paul Matthews case?'

'Yeah. Looks like they got the fucker who did it. And don't give me that "innocent until proven guilty" bullshit, not for him. You know the police wouldn't arrest one of their own unless they were sure. Won't help Paul, though.'

'At least he's still alive.'

'What kind of life is that?'

'Anyway,' she continued, 'the police officer accused of doing it wanted me to defend him.'

David laughed. 'Yeah, right. He'd be lucky.'

But when Lee didn't reply, she could feel his torso shifting as he turned to look at her. 'You're not going to do it, though, are you?'

She was glad it was dark. When she next spoke, all the words came out in a rush. 'Yes, I am. I have to, David. I'll get disbarred if I don't.'

She was glad she couldn't see his face. The rigid tension in his body told her enough.

'So you're going to defend him,' David concluded tonelessly.

'I gave it a lot of thought, David. I didn't –'

'Wait,' David interrupted. 'This boy's father is the minister at your mum's church, and you're *still* taking it on?'

'She encouraged me to take it on, though that wasn't the reason.' She stopped. She sounded like she was justifying her position. She'd never done that before and she didn't want to start now, not even to him. 'Anyway,' she continued, 'I wanted to tell you because at some point soon it'll be all over the papers again. Remember the Omartian case? You were on tour when that was bad. I think this will be worse. I wanted you to hear it from me first.'

Silence. She turned to face him in the dark. He looked like a bitter chocolate god.

'David?'

'So all that stuff I said in the pub, about you having too much integrity to do a case like this. And you agreed. Just words, then.'

'I can't explain it, David. You wouldn't understand.' Lee realized what she'd just said. 'Shit, I don't mean that. I'm sorry . . .'

David switched the bedside light on. She blinked in the sudden brightness, but he didn't. He was angrier than she'd ever seen him. 'What did you just say to me? I don't have a degree, Lee, but I've got a fucking brain! No, wait – there *is* one thing I can't understand. Is this why you went to the Bar? So you could defend people who come into our community and attack us? God knows you don't need the money. Help me understand that. Because when someone starts

174

chatting shit about you and I have to sort him out, I need to know why I'm defending your right to defend Lambert.'

Lee moved towards him, but he pulled away. 'I'm never going to let anyone say or do anything bad to you, Lee, but if you can do this, I don't know you. I think he did it, and if I ever met him face to face I would kick the living shit out of him. I don't know why Tony hasn't killed him yet. I would, if it were me.' He turned his back on her and got out of bed.

23

Satyr was an upmarket club for Ray to be working the door. Much higher than his usual standard. He would have got those in the old days, no question, but with a face like his he knew better than to expect the plum jobs. He had a certain freak show appeal for Trojan Security, which helped with the rougher jobs, but this? They must have felt sorry for him because he hadn't worked in a while. His gratitude, and the money, would insulate him from the stares he was certain to get from the clientele.

Dilla was also working the door. Dilla was a street name; Ray didn't care to know what his real name was any more than Dilla would have been prepared to tell him. They were acquaintances and got on well, but real names were for real friends only.

Ray made sure he stood as he always did, so that the light from the entrance would fall on the right side of his face, leaving the other side in shadow. The side which had been savaged by Omartian's dog, destroying the muscle in his cheek, jaw and neck. That was the last time he had tried to help Lee Mitchell. The last time he had seen her. Or wanted to.

For the most part Ray and Dilla worked in companionable silence, which was fine with him. He watched the crowd which, as hours passed, grew from a trickle to whole groups arriving at once. High-end, like the venue. He watched Dilla deal with the guest list and take invitations from those arriving. Occasionally he dealt with the overflow, but mostly was there as back-up muscle. He preferred it that way. Stares were stares, no matter how disguised or discreetly done.

About midnight, there was a rare lull. Without taking his eyes from the street or those approaching, Ray asked, 'So what time did you start? Boss told me to get here for seven.'

'Six,' Dilla replied. 'They have a few extra-special guests who came early. Not on this list.' He waved the clipboard.

'Private party, then. Whose is it?'

'Don't know. Rich queers, mostly. A lot of the guys wouldn't do it for that reason.'

Ray nodded sagely. So that was why he was offered the job.

'Doesn't bother me, one way or the other. These people pay well. Besides,' Dilla laughed, 'can you imagine any of them being brave enough to feel up my arse? They might like you, though. Dressed like that, you look like the last James Bond. You know, the blond one.'

'Fuck off,' Ray said amiably. 'Nah, not pretty enough for them, mate, not any more. Not that I'm interested, mind,' he added quickly. Suddenly his mood changed, as he saw a familiar figure approach. 'Hang on,' he muttered under his breath to Dilla. 'I know him.'

'Well, well, Ray Willis. Bit smart for you, this place, isn't it?'

'Look, one of the Met's finest. You know, I've always wanted to say this: if your name's not down, you're not coming in.'

Wallace flashed his warrant card at Ray, and then, as an after-thought, at Dilla. 'Very funny. I'm on official business, mate.'

'Not dressed like that you're not. Or do you always wear Italian shoes and designer gear to work?'

'Yes, you were always observant. That's what made you such a good crim. You were making more money back then, that's for sure. Anyway, I don't know why you're giving me attitude. I've nicked Lambert. That keeps him away from you. For a while at least.'

'So what? One of you lot will always be on my back. If you want gratitude, talk to me if he's convicted. And when you start looking at him for JT's death. But no one's bothered about that down at Miller Street, are they?'

'Oh, we're looking at him. Every murder matters on our patch.' Wallace's words sounded hollow, even to himself. 'Anyway, I need to get Lambert on this first. That's the way CPS wants to play it. Go with the stronger case first.'

'You mean the one where the jury has a victim they like. What exactly have you lot done about JT's murder?'

Wallace didn't answer that question. Which told Ray everything.

'Look, it's been a long time coming, but Lambert's going to get his. That's why I'm here.'

'Who are you here to see?' Dilla asked, checking his clipboard. But Wallace didn't even glance at the list as he walked past him.

'His name won't be on that list. And I wouldn't tell you even if it was.'

Wallace wondered if you could have a VIP area when everyone in the place was a VIP. But there was always a smaller, more select group wherever you went; this place would be no exception. He went up to the manager and showed his warrant card again, more discreetly this time.

'I need to speak to Hugo Cunningham.'

The manager looked at him a little too admiringly for his taste.

'Of course, Detective. You can use my office if you want more privacy.'

Wallace thought about people seeing him and Hugo Cunningham disappearing together into a private office and shuddered. 'No, out here's quiet enough. It won't take long.'

The manager disappeared and returned a few minutes later with Hugo before excusing himself. Wallace thought for a moment, then produced his warrant card. Of course Hugo knew who he was, but this wasn't like the other times – this was official. He addressed him formally before Hugo could say anything. 'Mr Cunningham, do you know Tony Matthews?'

Hugo giggled. 'Why, officer, all business tonight. Even though –' Hugo looked him up and down – 'you look good out of uniform. As always.'

Wallace could feel his whole body freeze. For a minute, he said nothing, then leaned in close to Hugo. 'You can't be that caned or that pissed,' he said in a low, menacing voice. 'Shut the fuck up or I'll arrest you for using. Class A, knowing you.' He stepped back. 'Perhaps you misheard me, Mr Cunningham. I'll ask again. Do you know Tony Matthews?'

'Yes, I do.'

'What's your relationship with him?'

'He came to see me at my last surgery. I'm his local councillor.'

'Any other connection?' Although he had been steady on his feet as he approached, up close Wallace had noticed Hugo's eyes were glazed and slightly unfocused. No point in asking him any more questions, then. Especially not in a place like this.

'Don't worry. We'll speak another time.'

Wallace left the club, walking past Ray and Dilla without saying a word. Ray watched him go. It must be pretty serious for him to come down here officially. For the first time in a very long while, he wondered whether he should contact Lee, tell her what he'd seen. He would have done, in the old days. But if she could defend scum like Lambert, she could fight her own battles. He touched his mangled and disfigured cheek. He had paid a very high price for helping her out last time.

24

Walking across the Temple into Chambers, Lee noticed how chilly it was, even for the time of year. Much like the atmosphere at home, she thought glumly. Since she had accepted the Lambert brief, she was amazed at how quickly news had spread around the Temple – largely due to Tom, she was sure. Her colleagues had spoken to her with a mixture of congratulation and envy. Her mother was supportive, but even she had the good sense to know that only other lawyers would see it as a career-advancing case. However, since she had told David he had pointedly avoided all mention of it. Ironically, he wasn't avoiding her – he went to gigs, sessions and rehearsals no more frequently than usual. But his brooding presence when he was home made her almost wish he wasn't.

She walked into the Clerks' Room and caught Tom at his most businesslike and urbane on the phone.

'No, of course she won't be making any comment. You know barristers don't do that, especially before a trial . . . well, I don't care what that Chambers does. Maybe they need to drum up business. We don't . . . try the solicitors; it's different for them. Goodbye.' He put the phone down and looked up at her. 'Three guesses what that was about.'

'I met two people in the Bar Mess who asked me about it today. One wanted to know the size of my brief fee; the other kept pointing out how hopeless it was. What have you been saying, Tom? You're not going to deny it's you.'

'Of course I won't. If your profile is raised, you get more work and so will Chambers. Everyone benefits. Of course,' he added thoughtfully, 'it would be even better if you could win, but no one really cares about that. By the way, Mr Donnelly called about the conference he'd booked for you. Apparently someone tried to run his client over. Nearly got him too.'

'What a shame,' Lee said, sarcastically.

'I wouldn't let anyone else hear you say that,' Tom said, reprovingly. 'Not now. Anyway, he wants to bring the conference forward.'

'To when?'

'End of the week.'

'Well, in case Mr Donnelly – or his client – has forgotten, I still have other cases. Anyway, I haven't had the rest of the papers yet, and I don't like conferences late Friday afternoons.'

'Mr Donnelly's thinking of putting him into protective custody. It'll take a lot longer to see him if that happens. Plus, the extra papers came down this morning.' He patted the substantial bundle on his desk, tied with dark-pink ribbon. 'And about the timing – I know how you barristers feel about late Friday conferences, but you know it will be virtually empty here after five thirty. No gawping in Chambers from the pupils, and no journalist likely to tail him into the Temple. It won't interfere with anything else you've got on. I've put it down for two hours. That should be enough for the first conference at least, and it won't cut into your weekend.' Pause. 'The only other alternative is this Saturday or Sunday. Your choice.'

Lee shook her head. This case was disrupting her life enough as it was. 'No, we'll go for Friday.'

*

Tom was right. By 5.30 p.m., like every other Chambers in the Temple on a Friday night, Maple Court was almost deserted, save for the clerks; a very keen pupil eager not to put his foot wrong in order to get an edge over the two hundred other applicants who were applying for tenancy; and his pupil supervisor, whose successful practice had grown in inverse proportion to his disintegrating marriage, so that he had nothing to go home to, even at the start of the weekend.

Lee would usually have conferences in her own room, but this time she chose the Chambers library. No one could fail to be over-awed by the long, oak-panelled, high-ceilinged room, lined floor to ceiling with law textbooks. A lot of money had been spent fitting out this room, and it showed.

She sat at one end of the long conference table. Brendan and Lambert were already twenty minutes late. Still, the later they were, the less chance of anyone seeing them – and besides, if they were half an hour late, she could legitimately cancel the conference.

No such luck. Almost on cue, Dean, the Junior Clerk, put his head round the door.

'They're here, Ms Mitchell.'

Showtime. Lee stood up and straightened her jacket. 'Okay, Dean, bring them in.'

No sooner said than done – evidently Brendan and Lambert had been right behind him. Lee stood up, but did not move from her position at the head of the table as she watched Brendan Donnelly help a limping Jack Lambert into the room. His right foot was heav-ily bandaged and, as he turned towards her, Lee could see his face was puffy and bruised. The bruises were starting to fade, but still looked pretty bad. Clearly, Tom hadn't been exaggerating. Still, she noticed he had a walking stick. Leaning on his solicitor was, there-fore, a clear play for sympathy. Lee felt her early stirrings of compassion disappear. She stood watching, expressionless, as solicitor and client hobbled and shuffled to the table, Dean moving ahead of them and arranging chairs to make Lambert comfortable. In the frigid atmosphere Dean looked both morbidly fascinated and deeply uncomfortable, as if he couldn't wait to leave, which he did as soon as he was able.

Once they were both seated, Lee sat down and looked pointedly at the clock and then at Lambert.

'Mr Donnelly, Sergeant Lambert, shall we get on?' Her tone was brusque to the point of rudeness but, for the first time in her professional life, she didn't care. With any luck, by the end of the conference Lambert might have changed his mind about her representing him.

'Well, nice to see you too.' Lambert's voice was thick and heavy.

'I'm going to be a lot more effective representing you if I don't have to pretend I like you as well.'

'Look, if that's how it's going to be –' Brendan began.

'Yes, it is,' she interrupted, curtly. 'If this is going to be a problem for your client –'

'No, it won't be.' Now, it was Lambert's turn to interrupt. He looked at Lee. 'I don't give a shit whether you like me or not. You're defending me, aren't you?'

Lee stared back at Lambert. 'Are you fit enough to have this conference? To give me proper instructions and to tell me, in your own words, what your defence is?'

'I thought you weren't going to be nice to me.'

'Don't flatter yourself. You've had a head injury. I just don't want you to say, if or *when*' – she subtly emphasized the last word – 'you get convicted, that I made you meet with me and forced you to tell me what happened when you couldn't think clearly.'

'I've seen worse.' He grinned and winced at the same time. 'Given people worse too, on the job.'

Lee stared at him. 'Only when they deserved it, right?'

Lambert stared back. 'Never bothered to ask, love.'

'Maybe that's what you did with Paul Matthews.'

Instantly, Lambert's expression changed from sneering to defensive. 'No.'

'I don't believe you.'

'Well, ain't that a surprise. When I got nicked, my own workmates didn't believe me, a fellow copper. So why should I expect some gun for hire to do that?'

Lee put her pen down and folded her arms. 'Okay. Tell me what happened, then.'

'It's in my statement. Haven't you read it?'

'I want to hear it from you.'

'I'm not playing this game. Do your job and read it!'

'What's the problem?' She glanced at Brendan, who was, literally and figuratively, keeping his head down, then back at Lambert. 'Afraid you can't remember what you've been coached?'

'That's enough!' Brendan said. He stood up and looked at his client. 'Come on, Jack. We don't have to take this.'

Lambert remained seated. 'Fine. You go, then.' He turned back to Lee. 'If you think you're going to insult me so much I'll be pissed off enough to sack you, you're dreaming.'

'Fine. But if you want me to do this, don't even think about telling me how to do my job again. I'm not your "love" either.' Lee jerked her head in Brendan's direction. He was still standing, embarrassed and unsure of what to do. 'What you do with him is up to you.'

Lambert shrugged. 'He needs me, and I need you. That's how it is – until this is over.'

'I'm still in the bloody room, you know,' Brendan said.

'Then sit down and start earning your fee,' Lambert snapped.

As Brendan slowly sat down, Lee picked up her pen again. 'So, Sergeant, you were going to tell me your side of the story.'

'I wasn't there, so I didn't do it. End of.'

'Where were you?'

'At home, drinking. Or sleeping it off. Alone.'

Of course alone, Lee thought. 'You have a landline?'

'Yeah.'

'Anyone call you on it at home during that time?'

'Not while I was awake. Don't know what happened after I passed out. I doubt it, though.'

'We can get those phone records.' Lee looked at Brendan, who was taking notes. He nodded. 'Do you always drink alone?'

'I prefer it that way.'

'Anyone see you buying alcohol that night?'

'Not that night, no. Got enough cans at home.'

'How long have you had a drink problem?'

'I'm no alcoholic! Drinking's not a problem for me. I don't care about anyone else.'

His answer highlighted their first big problem. 'So, no alibi?'

'That's right.'

'Do you know Paul Matthews, or anyone connected with him?'

'Just his brother, Tony; everyone knows I've nicked him before.'

'Where you live – how far is it from where he was shot?'

Lambert shrugged. 'If you walked, about fifteen minutes. No, that's from the church.'

'Which church is that? The one his father runs?'

'Don't know. I'm not a churchgoer.'

'So why mention it?'

'It's just a landmark round my way.'

Lee rifled through the documents in front of her, finally pulling one out. 'I heard about Jimmy Thomas on the news. What's he to you?'

'What's that got to do with this case?' Lambert replied.

'Well, the CPS must think it matters; a woman claims to have seen a man matching your description with Thomas about five, ten minutes away from the church on the night Paul was shot. It was stapled to the back of DCI Wallace's statement.'

'Stapled to the back of his statement? An accident, I'm sure,' Brendan remarked, drily. 'Anyway, that's nothing to do with this shooting. CPS can't use that in this trial.'

Lee already knew that, of course. But the fact that Lambert hadn't answered her was significant. 'Ten minutes could make all the difference,' she continued. 'You could have gone to the church, spoken to Mrs Matthews, and then shot Paul, all within the prosecution time frame. What do you say to that, Sergeant?'

'I'd say prove it.'

'Oh, I think they can, with the statement they've got from Mrs Matthews saying you were there that night. Plus, there's another statement which says the police collected CCTV tape from the security system outside the church. It puts you at the back of this church the same night Paul was attacked. They're getting it enhanced, so we don't have a copy yet. Not just a landmark, then.'

Lambert didn't look in the least bit bothered. 'Sign of the times, security cameras on churches. Wasn't like that when I was growing up. But a lot of things were different round here back then. Could almost be the Dark Ages. Mind you, we're in the "Darkie" Ages now. Can hardly find a native English speaker round my way.'

'Jack . . .' Brendan warned.

'Don't bother to stop him,' Lee said. 'I know what he thinks. It's that attitude that has him on this attempted murder charge.'

'Can't be convicted for my attitudes, though.'

'So, what were you doing at the church? What possible business could you have with Mrs Matthews?'

Lambert paused before he answered. 'Looking for Tony.'

'Paul was wearing his brother's jacket and had Tony's mobile. Plus, Tony doesn't live there. You know that.'

Lambert shrugged. 'So they say.'

'Why were you looking for Tony?'

'There's been even more crack and coke round here than usual the last few months. Knowing Tony, if he's not dealing, he knows who is.'

'Thought you were off-duty.'

'So?'

'Anyone back at the station know about this?'

'My Super? He hasn't been out from behind his desk in years. Besides, he doesn't live in the area. I do. I've been here man and boy. I hear about things long before anyone back at the nick does.'

'So, you made an unauthorized visit to see Tony Matthews; what were you going to do? Have a chat over coffee?'

'I was going to get him to stop!' Lambert's voice was raised now. 'I'm not going to stand by and watch my manor go down the shitter!'

'If it was him, of course.'

'I know it was him!'

'You know it was him,' Lee repeated, dispassionately. 'Tell me, was Tony Matthews ever convicted as a result of any arrest you made?'

'Twice. All the other times he had some high-paid fancy lawyer like you to get him off.'

'And now it's your turn.' Lee watched his face slowly flush. 'After you were arrested, did you tell this to anyone at the station?'

Lambert remained sullen and silent, no doubt the way he had looked and behaved after his arrest. Lee sighed and glanced at the clock. It was getting very late, but the more she could do tonight, the more she could minimize the number of future conferences with Jack Lambert. She leafed through her bundle of documents until she found the expert reports from the surgeon, Malcolm Weir, and from ballistics and forensics.

'Let's talk about the gun. According to the surgeon, "*The injury was caused by a single shot to the side of the face, causing blindness to the left eye, permanent brain damage and cosmetic disfigurement. This is a life-altering injury. The victim remains comatose. The prognosis is poor.*"' Lee paused and looked at Lambert before continuing.

'The expert reports say the bullet that was removed from his face matches a Glock 9mm. A gun that had a partial print from you on it. A gun that was involved in another shooting two weeks later, just before it was handed into Miller Street station.'

'The report says there were three other sets of prints on the gun too, two of which they could identify as belonging to Tony Matthews and Jimmy Thomas,' Brendan interrupted.

Lee turned to face Brendan. 'I'd much rather hear from Sergeant Lambert. Or are you planning to give evidence for him too?'

'I don't have to prove anything.' Now Lambert spoke. 'I'm innocent, remember, and will be until the day they find me guilty. Which they won't. Three sets of prints as well as mine on one gun should help with that. You know as well as I do – these guns, they get around.'

'Doesn't explain yours, though.'

'I took the gun off JT. Little shit had no business having it in the first place. But that's got nothing to do with this. I want to keep all references to him out.'

Lee shrugged. 'If we can,' she said.

For the first time since they met, Lambert looked worried. 'If the jury hears about JT, I'm fucked, good and proper. Maybe you should remember whose side you're on.'

'Not on the side of anyone who could shoot someone in the face.'

'Well, that's good, then, as it wasn't me.'

Lee turned to Brendan. 'I need to see that tape. If it's got times on it – and your client can remember if he was there – we might have some kind of alibi. We also need those phone records we spoke about before.' She looked at Lambert. 'Reasonable doubt, that's your best chance. No jury will ever be sure you didn't do this.'

'Well, that's good enough for me.' Lambert yawned and stretched his arms over his head. 'How much longer? I've got to be somewhere.'

'That's enough for now. Brendan will let you know if I need to see you again.'

Lambert scraped his chair back and got slowly to his feet. He limped towards the library door. Brendan followed close behind him. As his client went through the door, Brendan called out to him, 'Be with you in a minute, Jack.'

Brendan closed the library door and leaned against it. He put his hands in his pockets and lowered his head. 'So, what do you think?' He was facing Lee but couldn't meet her eyes.

'I'm not having any communication with you that can't be evidenced, Brendan. So, you either email or write to me, or speak to me in front of your client. Other than that, I've got nothing to say to you. Now,' she reached behind him and opened the door, 'don't keep your client waiting.'

25

Anyone who knew Lee outside of a courtroom would not describe her as aggressive or adversarial – words often used, wrongly, to describe Black women or anyone who was in places where traditionally it was felt they didn't belong. But she was a fighter; Tom was right about that. She never, ever backed away from a confrontation. She always met that head on. It was what made her so effective as a trial advocate. And, as she pulled up outside the Law Centre, she wasn't going to back away from one now, even though she knew this could get really ugly.

This was the regular scheduled monthly board meeting. She had thought, briefly, about not going; after all, she could have said she had too much work on, which was true. But she hadn't been on the board long enough to start missing meetings. She also knew that it would be seen as cowardice – that she didn't have the guts to face them now she was representing Lambert. Or to be in Lower Rick at all. For the first time ever she wondered whether her car would still be in one piece at the end of the night.

The first person Lee met was Claudine, who buzzed her in. As Lee looked at her, it occurred to her that Claudine would either be a terrible poker player or a dream of a witness to cross-examine to devastating effect: her emotions were all over her face. Not unfriendly, though her smile was not as fulsome as it usually was; more puzzled, and bursting with questions.

'Hi. Kofi and the others are all inside. You're the last to arrive.'

'Still on time, though.' Lee smiled, trying to ease the tension. It didn't work. It stretched taut as a rubber band between them until Claudine could contain herself no longer. She touched Lee's arm.

'Before you go in, is it true? It's not in every paper and I know how they can get things wrong . . .'

Lee took a deep breath. 'Yes, Claudine, it's true.'

The tension between them slowly ebbed away – not, as Lee expected, to be replaced with anger, but with something far worse. Real disappointment. It was evident on Claudine's face and from the sudden sag of her shoulders. She shook her head but said nothing more.

The door to Kofi's office where the meeting was to be held was slightly ajar. Lee could hear the low murmur of voices. Three guesses as to what they were discussing. She squared her shoulders and pushed the door open. 'Good evening, everyone.'

As she entered the room, all eyes turned in her direction and the conversation stopped cold. Scanning their faces, she was glad that years of trial advocacy had taught her to hide her feelings better than they were clearly able to. Or maybe didn't want to. There was fascination, as if for a specimen they had never come across before. And bewilderment. But, most of all, animosity, bordering on rage, which crashed over her like a wave.

Lee could feel herself curling up inside as if to protect herself from its almost physical force. For a moment she was tempted to look down, unable to face them. But that was no way to defend herself. She felt certain that, at some point tonight, board business or not, she would have to.

Except for Kofi. He had been a barrister too. His face, a mask of impassivity, was the only one she couldn't read.

'I'm surprised you have the front to come here.' It was Leon, whose record of attendance was so spotty Kofi had spoken seriously about kicking him off the board.

'I'm surprised you're here too, Leon. How many meetings have you missed in a row? Three? Four? Anyway, I'm still a member and I guess I'll keep coming until that changes.' She glanced at Kofi, who deliberately avoided her gaze.

It wasn't just Leon's face that was easily read. His body language was leaky too. From the tension radiating from him and the tight, controlled way he was sitting, Lee knew that the main, if not the only, reason he had come here tonight was to have a showdown with her.

Kofi held up his hand.

'We have a full agenda, people, and Marianne's Treasurer's Report is particularly detailed. Let's not forget why we're here. I know what you all want to talk about but that will have to be under Any Other Business – if we have time. And,' looking at Lee for the first time, 'if Lee's still here.'

Lee nodded. 'I'll be here.' It worried her that she still couldn't read Kofi. She'd known him for twenty years. She'd seen him do this with other people. Never with her.

It was a full agenda. A few of the members wanted to rush through it with minimal discussion but Kofi was having none of that. Lee wondered whether he was giving her time to marshal her arguments, to try to give him, and all present, at least one reason they might understand as to how she could agree to defend Lambert.

The minute hand seemed to crawl round the clockface. Finally, it was time.

'Okay,' Kofi began. 'Going round the room – Marianne, any other business?'

193

Marianne shook her head, apparently deciding, wisely, that this wasn't her fight.

'Leon.'

'How the fuck could you do it?' It wasn't the expletive that was shocking, but the venom in the question, the force of it landing like a punch.

'You haven't even asked her if it's true.'

'Yes, it's true.' It wasn't Lee who replied, but Claudine.

'I knew it! What,' Leon sneered, 'you didn't have enough money? House on The Hill and fancy car not enough for you, is it? You still need your thirty pieces of silver to defend shit like Lambert? A fucking racist!'

'I didn't do it for the money. If I was in law for the money, I wouldn't be doing crime.'

'What I don't understand, Lee,' it was Claudine speaking now, 'is your mum's a member of that church. She's been going there since she first came to this country. Do you know just how hard it will be for her now to go there every week? And even after the trial is over? She's an Elder in that church; she loves it. And she's a widow. You would ruin that for her?'

Lee felt tears prick the back of her eyes. Oh no. Not here. Not in front of these people. But it was too late.

'Yeah, crocodile tears. You're not fooling me. Think of Paulie's mum's tears.' Leon was on a roll now. 'You see, this is what happens to Black people. They get a bit of White man's book learning and it fries up their brain.'

'That's enough!' Lee banged her fist so hard on the table that it surprised everyone, including herself. She dragged the back of her hand across her face, wiping away her tears, smearing her mascara, ignoring the tissue Claudine had held out to her. 'Claudine, I know you mean well but leave my mum out of this. And you,' she turned her anger full force on Leon, 'you've lived here two minutes and you think you know everything? You think you know me? I was born here. I fucking grew up here – right here, in Lower Rick! I'm not some blow-in, like you!'

'But you don't live here now, do you? You just come back here slumming, breezing in here once a month doing your bit "for the community" just long enough to ease your conscience before you hightail it out again.'

Lee thought back to the discussion she'd had with her Senior Clerk that day in Chambers before she was forced to take the Lambert brief. They didn't need to know about that, but they did need to know about something else.

'You want to know how I got this case? The cab rank rule. If a barrister is instructed on a case, and they are available and have the experience to do it, they have to take it. You know how many Black people would be without representation, every day, if it wasn't for that? *That's* the reason I had to take it. But if this is about me apologizing for what I've achieved and how I live, then fuck you! Never!'

In the silence that followed, Claudine passed her a glass of water, which she gratefully accepted. Then Kofi spoke.

'Lee's right about the cab rank rule. I know her. I know she wouldn't have taken this case if she'd had any other choice.'

Leon stared at him. 'You defending her, Kofi?'

'No, I'm telling you straight facts. That's one of the reasons I left the Bar. But that was my choice. I don't agree with her doing this case. At all! But look at all the other cases she's been involved with over the last ten years, as well as her connection to this place. We need people like Lee at the Bar; those of you who've known her for some time know that's true. Look, feelings are going to run hot for a while. Does anyone else have anything new or different to say that they need to get off their chest tonight? No?' he asked, looking round the room. 'Well, I'm glad because it's late and, frankly, I'm tired. See you all next month. Don't worry, Claudine; I'll lock up. Lee, just give me a few minutes, please.'

They both sat in the room in silence until the last person left the building, slamming the heavy front door behind them. It was Lee who spoke first.

'So, are you kicking me off the board?'

'Not unless you want me to.'

'Thanks for sticking up for me.'

'I wasn't intending to. But most people don't know about the cab rank rule: they think you can just turn down cases you don't like. But I can't tell you how much I hate the fact you're defending Lambert. *Defending* him! I really fucking hate it. I knew you were Lambert's brief even when the others weren't sure. I still know people at the Bar.' He shook his head, almost in disbelief. 'I was so angry with you when I first heard . . .' He looked at her, properly now. 'How does your man feel about it?'

Lee looked away. 'He hates it too. It's bad at home – when he's there,' she added.

'And your mum?'

'I don't want to talk about her, Kofi.'

It was a while before either of them spoke.

'Okay. As far as I'm concerned, everyone's had their say. I won't let them bring it up again in future meetings or any time you come into the Centre. You'll have to deal with what happens outside on your own – but then, you had to know that when you took this on. Promise me one thing, though, Lee.'

'What?'

'I know you. Don't try to win.'

26

Plea and Trial Preparation Hearings were usually fairly routine affairs. In an average criminal case, it was often the first appearance at a Crown Court and the last opportunity to tie up any loose ends before the trial. Straightforward, in-and-out jobs. A judge could hear half a dozen in a morning's sitting.

But *R v Lambert* was never going to be one of those.

As Lee rounded the final corner on the approach to Southwark Crown Court, her worst fears were confirmed. There, on the steps of the court about three hundred yards ahead, were half a dozen reporters and photographers, drinking coffee out of Styrofoam cups on this bright but cold Friday morning. Of course, they could have been there for another case but, somehow, she doubted it.

Lee ducked back round the corner and rummaged in her bag until she found her sunglasses and mobile phone. It really was a beautiful early April day, the sun already bright at 9 a.m. Far too nice to be working, let alone in a formal black suit. She thought about the prospect of being fully robed in a hermetically sealed courtroom and groaned inwardly as she dialled Brendan's number.

'Are you there yet?' she asked as soon as he answered.

'Got here at eight. Only people here then were security and the cleaners. Even the canteen wasn't open. We knew we'd have to hang around for two hours, but it was better than running the gauntlet.'

'Okay. I'll be there in a minute.'

Lee jammed the phone back in her bag, put on her sunglasses and turned the corner purposefully towards the court building. At least her shades didn't seem out of the ordinary in the bright sunlight. She plugged her headphones into her phone and pretended to be listening to it. One of the reporters looked over curiously as she approached the first step. Out of the corner of her eye Lee could see him nudge the photographer.

''Scuse me, are you . . .'

Lee kept going, thankful to be finally swallowed up by the sliding glass doors at the top of the steps. It was quiet and cool – though evidently not cool enough for the security guard, mopping his florid face with a large handkerchief. She could see Brendan straight ahead, by the lifts, looking at the court listings, and once she had passed through security she headed straight towards him. He looked at her warily as she approached. Though they had been in regular professional contact, it had been by letter and email; they had not spoken face to face since the conference in Lee's Chambers.

'Good morning. So,' she said, looking over his shoulder, 'where is he?'

'In the cells downstairs.'

'Why? What's he done now?'

'Nothing!' Brendan's tone was reproachful. 'It's just the safest place for him – at least, here it is. Even he agrees.' He jerked his head towards the court listings. 'Look – "*R v Lambert, Court One*". Might as well hang a fucking sign around his neck. You think I want them out there finding him? Or paying someone to do it? There are fifteen courtrooms in here. Let them hunt for him in all of them.'

'How'd you manage that, seeing as he's on bail, and today's bound to be busy for them?'

'If you come here often enough there's always someone who will do you a favour. I'm going to get a coffee. You want one?'

'No, I'd rather just get started.'

'Of course,' Brendan said, drily. 'How stupid of me to think this was going to be friendly.'

She hesitated. Praise where praise was due. 'We still work well together; that hasn't changed. I'm happy to leave it at that. Get one for yourself if you like. I'll see you downstairs. Good idea, though, the cells.'

There were two things all Crown Court holding cell areas seemed to have in common. The first – and the first thing you noticed – was the smell, a peculiar mix of cheap disinfectant and unwashed fetid bodies straight from prison. It rose up the stairs and through the wicket to greet you. The second was the custody cell staff – disaffected, and longing to be anywhere but where they were. For the length of their shift they were as much prisoners as those they guarded. In fact, Marlon, the man in charge, had been doing this so long he was almost a lifer himself. He smiled at Lee as he let her in.

'Morning.' In his regulation uniform, the tall Black man was as crisply turned out as ever. He looked at the clipboard in front of him. 'And who have you come to see today?'

'I don't think he'll be on your list.'

'Ah yes, our "special guest". He's been here a while. I've got him back in one of the female cells; that block's empty at the moment. You want to go through?'

'Not yet, thanks, I'll wait for my solicitor.'

'Suit yourself, but if it gets busy, you might have to wait for one of us to take you through. You know what Fridays are like here.'

But in the end it was only a few minutes before Brendan joined them. Strangely, Marlon was smiling more broadly now. 'Bet you both can't wait to get started on this one.' He jangled his keys. 'Follow me.'

'You can't be this happy just because it's Friday,' Lee observed as she fell in step behind him.

Marlon didn't reply until he reached Lambert's cell door. 'It's your client. Don't even think he remembers me.' He peered through the hatch at his prisoner as if he were a fascinating specimen at the zoo, then leaned against the heavy cell door and folded his arms. 'He nicked me when I was a youngster – what, twenty years ago? I was fifteen, sixteen at the time. Beat me up, then tried to fit me up. Didn't work, though. Some old white lady was looking out of her bathroom window and saw what happened. The court didn't believe me, but they did her. Luckily.' He shook his head as if trying to dislodge the memory. 'Anyway, long time ago. Now, I'm this side of the door, and he's in there. So yeah, I'm very happy this morning.'

'Did you make a complaint to the police?' Brendan asked.

Marlon looked at Brendan, then Lee. 'He's having a laugh, isn't he? A Black kid? Against the police? No. Different times, mate.'

Lee's stomach lurched at the thought of how Marlon's life could have been so very different, but also at the prospect of this respectable, much-admired head custody officer giving evidence for the prosecution. 'What about now?' Lee added quickly. Marlon looked at her, puzzled. 'Would you tell the court about that if they asked you? I mean,' she continued, hesitantly, 'it could prejudice the case . . .'

The affable look on Marlon's face faded. 'I know what you mean, Counsel,' he interrupted. His tone was as formal as his address to her. 'I've got calluses on my hands, not my brain.' He put the key in the lock and opened the cell door with a flourish. Lambert was half sitting, half lying on the wooden bench. He looked up malevolently as the three of them entered. 'You don't remember me, mate, do you?' Marlon asked as casually as if he were asking for directions.

'Why should I?'

'See?' Marlon said.

The sound of the door banging shut as he left echoed round the cell. Lambert was the first to break the silence. 'Fucking stinks in here. I'm not on remand; I shouldn't have to put up with this. How much longer do I have to stay in this shithole?' When no one answered, he stared at his lawyers. 'What?' he demanded.

Lee walked to the furthest corner away from him, hoping her disgust didn't show, but past caring.

'So I didn't recognize him. I probably nicked him. Big fucking deal.'

'And how many people have you arrested who are Black and claim you beat them up when they were the same age as Paul Matthews is now?'

'Oh, so that's it. Well, that's his story. It's got nothing to do with my case.'

'You don't deny it, though.'

Lambert shrugged. 'Well, he's not fifteen now, is he? CPS don't know about him, or they would have told us.' Lambert stared at Lee. 'I'm going not guilty, and the only way you're going to get rid of me is if you get me off.'

'Or you get convicted.'

'Then guess who I'm coming to with my Appeal brief.'

'I don't think you need me down here, Brendan,' Lee said. She pressed the buzzer to be let out. 'His plea hasn't changed. You can explain the rest of what will happen today. I'll see you both upstairs.'

Lambert was right about one thing: the cell did stink and it lingered on her suit. Good job she wasn't wearing her robes. When she got to the front counter, Marlon was double-checking all the prisoners. Without looking up, he called to one of the staff. 'Pete, Counsel's leaving.'

Nine fifty a.m. She had already been there nearly an hour and court business hadn't even got under way yet. Brendan tugged at her robe to indicate his place in the row behind her.

'Our client's on his way up. Don't worry about Marlon; you were right to ask. He'll get over it.' Lee half turned towards him. He looked as cheerful as he sounded. 'Shit, I'm glad you asked. Pure instinct, Lee. You wanted to give yourself a fighting chance. I know how much you hate to lose; that's what I'm counting on. So's our client.'

There was nothing she could say. It was the truth, and Brendan of all people would know it. 'I didn't get a chance to speak to the prosecution,' she said, changing the subject. 'It's the usual scrum; too many other briefs trying to do the same thing.'

Brendan jerked his head towards a tall, professional-looking Black man who had been speaking to Prosecution Counsel for some time. 'Seems like CPS sent down someone more senior than usual to hold Counsel's hand. Looks familiar. Do you know who he is?'

The Crown Prosecution Service rarely had enough people to attend court with Counsel on pre-trial hearings, even one as big as this. Lee stiffened. 'He's not from CPS. That's –'

'All rise!' the court usher announced as the presiding Judge entered.

27

Meanwhile, outside the main entrance, Fee Smith, small and pale, leaned against the barriers that had been erected along both sides of the walkway to the court steps. She had arrived so early this morning she had seen the court security staff putting them up. Clearly, they thought there would be trouble. There had been no one else there then, but they weren't wrong. She had experienced enough of these to know that, with a case like this, anything could happen at any time.

She had been there for well over an hour, watching as people arrived for the business of the day. Watched as the gentlemen of the press gathered immediately to the side of the main entrance to the court. Not a large number; just a couple from local papers and a few photographers. Only one from the nationals; but then they wouldn't normally bother with a case at this level unless it was going to be discontinued. That was never likely in Lambert's case, and everyone knew that. Once the trial started, they would be out there in force. She saw people arriving for their own court matters; registering their surprise when they realized journalists were present. Some were clearly embarrassed, trying to hide their faces. Others strolled by, treating the narrow area between the barriers leading up to the court steps as if it were a catwalk. But the press were clearly disinterested in them. She knew, and they knew, there was only one story worth reporting here today.

It was clear, though, from the hostile way some of them were staring at her, that they also knew who she was, by reputation if nothing else. She had certainly criticized their profession in the past. She'd feel a lot better when the others arrived.

'I see the scum are here already,' said a voice from behind her. The woman jumped and turned round.

'Where the fuck have you been, Brian? And where is everyone else?' she added as she looked behind him. 'I told them to get here early.'

Brian Gibbs put up his hands in a mock-defensive gesture. 'Christ, Fee, you're lucky I made it here at all. And if the others have hangovers anything like mine, you'll be lucky if any of them turn up. Besides –' he looked at his watch – 'it's only nine forty-five. You know this court won't start till ten thirty.'

She said nothing but turned back to the barrier. Brian leaned against it next to her. Glancing down at her, he could see the tension just from the way she held her body. It was always like this with Fee. If the others didn't turn up it would be that intensity, as much as anything, that would stop them. She was good for the cause, but Fee Smith was not a woman you could warm to.

'You should have come last night. We had a great time.'

Fee stared straight ahead. 'I was here at eight thirty.'

Of course you were, Brian thought. She was clearly annoyed, and that superior tone in her voice was beginning to get on his nerves. Typical of her class. She wasn't the only one who cared.

'The others will be here soon, don't worry.' It was as much an attempt to lighten the mood as to reassure her, but Fee made no reply or gave any indication at all that she had even heard what he had said, much less paid any attention to it. Her eyes were feverishly scanning the crowd when she spoke again.

'They'd want to deal with a case like this early. Remove the object of interest. Get rid of the press and the crowds in case anything kicked off.' She laughed, bitterly. 'Especially if they knew we were coming. But we can't do anything if there's just two of us now, can we?'

'Lay off it, Fee. You're not the only one who wants to see justice done, you know.' His tone was now equally short with her, but he didn't care. Then, out of the corner of his eye, he saw what they were waiting for. He nodded to his right. 'Look, there's the family.' He chuckled. 'Surprised Tony Matthews is here. Thought they'd want to keep him well out of the way. He's not gonna get the press on his side if he keeps looking at them like that.'

Fee looked at Tony. Their fuckfest had petered out almost as soon as it had begun, ever since Paul was shot. Not that she cared. It was never going to last, and neither would acknowledge the other in public. She got what she wanted from him that last time. 'I don't know what he's doing here. Half the people on my estate are hard-core users because of him. It's a shame he didn't get shot!' Fee spat on the pavement between them. 'And journalists? Who needs them anyway? What do they care? Vultures and bastards, all of them!'

Brian tried to hide the look of disgust on his face, then instantly felt guilty. Why shouldn't a woman gob if she wanted to? He thought he was beyond such sexism. But she didn't realize how telling that last statement was. Of course, the press didn't care about this case beyond the headline it would make the next day. That didn't mean they weren't needed. The fact that she didn't realize this, or what she had said, showed how different she was from them – how protected and cosseted she had been from the compromises the rest of the world had been making for years.

Brian looked back over at Tony and his parents. He watched him put his arm round his mother, who leaned in close to him. For a fraction of a second he hesitated, then raised his arm as if to do the same to his father, who moved away. Just a small movement, but it was enough.

The half-dozen wide concrete steps seemed like an unbreachable wall. Tony leaned forward, his voice softening as he spoke to his mother. 'I won't come in with you, Mum. But don't worry – I'll be right out here when you come out. I'm not going anywhere.'

'No, Tony – we've got to go in as a family –'

'Won't? You mean you can't!' his father said, addressing his son over his wife's head. 'The number of times they've seen us here with you . . .'

Mrs Matthews turned to face her husband. The depth of anger on her face was clear for all to see. 'You're going to bring that up here, Desmond? In front of all these people?'

Tony looked at his father in amazement. 'Us? Us? Since when did you . . . ?' He took a deep breath in to calm himself. 'You know what? I'm not dealing with this here. This can't be the news story.' Turning to face his mother, he held both her hands in his. 'Mum, you know that wouldn't stop me from coming inside with you. All these police round here, you think they don't know who I am? I don't want it to be about me. I want them in there to focus on Paulie. Don't worry. I promise I'll be right here when you come out.'

Mrs Matthews put her hand gently on Tony's cheek. She stared at him for the longest time, her eyes searching his face. Tony could see the doubt there. He was hurt but wasn't surprised. The number of times he'd been to places like this, what reason did she have to trust him now? They both knew what his father had said was right.

Then she squeezed his arm. 'All right, Tony.'

Tony watched his mother as she climbed the steps of the

courthouse. Even now, it still surprised him to see that she was actually three or four inches taller than her husband, because he was always the more dominant presence.

It was a long wait. No one mentioned it at home, but he knew that bullet had been meant for him. Any number of people might want him dead. It was an occupational hazard. Even here, outside the court building. There were so many people, but if anyone tried again now, it would have to be a junkie. Only one of them would be crazy enough to do it here. Scanning the crowd, he noticed Fee Smith staring at him, but dismissed it. Scrawny bitch.

Waiting also gave him too much time to think about family. As bad as things always were between them, his father had never spoken to him like that in public before. He was under no illusions that their relationship was ever going to get better, but family business was just that – for family. His father had never been known to make such matters public knowledge; he cared too much about what people thought for that. He would never have spoken like that to Paul – but then, he thought ruefully, he wouldn't have had to. He'd never been nicked, for one. And everything used to be different between those two, like a circle he couldn't get into . . .

Suddenly the crowd surged forward.

'Here he comes!'

28

Inside Court One, there would not have been a single person present that day who hadn't heard of His Honour Judge Harris, either by reputation or direct experience. He had been a judge for twenty-two years, and the most senior judge at that court for the last five. That, plus an earlier distinguished career at the Bar, had produced a man who was, according to court staff, 'a real handful' – equal parts brilliant jurist and mercurial, self-entitled teenager. He bustled in, brisk and businesslike, put on his glasses and looked at the list in front of him. He then leaned forward to speak to the Court Clerk. After a brief discussion, he peered over his glasses at the serried rows of Counsel before him in the well of the court.

'Are all parties in *Lambert* present?' he asked.

Both Counsel stood up. 'Stephen Brooks for the Crown, Your Honour.'

'And Lee Mitchell for the defence.'

'Due to the sensitive and unfortunate nature of this case, I have decided to deal with this first. Only the parties to the case will remain in court during this hearing. No doubt Counsel will be making representations about reporting restrictions at some point. Is the Crown ready?'

'Er . . . might I take instructions, Your Honour?'

Judge Harris looked up sharply. 'I thought you said you were ready, Mr Brooks.' He had a round of golf booked for that afternoon. He was damned if he would miss it. 'Well, if you must, though I would have thought that was a very elementary question.'

Lee noticed the prosecutor turn briefly to the Black man sitting behind him before replying, 'We're ready, Your Honour.'

'Good. Dock Officer, please have the defendant brought up. Whilst this is being done, madam usher, please clear the court.'

Everyone doubted he had the authority to do that, as there were no reporting restrictions in place, but none of the lawyers wanted to get on his bad side for a case that wasn't theirs. As everyone trooped out, it was several minutes before they were able to continue. Then, at the back of the court, there was the sound of a steel door being opened, and some low voices. Lee didn't have to look behind her to know that Lambert had been brought into the dock.

The Court Clerk stood up and addressed him directly. 'Are you John Alfred Lambert?'

'Yes.'

'Mr Lambert, you face an indictment containing one count. On Count One, it is alleged that on the fifth of February, you attempted to murder Paul Matthews, a minor aged fifteen years. How do you plead?'

'Not guilty.'

Prosecution Counsel stood up. 'Your Honour, the Crown is considering whether to add a further count of Grievous Bodily Harm. Separate from that proposed count, Paul Matthews is still on life support in a coma. Should he . . .' Stephen Brooks glanced over at where Reverend and Mrs Matthews were sitting before choosing his words more carefully. 'Should that situation change between now and the end of the trial, the prosecution will seek to amend the indictment to reflect the appropriate charge.'

'Both Counsel should know I already consider this case of suffi-
cient seriousness to reserve the trial to myself. Mr Brooks, as I already
have your written submissions, please – briefly – outline the case
against the defendant.'

'The Crown say that on the date in question, a passer-by, Mr Morris, was walking his dog when he came across a person collapsed in
an alley leading to Havant Road. This person was later identified as
the victim, Paul Matthews.'

Lee half thought about objecting to the characterization of Paul
Matthews as a victim, with the implication that Lambert was the per-
petrator, but decided against it. After all, there was no one present
who wasn't already connected to the case – and, whichever way you
looked at it, Paul Matthews was indeed a victim.

'The Crown say the defendant attacked Paul Matthews and that
he had one of two possible motives for doing so. Firstly, the victim's
older brother, Anthony, is well known to the defendant, who had
arrested him several times previously. On the night in question, the
victim was wearing a jacket which Anthony Matthews has identified
as his. Anthony Matthews also identified his mobile phone, which
was found near the victim. The Crown say this was a case of mistaken identity – the defendant attacked Paul, thinking it was Anthony.'

Lee rose to her feet. 'Your Honour, if Tony – sorry, Anthony –
Matthews is as well known to the defendant as the prosecution
claim, he would not have mistaken one for the other – particularly
as Paul Matthews was shot at close range. There's a big difference
between a stocky, well-built man in his twenties and a fifteen-year-
old boy.'

'Jury point, Ms Mitchell.'

'But one I wish to flag up now, Your Honour.'

'So noted. Mr Brooks, what is the other alleged motive?'

'On the night Paul Matthews was attacked, the Crown have CCTV evidence that the defendant was seen loitering at the rear of the Church of God Ministry around the time of the attack. This church is not only run by Reverend Desmond Matthews, the victim's father, but is less than half a mile from where the victim was found. The Crown also allege that this was the same night the defendant came to extort money from Mrs Matthews and threatened her if she didn't pay up.'

Extortion. So this was how the Crown hoped to play it. Lambert hunting for the local drug-dealing gangster was one thing, even if you shot his brother by mistake. Blackmailing a middle-aged preacher's wife was another thing entirely. The jury were guaranteed to hate him before he even opened his mouth.

'Threatened her with what, and why?' Judge Harris asked.

'So far, Mrs Matthews has refused to say. But she is adamant that both the demand for money and the threat were made. And shortly afterwards her youngest son was found in the street, having been attacked and left for dead.'

Judge Harris was unimpressed. 'I'm sure she doesn't want to say. No doubt this was exactly the reason why he sought to blackmail her in the first place. But these are very serious charges, where the defendant will face a substantial prison term if convicted. If you wish to rely on this evidence the witness must be prepared to state precisely what happened, and why, and be cross-examined on this point by Defence Counsel. I will not let the Crown open on this basis unless this is the case.'

'I understand, Your Honour.'

'I'm sure you do. Just make sure Mrs Matthews does too. Now, I haven't heard representations from either Counsel on this but I am imposing reporting restrictions on this case, which I'm sure will please both Counsel. Ms Mitchell would want this to protect her client, and I'm equally sure the Crown would want to prevent a successful abuse argument by the defence that the proceedings have been prejudiced by adverse publicity. Do either of you object?'

Both Lee and Stephen Brooks shook their heads.

'Any further applications by the Crown, Mr Brooks?'

'Yes, Your Honour. I have been instructed to invite the court to reconsider the bail position.'

'What?' Lee blurted out. She stood up. 'Your Honour, the defence has had no notice whatsoever of this application.'

'I apologize to my learned friend, but I was only instructed to take the point this morning. I appreciate it's unusual, but I would ask the court's indulgence on this matter.'

'You can't deliberately put the defence at such a disadvantage, Mr Brooks. I'm disinclined to hear it.'

'Your Honour, I'm firmly instructed to make the application. Normally, I wouldn't seek to do so without notice, but perhaps it might be better if you heard from the officer leading the investigation. He is in court today.'

'The gentleman behind you?'

'Yes, Your Honour.'

'What do you say, Ms Mitchell?'

'Your Honour, for the Crown to seek to make an application on such an important point in this way beggars belief. The defence have had no notice whatsoever.'

'Yes, you've said that. All the same, once pleas have been entered, it's an appropriate time to reconsider bail.' Judge Harris was silent for several moments before stating decisively, 'I'll hear from the officer. No promises, Mr Brooks. Ms Mitchell, I think your lay client wants to say something.'

Lee looked over her shoulder to see Lambert gesticulating, red-faced with rage. She whispered to Brendan. 'Go and see what he wants.'

Stephen Brooks said, 'I call DCI Daniel Wallace.'

Wallace didn't acknowledge her in any way. After he had been sworn in and stated his name, rank and role in the case for the court, the prosecution asked him, 'Although the defendant is currently on bail, you are asking the court to consider withdrawing this?'

Wallace addressed the Judge directly. 'Yes, Your Honour.'

'Please give your reasons for this to the court.'

'Yes, please do,' added Judge Harris.

Brendan came back and whispered to Lee. 'Our client is urging you to resist this application and to make the strongest possible representations on his behalf. Only he didn't put it quite like that.'

'Ms Mitchell, if you're quite finished,' Judge Harris said icily. 'Please continue, DCI Wallace.'

'Your Honour, the defendant is a police officer who has now entered a "not guilty" plea on a very serious count. He, more than most, would know he would face a substantial prison sentence if convicted after trial – far longer than he would get if he had pleaded guilty – and that police officers have a more . . . difficult time in prison than the average offender. All this makes him an increased flight risk.'

'Thank you, DCI Wallace. Ms Mitchell,' Judge Harris said as Lee rose to her feet, 'I don't need to hear from you. I don't believe the defendant is any more of a flight risk now than when he was first arrested, and I am most unimpressed that the Crown did not give you at least some notice of the application they intended to make. In addition, whilst not giving the defendant special treatment because of his profession, the fact that he is a long-serving police officer would make life very unpleasant indeed whilst on remand. Bail on same conditions as before.'

'Thank you, Your Honour,' Lee said.

'In any event, if he did abscond, he would find it difficult to hide. He's rather notorious now, unfortunately for him. Which is why I'm surprised reporting restrictions weren't imposed before. However, Ms Mitchell, you know that under normal circumstances the defendant would most certainly not be on bail for matters as serious as this. Also, the shorter the period of the reporting restrictions, the more effective they are. I've had a long fixture in my diary which has just been vacated. I'm therefore minded to list this trial to start in four weeks.'

Lee and Stephen looked at each other. Judge Harris raised his hand.

'I know this is sooner than either of you would have expected, but is there any reason why this can't be done?'

Lee got up to object. After all, she had other cases, other trials, which were listed for the same time Lambert's trial was now due to start. Their cases might not be as serious but they were just as important to those defendants as this was to Lambert. But she couldn't think of a single reason to do so. Someone else could do those trials. For better or worse, she was committed to this – to the end. And the sooner it was over, the better.

'No, Your Honour, we've had most of the disclosure. If the Crown can comply with the rest within seven days, that won't be a problem.'

'Mr Brooks?'

'That doesn't give us much time, Your Honour.'

'Then I suggest you get cracking straight away. Remaining disclosure within seven days. Trial date three weeks thereafter. As there are no other applications, I will rise for ten minutes before we continue with the rest of the list.'

As soon as the Judge left court, Brendan exclaimed, 'Only a month! Jesus!'

Lee was about to reply when the court usher interrupted them. 'Ms Mitchell, Mr Donnelly. We've had reports that there is a great deal of press outside the main entrance – even more than we're used to seeing here. We believe a photographer has slipped past security and is heading up here now. It's only a matter of time before they get here. I suggest you get your client out of the building – fast.'

'Right. Thanks,' Lee said. 'Brendan, you'd better get him out of here. If the trial's in a month we need to speak as soon as we get the rest of disclosure.'

Brendan nodded and left. As Lee gathered her books and papers, she could see the prosecutor approaching her for the first time that day, smiling sheepishly. 'Lee, I –'

Lee glared at him. 'You could have warned me, Steve. Trying to revoke bail, without notice?'

'Look, I'm sorry. But if you'd come up earlier, so we'd had a chance to speak before we started –'

'Don't give me that. Whatever happened to professional courtesy? You know you should have let me know well before – not on the morning of the hearing. You could have asked for a short adjournment to speak to me before we were called on – you didn't even do that.' DCI Wallace had now approached and was standing a few feet away. Lee knew she hadn't been mistaken. For some reason that made her even angrier. She jerked her head in Wallace's direction. 'Did he put you up to it?'

'Hey!' Stephen Brooks protested. 'No one put me up to anything! I was acting on instructions.'

215

'I was the one who suggested making the application,' Wallace said. 'I cleared it with CPS. That's why I'm here.'

'So the police are running trials now, not the lawyers.' Lee folded her arms. 'Good thing you didn't win. I'd have gone straight to the Court of Appeal. My client would have been out in hours and I'm sure they would have had something to say about Prosecution Counsel's conduct.'

'You don't seriously think he deserves to be on bail?' Wallace blurted out.

'DCI Wallace . . .' There was a warning note in Stephen Brooks's voice.

'I don't have anything further to say on this, especially not to the man trying to put my client behind bars.' Lee picked up her things. 'Excuse me.'

When she got to the robing room, it was empty, which was unusual for the time of day. She sat and buried her face in her hands. In one morning she had truly surprised herself. She had never represented someone she personally disliked so much before, yet she had sprung to his defence not once, but twice. However, hiding here wasn't an option. She too had to get out fast.

She jabbed repeatedly at the lift button until finally it opened on her floor.

'Oh no, not you again.'

Wallace was inside, holding the lift door open as if nothing had happened, not the last twenty minutes nor the last eighteen years. She stood stiffly next to him, staring at the door as it closed. 'You can't really think he deserves bail, Leanne. If he was anyone other than a copper he'd be banged up for sure.'

'And if he was anyone other than a copper he'd have a fighting chance of staying alive in prison until his trial. I won't take that chance.'

'That's because he's a shit, not because he's on the job. You know, even the Fed won't help him. That must tell you something.'

Lee paused, then turned to face him directly. 'Look, I'm sorry for how I behaved at the school. I was rude right out the gate; you didn't deserve that.'

'What? Oh yeah, that.' He grinned as he remembered. 'It's usually only the people who see me every day who give me grief.'

Lee looked him up and down. 'You know, you were the last person I thought would join the police.'

Wallace grinned again. 'Yeah. I'm still surprised myself. I bet you thought if you ever saw me again, you would be defending me – and you were very nearly right.'

'You?'

'Story for another time, perhaps. Do you want a coffee?'

The lift opened on the ground floor. Through the glass entrance doors immediately in front of her, Lee could see that all the reporters had gone. To her left, on the Court List next to '*R v Lambert*' was now clearly marked 'Reporting Restrictions'.

'You know I can't do that.'

'After the case, then? It's good to see you again, Lee. I've been following your career, believe it or not. I'm the only copper I know who doesn't chat shit about you.'

They were outside now, standing close together at the top of the court steps. Too close. He was just as attractive as he'd been when he was her schoolgirl crush. Lee turned away and squinted into the bright sunlight.

'Not a good idea, Danny.'

He shrugged. 'Okay.' He turned to go back inside. 'Got a mate in another case; said I'd wait. See you at the trial, then.'

*

'Fuck! We can't sneak out. We'll have to make a run for it.'

'All right, mate. You see where the van is?'

Standing in the shadows, the younger of the two uniformed officers leaned forward as far as he could without being seen. Lambert grunted in assent. 'That's where we're headed,' he continued. 'Christ, they could have got it a bit closer. What's the point of being Old Bill if you can't drive right up front?' Gingerly, he leaned forward again. His stocky, muscular build was at odds with the note of terror he was trying to hide in his voice. 'Bloody hell! They'll eat us alive!'

'Okay, that's enough of that,' his older colleague said, sharply. 'If you can't cope with it now, how will you manage when the trial proper starts? It'll be twice as bad then.' Turning to Lambert, he said, 'Better pull your coat over your head, mate.'

'You must be fucking joking! I'm not a criminal! Come out like some bloody nonce? No chance!'

'Look, I'm not arguing with you. As far as the court's concerned, a criminal is just what you are.'

'And what do you think?' Lambert turned to face the older officer directly. 'Come on, you're on the job, same as me . . .'

'Doesn't matter what I think. Right now, we're responsible for your safety –'

'And that's not just press out there, you know,' the younger officer interrupted. 'There's all sorts, and they want blood. Besides, when they start lobbing bricks – or worse – it won't just be you that gets hurt.'

'Come on, mate.' The older officer spoke to Lambert, his tone softer now. 'You know it's for the best.'

Lambert stared at them both, his contempt plain to see, before pulling his shabby raincoat over his head.

'And make sure you hold on to it,' the older officer said to him. He looked at his younger colleague. 'Okay. You ready?'

He nodded.

'Go!'

'Here he comes!'

Two police officers flanking a man with a coat over his head ran down the steps, almost pulling him down as they did so. They couldn't have advertised Lambert's presence better than if they'd held a neon sign over his head.

Press and protesters seemed to move forward as one. The sudden surge of the crowd, the noise, the camera flashes caught Tony Matthews momentarily off-guard, but standing where he was, he didn't have to move far. He doubted anyone else there knew this place as well as he did. He had specially chosen that spot at the foot of the steps, where the metal barriers didn't quite meet the concrete supports. A quick burst of speed – and there he was, three feet from Lambert.

It was a confrontation long overdue, one they had both wanted and feared in equal measure. But here in full view of dozens of people, neither of them could do anything about it. For a moment, everything else faded away as if they were in the still centre of the noisy crowd swirling around them.

'Watch out! He's got a gun!'

The taller officer pushed Lambert down, using his greater size to shield him; the other swung out at Tony Matthews, the force of the blow catching him across the chest, knocking him to the ground. He removed a small canister from his belt, held his arm out in front and moved towards Tony as he struggled to get up.

'No PAVA spray!' shouted his colleague. 'Too many people.'

'He hasn't got a gun,' said Lambert, picking himself up. 'If he had, I'd be dead by now. You too.' He shouted over to Tony in a mocking voice. 'You're not armed, are you, Tony?' Turning to face the officers, he added, 'If he's going to kill me, he won't do it here.'

'You *know* him?'

'Yeah, I know him. If you don't, you're definitely not from round here.'

The wail of police sirens at close quarters was a welcome sound. Everyone turned towards the police van slowly making its way through the crowd, closer to the steps.

'Thank Christ! Let's make a run for it!'

The van door slid open just as the three men reached it. Lambert was bundled inside. As the banging and hammering started on all sides of the van, it was clear to Lambert that the younger officer had never experienced anything like this before. For his part, it hardly bothered him. If he had been kept in custody – a police officer on remand – he would have been better off dead, and probably would have been within a week. He thought about Tony. So close. At least he had lived to fight another day.

29

Since she had accepted the Lambert brief, Lee had been working flat out to get the case trial ready. Four weeks was a very narrow margin, but she knew better than to go back to court to apply for an adjournment that would almost certainly have been refused. Also, the sooner Lambert was out of her life, the better.

It was almost two weeks before she realized she hadn't spoken to her mother. Verna Mitchell had been leaving her daughter very brief messages when she knew she wasn't home, but she hadn't seemed her usual self. She hadn't even made any cracks about David. Something was seriously wrong.

So, on instinct, Lee found herself outside the Church of God Ministry at what she estimated would have been the time the service would finish, so she could collect her mother and surprise her with lunch. She had no intention of going inside – she'd left that church at sixteen and hadn't looked back – but she had dressed with more care than she otherwise would on a Sunday morning: still in jeans, but with Louboutins, her most expensive coat and a designer handbag she had been on a three-month Bond Street waiting list for. She knew her mother would appreciate the effort, but it was more than that. People had known who she was even before the Lambert case. This was still a largely Black, working-class neighbourhood. If you were successful, people expected to see that success – particularly if you were now Public Enemy Number One.

In the event, she was out by almost an hour. She sat in her car and waited, playing a rare New Orleans blues CD David had given her for her birthday. The plaintive wailing of the usual bluesman's lyrics of love gone wrong was a little too close for comfort, but she left it on. For weeks, David seemed to have been accepting every job that took him outside London, including abroad, so he had been away most of the time. He was due back later today, in fact, but she didn't know whether to be glad or sorry.

The noise of the congregation finally spilling out on to the streets grew increasingly louder, drowning out the music in the car. Lee wound the window down and scanned the crowd. For a tiny woman, her mother was easy to spot. Easy because, as she walked down the short flight of stone steps on to the path leading to the main gate, the crowd divided and rolled away from her, like a sick parody of the parting of the Red Sea.

Lee watched as her mother attempted to engage a woman of similar age in conversation, only for her to get the briefest of coldly polite responses before the other woman moved away. The slump of her mother's shoulders at that rejection, even as she tried to keep a brave smile on her face; the nervous way she protectively clutched her tortoiseshell-framed leather handbag to her chest as she tentatively picked her way through the mass of people – Lee felt as if someone had reached into her chest, grabbed her heart and twisted it. Then she got angry.

She got out of her car, deliberately slamming the door. Some people looked up and across in her direction as she drew herself up to her full height and strode purposefully across the road. As she approached, the looks she was getting were as varied as the people in front of her. A few didn't recognize her; others were hostile; the younger girls were checking out her bag and shoes; still others were frankly curious, as if they were in the presence of a minor celebrity. But as she stepped from the pavement on to the church path, the only person there she cared about seemed rooted to the spot as she watched her daughter bearing down like an avenging angel.

'Leanne, what are you doing here?' her mother whispered.

Lee could hear her mobile ringing in her bag. That could wait. She realized how quiet it had become, even with all these people around, if she could hear it so clearly.

'Thought you might like a lift home, Mum,' she replied, so everyone could hear. 'I could buy you lunch too, if you like – saves you having to cook.'

Verna looked up at her daughter. Her eyes were moist. 'You're a good girl, Leanne. A good daughter to me . . .' She stopped, clearly trying to collect herself. When she spoke again, her voice was firmer, her smile genuinely bright. 'You remembered I hate to wait for the bus.'

Once inside the car, Verna Mitchell turned to her daughter. 'On second thoughts, you know I prefer my own cooking to any of those fancy restaurants you take me to.'

Lee sighed. 'It's good to try new things sometimes, Mum.'

'Girl, at my age, there's not much that's new. I know you want to look after me, and I'm glad you came today – very glad. But now,' she pulled her coat around herself more tightly, 'I just want to be in my own home. Somewhere I feel comfortable.'

Lee stared at the last of the worshippers huddled by the iron church gates. 'How long has that been going on?'

Her mother shrugged.

'Now you see why I don't go to church. They might hate me doing this case, but they know you. You've been attending since before some of them were even born and they treat you like that? Bunch of hypocrites!'

'It's not usually like that, Leanne. I've found a lot of comfort and support there, especially after your father died. And the baby, all those years ago. It can't stay like this forever. Once your case is over, it'll get back to normal sooner or later. Don't worry, I'll be there next week as usual. Nobody's going to run me out after all these years. I was there even before Desmond Matthews came to lead our church! And don't you think about losing to make things easier for me. You just do what you have to do.'

Lee shook her head. 'The rate things are going, I don't think I'll have to try and lose it. Anyway, this time next month, it'll be over.' She turned on the ignition. 'You sure you just want to go home?'

'Oh yes,' Verna replied. She was looking more comfortable and relaxed by the minute. Just then Lee's mobile rang again. Three missed calls, number withheld. But a message. From Lili.

'Lee, I can't get hold of you. You better get down here quick as you can. It's David.'

Lili was unflappable. You had to be if you owned and ran a South London pub. But she had sounded really scared. Knowing that, it was hard to drive within the speed limit, but the last thing Lee wanted was to be done for speeding by Miller Street police. Thankfully, it was fairly close to her mother's house, and the Sunday lunchtime roads had little traffic. She turned a corner and could see the pub at the end of the road when a police car screamed past her, lights on and sirens blaring. Her stomach lurched as it paused momentarily outside the Lily Langtry, but then it did a sudden sharp left and disappeared into the sprawling council estate. She screeched to a halt on a double yellow line right outside the pub, put her hazard lights on and ran inside.

The inner door was locked. She rattled the handle and banged on the door. Lili opened it. She looked pale and drawn, and her eyes were red as if she had been crying.

'God, Lili – are you all right? What's happened?'

'Do I look as if I'm fucking all right?' She jerked her head back over her shoulder. 'He's in there.'

The scene inside stopped Lee in her tracks. No wonder Lili was upset. Even though it was still bright outside, the harsh overhead lights were on. The area immediately in front of the bar looked like a scene from a TV Western saloon brawl. Two of the round tables were overturned, their heavy clawed iron feet pointing bizarrely upwards. Lumps of broken glass from pint mugs were embedded in the carpet, mixed in with the tiny twinkling shards of shattered wine glasses.

David had his back to her when she entered. Although he had to know that she was there, he didn't look round. He held his right arm bent in close to his body, and was trying to pick up one of the over-turned tables with his left hand. Strong as he was, he wasn't having much success. Even standing behind him, Lee could tell he was in pain. She moved closer.

'What happened, D?' She reached out to touch his right arm, but he pulled away, wincing as he did so. Eventually, he managed to haul the table upright. He sat down on it, facing her, and Lee was able to have a good look at him for the first time since she arrived. He had a nasty bruise above his right eye which would be even worse tomorrow. There was blood on the front of his sweatshirt and on the right sleeve, which had a jagged slash across the forearm.

'Oh God! You've been stabbed! Let me see.' She gingerly opened up the torn fabric. Blood was oozing from a fresh wound. It didn't look too deep, but it was nasty, nevertheless. Then her eyes travelled down to his hand. It was badly bruised across the knuckles and grotesquely swollen.

'Terry tried to glass me. Good thing his aim was off.'

'Over what?'

David stared at her. His eyes were frighteningly cold. Even when he had been angry with her before, she had never seen that look.

'Take a wild guess.'

'It wasn't just that.' Lili had come into the bar now. She surveyed the wreckage of the business she had painstakingly restored to its former glory and shook her head. 'Terry said some other stuff about you. What you did to get all these big cases. The kind of things no man would stand by and hear said about his woman.'

'Where's Terry now?'

'Terry?' Lili replied. 'Ambulance came for him. He needed it. David should go too, Lee. I'm no doctor, but his hand looks broken to me.'

'Lili,' David said, 'do me a favour. Get me my mobile. I need to cancel the rehearsal tomorrow –'

'Don't worry about that now,' Lee interrupted. 'I can do that. But first I need to get you to hospital –'

'I'm not going anywhere with you, Lee.'

This had been building up for weeks. Lee was prepared for shouting, swearing, raw naked anger. The icy calm of his voice was far worse.

'You can say what you like to me later, but I need to get you to A&E –'

'Don't say anything else to me, Lee. Just don't.' David was taking deep breaths, as if trying to keep his emotions under control. 'If I need a doctor, I'll get myself there. I've just defended your right to represent a racist. I think that's earned me the right to have you leave me the fuck alone!' He stood up slowly and, with difficulty, walked towards the back of the pub and disappeared from view.

Lee stared at her boyfriend's retreating back. She could feel tears pricking her eyes and blinked them away. She wasn't normally a crier, but it seemed to be happening more since she'd been connected to this case. And it was hard not to, especially when Lili was looking at her the way she was now.

Lili walked up and gave her an all-enveloping hug. That's when the tears came.

'Don't worry about David,' her friend said. 'I'll either get him to hospital or he can sleep it off here.' She waved her arm at the debris. 'At least I've got good insurance.'

'If you claim on your insurance, Lili, the premiums will bankrupt you, especially in this area. I'll pay for the damages.' She paused. 'Thanks for not calling the police on David.'

'I'd never do that. But this can't be worth it, Lee? For one case?'

Lee thought of her mother, of David. Of Paul Matthews. Marlon, the head custody officer. And then Lambert. 'No, Lili. It stopped being worth it a long time ago.'

30

Brendan thought he might as well state the bloody obvious. 'It's very unorthodox, you know, taking instructions from one's client in a pub.'

'Well, you wanted to see me at short notice.' Lambert sounded for all the world as if he were doing his solicitor a favour, rather than his lawyer trying to keep him out of jail. 'Here I am. Don't worry, no one is going to bother us here. I've still got *some* friends. There's one over there that used to be a mate. Collier. Now he works for the IOPC. Fucking traitor.' He took a sip of his pint, leaving froth on his upper lip before he wiped it away with the back of his hand. 'Remember Ray Willis? Used to work the door here sometimes, specially to pull in the ladies. Course, they don't need him now his face is all chewed up. Bad for business. So,' he slammed the pint on the table, 'what did you want to see me about?'

Brendan thought he'd better get this over with. He wasn't sure how much Lambert had had to drink, and drunken instructions would be worse than useless. 'I've got the extra disclosure. Nothing much: continuation statements and the like. I told Lee I'd get your instructions on the statements and ring her later. But what I really want to hear is some sort of defence. The trial starts Monday!'

'That's your job, innit? You and your "learned friend",' he said sarcastically. 'Make something up.'

'I'll pretend I didn't hear that.'

'Brendan, this is Jack Lambert you're talking to. I don't know about her – I suppose she's one of those "don't ask, don't tell" types, but I know you. I know you've done it before, and you're desperate enough to do it again. Why do you think I came to you?'

Brendan could feel his face flush. At least, in the dimly lit pub, Lambert wouldn't be able to see it.

'So what will happen when she calls you to give evidence?'

'Well, if I don't think what you're going to tell me to say will be convincing enough, I won't do it. I told you before when I went to her Chambers. Prosecution say I did this? Let them prove it. As I said before, I've got faith in our wonderful criminal justice system; it lets all sorts of guilty people off.'

Brendan stiffened. 'Are you telling me you did this, Jack?'

'We're all guilty of something, Brendan. But no, I'm not admitting anything. I've told you all along I didn't do it.'

Realization slowly dawned on Brendan. He was only shocked that he didn't see it before.

'It's Mrs Matthews. You *were* trying to blackmail her.'

'Careful. The PC police will nick you for using that word.'

'Stop pissing about, Jack. I can't believe you'd be so fucking stupid. A reverend's wife! Why?'

It was a long time before Lambert replied.

'Okay, okay. So I tried to get some money off her. Look, blackmail's one thing, attempted murder's another. You think if the jury heard about that I'd have any chance of getting off? That's why I don't want to give evidence.'

'So, what's she got to hide?'

Lambert drained his glass. He paused before replying.

'Has she said anything about it in her statement?'

'No.'

'Then I'm not saying.'

'Look, it's too late to get noble or to save your soul. I'd just con-
centrate on saving your arse if I were you.'

'Even if I went to jail – worst-case scenario – I'd be out at some
point. I can use it then. I might even get out sooner, thanks to her. She
might be persuaded to head up the campaign to free me, know what
I mean?'

'So you're not going to tell me what it is?'

'You mean, am I going to trust you with this information, the only
thing that might be standing between me and a stretch? What do you
think, Brendan?'

Brendan shook his head and gathered up his papers. As he got up
to leave, Lambert said, 'If you get it out of her, I'll give evidence. But
don't hold your breath. Either way.'

'So, nothing?' Lee asked.

'Nothing.' Brendan's voice sounded crackly on his mobile.

'I can hardly hear you. Where are you calling from?'

'Don't ask. I'm surprised you're still in Chambers.'

Lee looked at the clock: 11 p.m. 'What do you expect? The trial
starts Monday and we've got nothing, absolutely nothing positive to
put before a jury. No defence, no character witnesses . . .'

'Well,' Brendan said hopefully, 'he *is* a long-serving police officer,
and he's of good character.'

'Who never got further than sergeant. Besides, this is a Southwark
jury. Being a copper isn't exactly a recommendation. He's got no
convictions – that will help. But describing him as a man of good
character? Don't make me laugh.' She sighed. 'Well, no point me
staying here any longer. See you Monday.'

Lee looked out of the window. Late in Chambers on a Friday night was one of the loneliest, saddest places to be. She thought back to the recent past. She used to go home as early as she could on a Friday, straight from court – all the sooner to begin her weekend and spend it with David. She used to feel sorry for members of Chambers who would stay late, when really they had nowhere to go and no one to go home to. Now she was one of them. But having spoken to Brendan, there was nothing else useful she could do tonight. It was the last working day before the trial started on Monday; she would have to work over the weekend anyway.

Just then her mobile rang. She looked at the screen. Number withheld. She let it ring and go to voicemail. No message. When it rang again she was about to switch it off, then remembered the 'number-withheld' call she had received from Lili nearly two weeks ago. Suppose she had ignored that? And it might even be David. Lili gave her progress reports, but she hadn't seen him since that day.

She accepted the call, pausing at first to let the caller speak to get some clue as to who it was. Nothing.

'Who is this?' she said, finally.

'Well, at least your number ain't changed.' It was a man's voice, roughened by South London streets, and something else. When Lee didn't reply, he continued, 'Yeah, I know I sound different. Did you know your voice changes when your facial muscles are damaged? That's what a doctor told me. She was in bed with me at the time, mind. Slumming.'

'Ray?'

'Yeah. I'm outside your Chambers. Let me in. I need to talk to you.'

'What do you want? And how did you know I'd be here?'

'You told me you always used to work late leading up to a big case.

231

I took a chance. I wouldn't be down here if it wasn't important. I've got better places to be on a Friday night.'

It had been well over a year since she last had seen or had anything to do with Ray. She had represented him for years before that. He had put a lot of business her way, for him and his associates. She still acted for some of them. As different as they were, they understood each other. The fact that he had her mobile number was testament to that. But he had been a career criminal, and a year was a long time. While she doubted he blamed her for Omartian's dog disfiguring his face after he had tried to help her, tonight when she was alone late in Chambers was not the moment she wanted to find out.

'You're not going to go away, are you?'

'You know I'm not.'

The area immediately outside Maple Court was brightly lit. Chambers had security cameras, and there was a guard patrolling the Temple. Somewhere. 'Then I'll come out to you.'

She packed her things, but kept her mobile in her pocket, 999 on speed dial.

As she stepped outside, he was standing on the top step with his back to her, looking out. Force of habit, maybe; she had heard he was doing door security. Definitely more muscular, though, from the set of his shoulders and the way he stood. His hair had grown out from the severe crew cut just long enough not to be immediately threatening. As he turned to face her, his handsome profile was the same Ray she knew. Then he faced her fully, and she saw all of his face.

He stared at her intently, arms folded across his chest. He had a tattoo over the knuckles of his right hand, which was new, at least to her. She knew he was watching for the slightest hint of revulsion. She thought of photographs she had seen in court, of dead and maimed bodies. It helped to keep her face without expression.

'You look like money,' he said at last.

It was a compliment, coming from him, but Lee ignored it.

'It's late, Ray. What are you doing here?'

'Found out something I thought you'd want to know before your trial starts Monday.'

'I didn't think you'd want to help Lambert. Or me,' she added, quietly.

'I don't.' His voice was abrupt. 'I've come to trade. I want you to do something for me.'

'What's that?' Lee asked, warily.

'I know JT's dead because of Lambert. He shot him, got someone else to do it, or someone did it because they found out he was his grass . . . Whatever: it's down to him.'

'I'm not defending him on that.'

'I know. Too bad JT wasn't the son of the local saint. Someone else might give a shit then, apart from me. CPS won't bother to prosecute this. You and I both know how they work. Far as they're concerned, he's some petty dealer who got out of his depth and got what he deserved. They probably want to pin a medal on someone for getting rid of him.' He looked away into the middle distance. 'He wasn't always like that. He was no angel, but it was when he started using that things went downhill. I tried to look out for him . . .' His voice trailed away. When he looked back at Lee, his eyes were hard. 'I want Lambert to pay for this.'

'So where do I come in?'

'I was working the door at Satyr a couple of months ago. You wouldn't know it. Private gay club in Mayfair. Very discreet. That Black DCI – Wallace – came in. "On official business," he said. I didn't know what official business he could have had with a bunch of rich queers. So I did some digging. Turns out he came to see Hugo

Cunningham. You know him, right?' When Lee nodded, he continued, 'Cunningham's been a cokehead for years on the quiet. Tony Matthews is his supplier. JT told me. I know the gun used on JT and Paul Matthews turned up at Miller Street because Cunningham handed it in.' He held up his hand as if to ward off any questions. 'Don't bother to ask me how I know, neither. I think that gun came either from Tony or Lambert. Both of them are connected with you and Paul Matthews.'

'So?'

'So when the case starts I want you to make the link between Paul Matthews's shooting and JT's death. They were both shot with the same gun. Only Lambert could have done that.'

'You want *me* to do that?' Lee was astonished. 'You've come to the wrong person. I'm defending Lambert, remember – not prosecuting. That would ruin what little defence I have.'

'This'll help to ease your conscience, then. I'll never understand why you agreed to do it in the first place. I remember when Lambert saw me in the pub, boasting about how he was going to get you. I'd have bet my life you wouldn't do it. Especially because you know, win or lose, he'll always think of you the same way he does all Black people – as a nigger.'

Lee knew Ray was no racist, but that ugly word still had power, no matter who said it, and her reaction was immediate.

'You just watch your fucking mouth! I am so sick of everyone telling me how I should feel. I know what I'm doing, and why. I don't need some white boy coming down here telling me about my conscience!' She jabbed her finger in his face. 'It's *your* conscience that's got you here now. Your friend's dead and you couldn't protect him.'

'You're the only woman I'd ever let talk to me like that, Lee. But take your finger out of my face. If you were a man, I'd break it off

234

and shove it up your arse.' Ray's voice was low, quiet and deadly serious.

Lee could feel the tension swirling around them in the silence that followed. Finally, she said, 'I can't help you, Ray. If I did, I'd jeopardize Lambert's case. Go to CPS with what you've got.' She picked up her bag. 'If anyone asks, far as I'm concerned this meeting never happened – so you won't get into trouble for trying to lean on Defence Counsel. I'll just say you happened to be passing. Even though it's late, who's to say different? I've got to go.'

But Ray remained blocking her path. She looked up pointedly at the CCTV camera aimed at them, then back at the man in front of her. 'You're smarter than that, Ray. Better let me pass.'

31

Lee had always found it hard to sleep the night before a big case. She wandered around the flat restlessly. It seemed bigger than ever now it was just her. The fact that she had been smoking all day was a bad sign. An empty cigarette packet lay on the table, a silent reproach as she pulled the cellophane from yet another one. She'd have to start vaping soon if she carried on like this; she hadn't smoked more than twenty in a day in years.

She sat at the dining table where she had been working and looked through the French windows on to the garden. This view had been the reason she had bought this flat when she couldn't really afford it. The garden still looked lovely, but slightly neglected. Yet another item on the long list of things to do once this was over.

The night sky was beginning to get lighter. Time for at least a few hours' sleep. She would need every one of them today.

Way down on the Brighton coast, Wallace knew he wouldn't have any problem sleeping. Not now, because he had prepared for it. There was a lot riding on getting a conviction, and you could never tell with juries; Lambert was still a policeman, after all. He knew he would be wired and jumpy the night before. He could either smoke a spliff – not advisable in his line of work – burn off his excess energy at the gym, or burn it off some other way. Option number three. He looked at the sleeping body next to him. Normally he would kick them out, but they had worked their magic. And they weren't a snorer. He'd do it tomorrow.

Lee walked as quickly as she could from the train station to the court. She had overslept, and was still tired and foggy on nicotine and four hours' sleep – the worst possible start to any day, let alone a big trial. At this early stage what else could possibly go wrong?

Turning the final corner before the entrance to the court, her question was answered.

There was a group of protesters, small but vocal, standing directly opposite the court. *Black Lives Matter. Justice for Paulie. Racist Police Out.* She didn't need to read the placards to know who they were and why they were there. The last time she was here, she'd been able to hide behind her sunglasses. Not today, on this unusually overcast May morning.

Fee Smith was the smallest and most vocal. Lee saw her nudge a man standing next to her and deliberately point her out as she approached the steps. Suddenly, the protesters were shouting only one word: '*Shame! Shame! Shame!*' Fee's voice started it but was soon drowned out by the others behind her. Lee kept walking, looking straight ahead. Then she saw David, his right hand still strapped. He was standing back away from the protesters, silently observing. It was clear his sympathies lay with the protesters, but as Lee watched him scanning the crowd, when he looked at Fee he appeared both suspicious and completely unimpressed.

Lee wasn't worried about physical violence – the reassuring sight of the court security staff, as well as two police officers at the court entrance, meant this was unlikely. And even after everything that had happened between them, instinctively she knew David would protect her. But the venom directed towards her felt like a punch in the gut. As she neared the top of the steps, however, it suddenly fell silent. She turned round and saw Reverend Matthews. He was clutching a Bible to his chest, and his lips were moving, apparently in prayer. For a moment, she wondered where the rest of his family was, and then remembered that both Tony and Mrs Matthews were listed as prosecution witnesses and wouldn't be able to sit in the public gallery until they had finished giving evidence. In any event, he hadn't come alone – Hugo Cunningham was with him. For a moment, their eyes met. Then Reverend Matthews turned away and Lee headed into the building.

Ten twenty-five. Five minutes to go. The public gallery was packed, as expected. Lee arranged and rearranged the pens and trial papers in front of her, trying her best to hide her nerves. She always used good-quality fountain pens, the one barrister tradition she embraced, but now she also had her laptop with her. Ancient and modern – that was the English Bar.

Brendan was sitting directly behind her. She didn't have to ask how he felt; his anxiety was obvious. She glanced over at Prosecution Counsel. Stephen Brooks was studiously avoiding her gaze, but Lee was glad to see he was nervous too. In fact, looking over her shoulder to the dock, the only person who seemed calm was Jack Lambert.

The Court Clerk stuck his head through the door from the Judge's chambers, checking everyone was ready, and at 10.30 a.m. exactly the court usher said, 'All rise!', announcing Judge Harris's entrance into court.

'Are all parties ready?' he asked, as soon as he sat down.

Stephen Brooks stood up. 'Yes, Your Honour.' Lee nodded.

'Good. Madam usher, let's empanel the jury.'

Lee had been thinking about the type of jury most likely to acquit Lambert for weeks. She had hoped at least six of the twelve would be from the same demographic as her lay client – white, working-class men in their forties, or older, nursing a sense of grievance at the world. Worst-case scenario would be mothers, or any woman who appeared old enough to have a son – or worse, grandson – the age of the victim. And, of course, anyone Black. But as the names were called out, the jury slowly took shape as a mixture of all of these. A typical reflection of modern multicultural London, in fact, and with any other defendant, that would be ideal. Just not today.

Some of them clearly recognized Lambert, particularly when, once again, the indictment was put to him and he repeated his 'not guilty' plea. Once the jury was sworn in, Judge Harris addressed them directly.

'Members of the jury, you have heard the defendant's pleas. I am the judge in this case – the sole judge of the law on which I will guide and direct you. You are the judges of the facts. Together we will decide whether, after hearing the evidence, the defendant is in fact guilty or innocent. Now, no doubt many of you will have heard or read about this case in the press before reporting restrictions were imposed. You must put whatever you have heard or read out of your mind; that is not evidence, and the evidence you hear in this court must be the only thing upon which you decide this matter. Mr Brooks appears for the prosecution, and Ms Mitchell for the defence.'

At this point, Lee, who was sitting nearest the jury, gave them a half-smile. Some avoided her, and those who did not were at best indifferent, at worst hostile. Not a promising start.

'Mr Brooks,' the Judge continued, 'please proceed.'

Stephen Brooks stood up. Turning to the jury, he began. 'Good morning, ladies and gentlemen. As you have heard from His

Honour, I prosecute this case, and my learned friend Ms Mitchell acts for the defence. This will be a relatively short trial, but by no means a trivial one. You've heard the indictment that the defendant has pleaded not guilty to; the allegation is among the most serious known to English criminal law.

'But strip away the trappings of court – the lawyers, the wigs and gowns – and at the heart of this case lies a victim. A fifteen-year-old boy, his whole life ahead of him, shot in the face and receiving head injuries so severe that several weeks after the attack on him he is still in a coma on life support. The Crown will prove to you that the defendant, John Alfred Lambert, committed this vicious act.'

As Brooks went on to outline the evidence the Crown intended to call to support their case, Brendan, who was sitting behind Lee, passed her a note. '*Strong opening, pulling at heartstrings. No mention of motive?*' Lee had noticed that too.

Finally, Brooks concluded his opening speech. 'And with that, I call my first witness, Detective Chief Inspector Wallace.'

Wallace stood in the witness box. Tall, handsome and impeccably dressed in a suit that was, in every sense of the word, a cut above that of the average plain-clothes police officer, he exuded authority and credibility. He was a dream witness for the prosecution before he even opened his mouth. Lee glanced at the jury. Clearly, some of the women jurors thought so too. After he was sworn in and had con-firmed his name and rank, Brooks asked, 'You are the officer leading this investigation?'

Wallace addressed the Judge. 'That's right, Your Honour.'

'How long have you been a police officer?'

'Twelve years, and I've been a detective for ten.'

'Please tell the court about the type of work you've done as a police officer.'

'I've mostly worked on major crimes and murders. I've also worked as a close protection officer for visiting dignitaries. That was because of my Army expertise. I served for four years, seeing active duty before joining the police.'

'Where did you serve when you were in the Army, DCI Wallace?'

Lee knew where this was going. Brooks was trying it on. She had enough problems with this case without Wallace being made out as a war hero. She stood up. 'Your Honour. Relevance?'

'I withdraw the question, Your Honour. DCI Wallace, is it right that the day after Paul Matthews was found, you spoke to his mother, Eloise Matthews?'

'Yes.'

'And as a result of what she told you, you seized some CCTV footage showing the rear of the church above which she and her husband lived?'

'That's right.'

'Your Honour, I would now like to play this for the jury.'

'Ms Mitchell,' Judge Harris turned to Lee, 'surely you can have no objection to this?'

Lee shook her head. There was no point; it would only make the jury think Lambert had something to hide. 'No, Your Honour.'

The CCTV footage was, unfortunately for Lambert, very good quality. Although it was dark and raining and there was no audio on the tape, there was no doubting it was him. Worse, Mrs Matthews clearly looked frightened. The whole court watched in silence. When it was over, Brooks turned back to Wallace.

'DCI Wallace, the expert reports, which have not been challenged by the defence,' he looked sideways at Lee, 'state that the bullet that shot Paul Matthews was from a Glock 9mm. Is that correct?'

'Yes, it is.'

'And what type of weapon is that?'

'It's one commonly used by gangs and other criminals. It's a known street weapon.'

'Was there anything connecting the defendant to that weapon?'

'Yes. Forensics found a partial print on the gun, identified as the defendant's.'

As she cross-checked the forensics report, out of the corner of her eye Lee could see the jury looking at Lambert, then at her.

'Finally, DCI Wallace, please tell the jury where the bullet was recovered from.'

Wallace paused, making sure he had the jury's full attention. 'From the victim's skull, behind his left eye,' he replied grimly.

'Thank you, Chief Inspector. I have no further questions. Please wait there.'

Lee stood and faced Wallace. Clearly, the jury liked and believed him. This had to be undermined at once.

'Mr Wallace,' she began, stripping him of his title. Wallace frowned. 'Would you confirm the defendant is an officer of twenty-five years' service?'

Wallace looked at Lambert, then back at Lee before answering. 'Yes.' She wondered whether the barely concealed disgust in his voice was for Lambert, or for her.

'Thank you. Did your team do a trawl for any other relevant CCTV? For example, where Paul Matthews was found?'

'Yes, we did.'

'Did you find any?'

'Nothing of this quality.'

'That doesn't answer my question, officer. You found no other footage showing the defendant at all, is that right?'

'Yes.'

'Nothing showing him committing this attack?'

'That's right.'

'The partial print you found on the gun.' She held up the forensics report. 'Your own expert said it was just part of one thumbprint belonging to the defendant, isn't that right?'

'Yes.'

'One lift, or print, out of a maximum of ten.'

'You hardly ever get that many prints, even where the item in question is being held in both hands. I doubt that was the case here.'

'It's right these guns are often passed around, aren't they, Mr Wallace?'

'What do you mean?'

Lee knew he knew what she meant. He wasn't going to make it easy for her. 'Come on, you're an experienced detective. I mean, that one gun is often used in more than one incident.'

'That's right.'

'According to the report, the defendant's partial thumbprint was not the only one found on this gun, was it?'

'No, it wasn't.'

'Please tell the jury how many other sets of prints were found.'

Brooks was staring straight ahead. Wallace paused before replying. 'Three.'

'Three,' Lee repeated, driving home the point to the jury. Not such conclusive evidence now. She wanted him to say in front of the jury who they belonged to, but this was as far as she could safely take it. She had made her point. Two of them belonged to Tony Matthews and JT. She didn't want the jury to think that she was suggesting Paul Matthews was shot by his own brother, or that she was besmirching the parents' good name. Plus she wanted to keep JT's name well and truly out of this. She thought of Ray and what he'd asked her to do. It would be so easy.

'So, according to this evidence, potentially three other people could have shot Paul Matthews, isn't that right?'

Silence.

'Isn't that right, officer?'

'Yes.'

'Thank you. That's all I ask.'

Brooks stood up. 'Re-examination, Your Honour. DCI Wallace, what – if any – items did you find on the victim?'

'Some house keys, a few pounds in change, a receipt for some chocolates, a bus pass and two mobile phones, one registered to his brother. We found his brother's phone on the ground where he fell.'

'Thank you. Does Your Honour have any questions?' As Judge Harris shook his head, Brooks said, 'I call Mr Arthur Morris.'

After Mr Morris was sworn and the preliminary questions dealt with, Brooks began, 'Please tell us where you were on the night in question.'

'I was walking Bessie, my Alsatian.' Arthur Morris was a man in his late sixties, slightly stooped with a soft Scottish accent. 'I remember that night because it was raining heavily, as well as being cold. I didn't want to go out, but Bessie was making such a racket I had to take her. I didn't intend to be out for long, so I cut through the alley behind the shops.'

'Which one was this?'

'It's not far from Miller Street police station. Normally, I wouldn't go there. Too dangerous at night, especially at my age. But no one argues with an Alsatian.'

'Then what happened?'

'Then I saw someone – or rather, Bessie found him first. I thought it was a drug addict, but then I thought, out in this weather? Plus, he was all crumpled up; half sitting, half lying, you know? Then when I got nearer – I could tell it was a man or a boy by then – I saw his head. Or what was left of it . . .' Morris's voice trailed off.

Brooks paused before asking the next question, giving the witness time to compose himself but also letting the reply hang in the air for the jury.

'What did you do then?' he asked, gently.

'I called the police. Luckily, I had the mobile my granddaughter had given me. Then I sheltered in a doorway until they came.'

'That can't have been very pleasant for you. Why wait there?'

'Because the police are always in the area, so I knew they'd be quick! Besides, as I said, I've got grandchildren. I didn't want to leave him. When the police came, I told them what I've just told you.'

'Thank you, Mr Morris. Please wait there. There may be some questions for you.'

Lee stood up and faced the witness. Morris was nervous, but clearly he was telling the truth, a Good Samaritan caught up in something not of his making. She smiled at him.

'Mr Morris, I know Paul's parents must be very grateful. Your quick action almost certainly saved his life.'

Morris shrugged and smiled, embarrassed.

'When you found him, did you see or hear anyone else in the vicinity?'

'No, I didn't.'

'And did you see anything that could have caused the injury?'

'No. I remember seeing a mobile, and a bus pass I think, but nothing else.'

'Thank you. No further questions.'

'No re-examination. If Your Honour has no questions, I call Malcolm Weir.'

Malcolm Weir was sworn in. He looked tired, as if he had worked all night. Being an NHS surgeon, he probably had.

'You were the surgeon who operated on Paul Matthews?' Brooks began.

'That's right.'

'And saved his life.'

'I've helped to keep him alive so far, if that's what you mean. He's still on life support, however.'

'Both prosecution and defence have seen your statement, Mr Weir, but I wonder if you could explain, in layman's terms for the jury, the injuries the victim sustained, and his prognosis.'

Malcolm Weir went on to describe how Paul Matthews had presented when he came into A&E; the operation carried out that undoubtedly saved his life; and the weeks in which his life hung in the balance. When Weir described his future prognosis, so long after the attack, as 'very poor, with no expected improvement', there was an anguished, piercing sob from the public gallery which echoed across the courtroom. Everyone looked up to see Reverend Matthews, shoulders shaking, his face buried in his hands. Judge Harris opened his mouth as if to say something, but decided against it as the minister struggled to compose himself. It was some time before anyone spoke again.

'Thank you, Mr Weir. Please wait there.'

Lee stood up, deliberately avoiding catching sight of Reverend Matthews. 'I only have a few questions for you, Mr Weir. You say Paul Matthews was shot in the side of the face, through the left eye.'

'Yes.'

'Could you tell from the angle of the bullet whether the assailant was taller, shorter, or the same height?'

'No. I can give you a medical opinion on the weapon, not a police opinion.'

'So the attacker didn't necessarily have to be taller or bigger than Paul Matthews?'

'It's more likely. Paul isn't that tall.'

'But not necessarily.'

Malcolm Weir paused before replying. 'That's correct.'

'Thank you, Mr Weir. No further questions.'

'No re-examination. Does Your Honour have any questions?'

'No. Thank you, Mr Weir. You may go.' Before Judge Harris could continue, the Court Clerk stood up, turned and leaned over his desk to speak to him. After a conversation of some minutes, the clerk sat down as the Judge addressed the court.

'Counsel, members of the jury, there is an unexpected matter I have to deal with which doesn't concern this trial. It's likely to take the rest of the day.' He looked at his watch. 'I see it is almost lunch-time. I suggest we adjourn now and reconvene tomorrow morning at ten thirty. Although you will have the benefit of a free afternoon, I must warn the jury not to discuss the case amongst yourselves or with anyone at all outside the jury room. You have only heard part of the evidence so far, and nothing yet for the defence. Court will rise until ten thirty tomorrow morning.'

It was getting late. Eloise Matthews looked at the bedroom clock. Strange for Desmond not to be in bed by now. It had been a strained evening. He had hardly said a word since he'd come home, not even about the trial. Part of her hoped he would tell her what had happened today, but more than that she was worried about tomorrow.

She knew that, whatever the outcome of the trial, what she had to say would mean that her life, and her family's, would never be the same again.

She knew where he would be. She went downstairs, and then through the narrow corridors that separated their living quarters from the church he had led for over twenty years.

He was sitting in the front pew near the altar, staring into the distance, apparently lost in thought.

'Desmond?' she said, softly.

He looked up at her, his face both sad and angry. She went over and sat down next to him. She hesitated, then took his hand and squeezed it. He looked at their joined hands, as surprised as she was at this unaccustomed act of affection. Over the years, particularly after Paulie was born, they had been too busy loving God to love each other.

'How was it today?' she asked.

'They talked about how he was found; what the doctors did . . . anyway, I can't discuss it with you.' He withdrew his hand. 'You're going to be a witness tomorrow.'

He stood up and walked away from her. Eloise shrank back in her seat.

'Look at all this.' He waved his hands in front of him. 'Remember when there were only half a dozen people in the congregation, and they used to worship in our front room? I wanted to build something lasting for my family. Something clean and spotless. I thought, a new country, a new start . . . no one would know, and even if they heard a rumour, they would never believe it. Not Eloise Matthews. Not my wife. And now, after all these years, you're going to hold up your nasty, dirty past for all to see. Soiling and destroying everything I've built . . .'

'I helped build it too!'

Her husband whirled round, his face now contorted with rage and bitterness. 'You better not say anything to me. Nothing!' He started to cry. 'My son, my only son. Months I've been praying for him to get well, but nothing. He'll be a cabbage. The doctor confirmed that again today in court. All the things I wanted for him . . .' He tailed off. 'Well, at least he won't know what people will be saying about his mother after tomorrow. Have you told *your* son, yet?' There was no mistaking the emphasis.

'No. Why do you talk about Tony like that? You've raised him since he was a baby. Don't you love him, even a little?'

'I wanted you; he came with the package. That's what beauty and youth can do to a man, even a man of God. I knew a girl like you would have to have some blemish if she was prepared to consider a man so much older than herself. And you did: your belly full of another man's seed, and you had no idea who. I didn't find out the whole truth about you until I had my own son – when it was too late to rid myself of you.'

'But you can't forgive me, even after all these years? You preach about forgiveness all the time.' Eloise was crying openly. 'I've been a good wife to you, you can't deny that.'

'I don't deny it. And I could forgive you, as long as no one else knew. What I can't do is forget. And after tomorrow? Do you know what it's going to be like for me next Sunday when I get up to preach? Everyone looking, sniggering, laughing at me? One son nearly dead, his brother a criminal, and their mother –'

'Enough!' Eloise shouted. 'Would you prefer me not to give evidence? Not to tell of the threats that man made to me? And how soon afterwards our son was found face down in an alley, his life blood seeping away? No one saw him with Paulie. He could get off, and I know he did it.'

'And if he does get off anyway? You would have done it for nothing, and look what we would have lost.'

Eloise looked at him in shock. 'I can't believe you, or what you're suggesting. I know what I have to do.' She stood up and walked towards him, until they were almost touching. He refused to look at her. 'False pride, Desmond. That's a sin too.' Then she turned and walked back towards the corridor.

32

Tuesday, 8.45 a.m. Even though they were both going to court, Desmond Matthews couldn't bear to be in the same car as his wife, just as he couldn't bear to share their bed last night. He had considered sleeping in Paul's room, across the hall, but as soon as he opened the door he knew that would be impossible.

He wondered if his son would ever come home again, even if he couldn't be like before. That was what he was praying for; that was his bargain with God. However, if there was a chance, any chance at all, that his son could be restored back to full health, he would make a bargain with the devil himself and ask for Divine forgiveness later.

He had slept poorly in his study and had left early by taxi, leaving the car for his wife. Maybe she would drive to court; maybe she would call Tony and he would take her. He didn't much care. The floodgates were wide open now and it was all pouring out. Anger at his wife for matters he thought he had resolved long ago. Anger at himself for being unable to help his son. And shame – shame at what was about to become common knowledge, not just nasty rumours that could easily be dismissed. Now those gates were open, he wondered if they would ever close again.

And yet there was still something else there, bobbing up and down on that tide of rage. That was why he had asked for this meeting today, and, proud as he was, would have begged for it if he had to.

'Thank you for seeing me at such short notice, Mr Brooks. I know you're busy. This won't take long.'

'I really hope not, Reverend Matthews.' Like all barristers, Stephen Brooks had his own trial rhythm, and he didn't like it being thrown off. He didn't like unscheduled meetings of any sort mid-trial even with a victim's parent. As a seasoned prosecutor, he knew the families often didn't like it, but they would like it even less if he lost.

'It won't. It's about Eloise. I know what she's going to say when she gives evidence.'

Brooks glanced at the clock. 'And?'

'I want to say it. Let me give her evidence.'

'What? To let you say, under oath, that your wife was being black-mailed because of her –' he paused, trying to search for the least offensive word as the older man stared at him – 'past?'

'Yes.'

'I'm sorry. I'm not going to do that.'

'You of all people know how damaging this will be . . .'

'I'm sorry. I can't be concerned about your reputation.' Brooks gathered his papers as if to leave, but Reverend Matthews grabbed his arm.

'You think this is about my damn reputation? Or the work I've done around here – anti-crime initiatives that the CPS publicly supported? No, it's about my wife. *Her* reputation. We're men, Stephen. Times may have changed but we haven't. We can just about countenance not being a woman's first, but dozens before us? Maybe even more?' He squeezed his eyes shut as if trying to block that image from his mind. 'And the women on the jury will be worse – they'll think she's just an old whore masquerading as the preacher's wife. They'll all think I'm a fool for marrying her – and maybe I was. I'm angry and embarrassed for myself, yes – but I love my wife, despite everything. I want to spare *her* the shame, not me. From being asked nasty questions in cross-examination.'

'That's not Lee Mitchell's style. I've been against her before.'

'Every case is different. You don't know what she'll do here.'

Brooks looked at Reverend Matthews, overwhelmed with emotion but trying to keep his composure, and felt a wave of sympathy for him. But it was evidence that won cases. Untainted evidence, not sympathy.

'I'm sorry, Desmond. I won't do it. Your wife wants to give evidence, despite everything. What she has to say will be much more persuasive coming from her. A middle-aged woman who has turned over a new leaf, someone completely different than the girl she was decades ago; a woman who knows her teenaged son will never be the boy he was, or grow into the man she hoped he would be. You'd have to be made of stone not to sympathize with that. With her evidence, we'll get a conviction. Without it, I don't know. Neither of us wants that.' He gathered up the rest of his things, trying not to look at Reverend Matthews as the older man fought back tears – not of sadness, but frustration, anger and grief. 'Stay here as long as you like; I'll make sure you're not disturbed. And you don't have to come into the public gallery today.'

At 10 a.m. that morning, in another part of the building, Lee entered the consultation room next to the court. Brendan and Lambert were already seated at the table. She took her place directly opposite Lambert.

'Morning,' she said. She put her barrister's wig on the desk and started sorting through her papers, not looking up.

'You did good yesterday. Good start.'

She looked up, surprised.

'I never said you were a bad brief,' Lambert continued. 'Just didn't like the scum you represented.'

Brendan smiled triumphantly.

'We scored some points,' Lee conceded, 'but now we've got Tony and then his mum – and we still don't know what she's going to say.' She looked at Lambert. 'I don't suppose you're going to tell me?'

'Let's wait and see.' He leaned back in his chair, looking smug.

'Well, seeing as you're making yourself comfortable, have a look at this.' She slid a document across the table towards him.

'What's that?' Brendan asked.

'The most up-to-date list of Tony's previous convictions. I just got it from the prosecution this morning. Tell me if it is accurate, particularly if they've left anything out.'

Lambert read through the long list. 'Well, they've left most of his juvenile stuff out, but everything since age seventeen is right. He was suspected of a serious wounding . . .'

'Well, we won't be going there,' Lee said sharply. 'Innocent until proven guilty, or have you forgotten?' Lambert's face reddened. 'Anything else you want to tell me?'

'Tony's got a temper. Try and rattle him. That'll do half your job for you. Trouble is, he might be waiting outside court to knife you.'

'Thanks. That's reassuring.' She looked at her watch. 'Okay, let's get started.'

In another room near the court, Tony and Eloise Matthews were waiting to be called. Both were silent. Eloise looked at her son. She knew she was nervous, and that it showed. Tony wasn't – far from it; he crackled with pent-up energy. But then, court wasn't new to him. She would have told him now, she reasoned, but it would only distract him: his mind needed to be clear to give evidence in court. Yes, that was the only reason she wouldn't say anything now.

She looked at her elder son. 'What's it like, giving evidence? I mean, you've done it before.'

'Not too bad. It's difficult the first time, but then everything is.' He smiled at her. 'Don't worry, Mum. I'll be there with you.'

'No, you won't,' she replied, more sharply than she intended. 'I mean,' she went on, 'you're giving evidence too, so you can't hear mine.' She had asked the prosecution to let her go first for precisely that reason.

'Oh yeah, I forgot. But don't worry, I'll be there when you come out. I'll always look after you, Mum. You know that.'

She looked into her son's face, the tough-guy mask now gone, and tenderly stroked his cheek. He believed in her so much.

'Tony, whatever happens, I want you to remember that I love you. We don't say it as often as we should in our family. I hope – I hope you won't judge me too harshly.'

'Me? Judge you? After all the trouble and shame I've brought you? All the times you came to court, visited me in prison, even when you were angry with me? Me of all people, how could I judge you? And for what anyway?'

Just then, the court usher opened the door. 'Come with me, Mrs Matthews.'

Eloise got up, struggling to compose herself. 'I can't say it twice, Tony, I just can't.'

'Mrs Matthews, when did you last see the defendant?' Brooks asked.

'The night my son was attacked.' Eloise Matthews was gripping the front of the witness box so hard it seemed she was using it to hold herself up.

'And was that the first time he'd come to see you?'

Lee rose to her feet. 'Prejudicial, Your Honour. What relevance do previous visits – even if true, which is not accepted by the defence – have to do with what happened to Paul Matthews that night?'

'Shows a pattern, Your Honour, and why Mrs Matthews had every reason to take his threat seriously.'

'Overruled, Ms Mitchell. The witness may answer.'

'No, he'd come round for money before.'

Lee turned round quickly and whispered to Brendan, 'Ask him if that's true.'

'And had you given him money before?' Brooks continued.

'Small amounts, yes.' Mrs Matthews turned towards the door, as if Tony were standing just beyond it. 'I wanted to stop him harassing my son.'

'Paul?'

'No, Tony. He's been in trouble before, I'm not excusing that, but Sergeant Lambert just wouldn't leave him alone. Wouldn't give him a chance to stay on the straight and narrow. Plus I . . . I suppose in the beginning I wanted to keep it quiet. From the congregation, I mean. At first, some people just gossiped, and that was it. But when I realized more and more people knew for sure, and Lambert was still picking on Tony, there was no point in paying, so I stopped and started avoiding him. Also, my husband didn't know about any of this, and I was worried he might find out.'

'And on the night in question?'

'After I'd been avoiding him, he finally managed to corner me. He made the same demand for money. Said Tony would go to jail again. That had been such a long time ago; I couldn't bear the thought of him going back there. Then, he said something else . . .' Her voice trailed off.

'What was that?'

Her grip tightened. 'I've been trying to keep it a secret for so long . . . this is so hard . . .'

'Mrs Matthews,' Judge Harris said in a voice more gentle than usual, 'you said that the defendant tried to blackmail you and that is connected in some way to what happened to your son. I'm afraid you'll have to tell the court why you think he was doing that.'

Mrs Matthews took a deep breath before continuing. 'It was two things, really, wrapped up into one. The first is . . . Tony is not my husband's child. I was pregnant by another man when he met me. When he married me, Tony was just a baby. Tony and Paul both look like me, so no one in the church knew. Not for sure.' She looked at the public gallery for the first time. So many faces she recognized. Too many. Everyone but her husband's. 'At least, not until today.'

'But that's not uncommon nowadays, Mrs Matthews. Do you think that was bad enough for the defendant to want to blackmail you?'

Mrs Matthews smiled, sadly. 'You're not a minister's wife. In my community, people are very conservative about sex – much more than people think. With church women like me, they expect high moral standards that they couldn't possibly keep themselves. But the other thing . . .' Again, she was silent.

When she next spoke it was all in a rush. 'I was twenty-three when I had Tony. For seven years leading up to that time I was a prostitute. Tony's real father must have been one of my clients – I have no idea who that was. When I knew I was pregnant, after all the backstreet abortions I'd had . . . I knew this time I wanted to keep him, and I wanted better for myself and him. It didn't happen overnight, but I got out of that life. I even started going to church. That was how I met my husband.' She was crying now. 'He said it didn't matter to him, and I believed him. That he would marry me, and we would move to England, and no one would know. After we came here, we established the church and, much later, Paul was born; again, my little miracle. My past was more than half my lifetime ago, and it still matters. Do you think I wanted either of my sons to find out about that?' She looked at the jury.

'Please, you have to believe me. I would never say all this if I didn't believe that man tried to kill my son!'

Judge Harris interrupted her. 'I can see you're upset, Mrs Matthews, but please don't address the jury directly.'

'Sorry, Your Honour.' She bowed her head, still crying softly.

'Mrs Matthews. Mrs Matthews,' Brooks repeated when Eloise wouldn't raise her head. She looked up. 'That's all the questions that I have for you. Please wait there.'

Lee stood up. 'Would Your Honour give me a moment?' She turned back to Brendan. 'Well?' she whispered.

He whispered back, 'Yes, he'd been there before.'

She glanced at the jury. Many of them looked as disgusted with Lambert as she felt. She turned back to the witness. 'I have no questions, Mrs Matthews. Thank you.'

'In light of the evidence we have just heard, would Counsel like a ten-minute recess?'

'For my part, no, Your Honour,' Brooks replied. 'I'd like to press on.'

Lee couldn't blame him. The jury was on his side and the dramatic tension was at its height. The prosecution had all the momentum. Why stop now?

'Ms Mitchell?'

Lee shook her head. Even she didn't think Lambert would stoop to blackmailing a woman over something like this. More than ever, she wanted this case over.

'Then call your next witness, Mr Brooks.'

'Your Honour, I call Anthony Matthews.'

Tony entered the witness box. He was the only person present not to have heard his mother's revelations in court. He was just about average height for a man, but compact and muscular. The old scar along his jawline didn't detract from his smart, suited appearance. The Matthews boys: both young and from a good home, but neither with any future in front of them – one through crime and the senseless violence he had inflicted, the other through crime and the senseless violence he had suffered. It was a sobering thought.

Brooks asked him to tell the court about his relationship with his brother, and the last time he had seen Paul before the shooting. As he did so, warm glimpses of the boy Tony was, and the man he could have been, came out. His voice ranged across the emotions, from the pleasure of having an adoring younger brother, first to protect and then, as he got older, to spend time with; to the sadness, shock and rage of that terrible night.

'I wanted him to turn out better than I did,' he concluded. 'We all did. He wasn't streetwise, not really. I liked that, in a way. He was a proper fifteen-year-old – he weren't no roadman, or some wannabe gangsta. I was already getting into trouble at that age. Maybe if he had been a bit more street . . .' Sadness and anger were clear on his face.

'Do you know the defendant?'

Tony looked at Lambert. 'Yes.'

'How do you know him?'

Tony stiffened. He knew what was coming. 'He's arrested me before. Nuff times.'

'Let's not beat about the bush, Mr Matthews,' Brooks said briskly. 'You have previous convictions. Quite a number in fact.'

Lee listened intently to what was coming. Normally, a jury wouldn't know if anyone giving evidence had previous convictions unless the Judge allowed it, which rarely happened. Now the prosecution was introducing it into evidence, Lee could ask Tony questions about his past she would otherwise be unable to.

'Yes.'

'And you've been to prison?'

Tony hesitated for a moment, then squared his shoulders and looked directly at the jury. 'Yes.'

'Was Lambert involved in all these arrests?'

'Not all, but in a lot of them. He also arrested me for things I haven't done. It got to a point when any time something happened, he was turning up at my door.'

'So why would he attack your brother?'

Lee rose to her feet. 'Calls for speculation, Your Honour. This witness cannot say what was in the defendant's mind.'

Judge Harris shook his head. 'No. The witness is related to the victim, and knows the defendant – very well, by his account. Overruled. I'll allow it. The witness can answer.'

'I don't think he was going for Paulie, I think he was after me.'

'Then why . . .'

'Paulie was wearing my jacket. I didn't know. He always liked it but I wouldn't let him near it. Too distinctive.'

The statement dropped like a stone, sending ripples all around court. Brooks let it linger in the air before continuing.

'Your brother also had your mobile phone?'

'Yes. It was in one of the pockets. I use it sometimes, but it's not the only one I've got, and it's old. I forgot it was in there.'

'Our records show that someone rang your mobile phone from your house. You know who that was?'

'Yeah, me.'

'Why was that?'

'Well, I wanted the phone back. Paulie had his own with him. But mainly . . . I thought I'd left some drugs in one of the pockets. If I had, I didn't want him to get stopped with that on him.'

'Drugs?' Brooks thumbed rapidly through the papers. 'There was no mention of . . . don't say anything else, Mr Matthews, especially if you're not certain.'

'Paulie didn't know anything about it. It was mine. Police are always stopping Black youth. I didn't want him to get pinched for something he wasn't responsible for.'

'Mr Matthews!' Brooks said sharply.

'Mr Matthews,' said Judge Harris, 'you are in danger of incriminating yourself. I have to caution you that you do not have to say anything, but anything you do say may be used in evidence against you. Do you understand?'

'I understand. You think I care about that now? I just don't want anyone to think it was Paulie's.'

'Thank you, Mr Matthews,' said Brooks. 'Wait there, please.'

Lee stood up and faced Tony. The drugs admission was a gift, especially when none had been found on Paul. Tony had made that admission for nothing and needlessly incriminated himself. However, it showed real loyalty to his brother; the jury might like that. She wondered what had happened to the drugs. She glanced over at Wallace. From the look on his face, he was wondering too.

What she was about to do was unpleasant, but necessary.

'The prosecution said you have "quite a few" convictions, Mr Matthews. In fact, you have seventeen.'

Tony said nothing.

She held up the list of his convictions. 'Convictions for violence, drug dealing, two spells in prison. That's quite a record for a twenty-five-year-old, isn't it?'

Again, Tony said nothing.

'We're not going to get very far if you don't answer my questions, Mr Matthews.'

'So what you want me to say to that? I've already said I've got form.'

She went for the jugular. 'Was your brother running drugs for you?'

'What? No!'

'It's fair to say you've made enemies in your line of work.'

'Friends and enemies, yes.'

'Jack Lambert being an enemy, according to you.'

'Yes.'

'Why did you give your brother your jacket to wear that evening?'

'I already said I didn't give it to him. He took it. I didn't know.'

'Even though it would be too big for him?'

'You may not be familiar with the streets,' the dig was intentional and Lee knew it, 'but that jacket? Trust me, it being too big wouldn't have been a problem. I was the only one round here with one. People would kill for that jacket.' He hesitated, then continued, his voice lower now. 'In fact, when I first heard what had happened, I thought that was the reason.'

'For a jacket?'

'People kill for less. Trust.'

'I may not be as familiar with the streets as you, but neither was your brother – you said so yourself. Yet you send him out in a jacket that people identified with you, a jacket people would kill for, with drugs in the pocket.'

'Are you deaf? I didn't know he was wearing it!'

'I don't believe you.'

'So are you saying this is my fault?'

'I am saying a number of people could have attacked your brother, Mr Matthews, thinking it was you. As to whether or not it's your fault, that's between you and your conscience.'

Someone in the public gallery hissed. The last remains of Tony's control snapped.

'Me and *my* conscience? You fucking turncoat bitch!'

Judge Harris interrupted. 'Mr Matthews! Any further outbursts like that and you will be in contempt of court.'

But Tony was now in full flow. He pointed at Lambert. 'I know it was him! I know it was him because he's a fucking racist! He's been hounding me from day one. And who does he arrest? Only bare Black mandem!'

Lambert stood up in the dock, clearly rattled for the first time in the trial. 'I'm not a racist! I'm not a bloody racist!'

'I should have killed you when I had the chance! And if you get off, I will!'

'Mr Lambert, sit down! Ms Mitchell, get your solicitor to control your client. And, Mr Matthews – I warned you once. Dock officer, have someone take him down to the cells. I'll consider whether he should face charges for threats to kill as well as for contempt later.'

It took three guards to remove Tony kicking and screaming from the court. Even Judge Harris appeared shaken. It took several deep breaths before he spoke again. 'Ms Mitchell, did you have any further questions for that witness?'

'No, Your Honour.'

The jury were clearly affected. Judge Harris addressed them directly. 'Ladies and gentlemen, that last outburst was not evidence. Please disregard it. In the light of what has just happened and the lateness of the hour, I suggest we retire until tomorrow. Court is adjourned until ten thirty a.m.'

But Lee knew it would be impossible for the jury to put that out of their heads. With the cross-examination of Tony Matthews, she had sown doubt in the jury's mind and had discredited him as a witness by causing him to lose his temper. Mission accomplished.

After the Judge left, the CPS lawyer sitting behind Brooks said, 'I didn't know about the drugs. There was nothing in the statements about it . . .'

'I know,' he replied. 'I'm not blaming you. But forget about that. "*I'm not a racist*," he says? We've got him now!'

33

Day three of the trial. Lee had woken up with a migraine, and it was still with her when she arrived at court at 9.30 a.m. She had an hour before the trial was due to resume. Apart from a few minor statements which she and Stephen Brooks had agreed could be read, there were no further live witnesses to be called by the prosecution. By mid-morning, Lambert would be giving evidence. She would need this hour to fine-tune what he was going to say, and to prepare him for cross-examination.

Twenty minutes later neither Brendan nor Lambert had arrived. She was just about to go downstairs and wait for them – and take the opportunity to have a smoke – when they burst through the door. Brendan was red-faced, breathing heavily and slightly dishevelled. But Lambert looked even worse. He had shaved, but not very well, and he looked suspiciously hung-over.

Lee stared at them. 'What happened to you?'

Brendan answered, 'When he didn't meet me at the office, I had to go to his place to pick him up. He'd overslept. I'm sorry, Lee. I know it was important to get an early start, today of all days.'

Lee continued staring at Lambert, shaking her head. 'You're a complete disgrace. Don't you think this case is hard enough without you turning up looking like shit? Did you even have a wash before you came here?'

At least Lambert had the decency to look sheepish. 'All right, all right. Don't rub it in.'

She pulled two £20 notes out of her wallet. 'Brendan, go round the corner and buy him a shirt. And some deodorant. As for you,' she turned to Lambert, 'we'd better start going over your evidence.'

'All rise.'

'Good morning,' Judge Harris said to the assembled courtroom. 'Let's hope today's proceedings will be calmer. Mr Brooks, are you ready to proceed?'

'Yes, Your Honour. There are two agreed statements to be read.'

The statements were non-contentious. Lee was polishing up the questions she was going to put to Lambert when her opponent said, 'Finally, Your Honour, I would like to recall DCI Wallace.'

Brendan leaned forward and whispered to Lee. 'What's that about?'

'Probably to do with the drugs. Or Tony really losing it yesterday.'

'DCI Wallace,' Brooks began, 'do you recall being asked to confirm the defendant's length of service as a police officer? Twenty-five years?'

'Yes, I do.'

'Has that service been without blemish?'

Something wasn't right here. Lee rose to her feet. 'Your Honour, where is this going?'

'Yes, I was wondering that myself. Mr Brooks?'

'Your Honour, the defendant told the entire court yesterday that he was not a racist. The Crown seeks to disprove this.' Brooks held up a document. 'I have copies for you and Defence Counsel.'

'Here, let me see that.' Lee snatched the document from his hand. But Brooks wasn't bothered. Rather, he looked smug and, as she read what she had just been given, Lee realized he had every reason to be so.

'A moment please, Your Honour.' She turned to Brendan and showed him the statement. 'Did you know about this?' she whispered.

'Fucking hell! No,' Brendan hissed. 'He's never said anything. Ever.'

'Go back and check if it's true.'

As Brendan took the document to Lambert, she turned back to the Judge. 'I'm just taking instructions, Your Honour. This is completely unexpected.'

'But your client did rather open the door for this line of enquiry with his outburst, Ms Mitchell. Nothing equivocal about what he said.'

'If it's true, Your Honour.'

'Well, I see your solicitor returning. You're about to find out.'

All Brendan could do was nod. The look on his face told her all she needed to know.

'So, are you in a position to object, Ms Mitchell?'

'No, Your Honour.'

'Then I'll allow this line of questioning. Mr Brooks, please continue.'

'Thank you, Your Honour. DCI Wallace?'

Wallace looked and sounded triumphant. He spoke directly to the jury. 'He has two substantiated police complaints against him. One for excessive force, the other for racially discriminatory conduct.'

Lee didn't need to listen to the details. The damage was already done. For the life of her, she couldn't see how an acquittal would be possible now.

'Ms Mitchell?' Lee looked up. Judge Harris was addressing her directly. 'Do you have any questions for the witness?'

She stood up and opened her mouth to speak but couldn't think of a single useful thing to say. 'No, Your Honour.'

'I have no re-examination. Does Your Honour have any questions?' As Judge Harris shook his head, Brooks concluded, 'That's the case for the prosecution.'

'Ms Mitchell, are you ready to proceed, or would you like a brief recess to take further instructions in the light of recent evidence?'

She turned and looked at the dock. Lambert wouldn't look at her. He had lied by omission to her and Brendan all along – about blackmailing Eloise Matthews; about the complaints against him, which showed him to be both violent and racist. The cleanest thing about him was the new shirt he was wearing. She could go and take further instructions; she could even choose not to call him to give evidence at all.

But then he stared back at her, as unrepentant and belligerent as he had always been. Something inside her snapped. She turned back to the Judge and said, decisively, 'No need, Your Honour. I'd like to proceed. I call John Alfred Lambert.'

Lambert's bulky frame seemed to fill the witness box. He confirmed his name, rank and the station where he was based. 'I've been at Miller Street the last twenty years, five as sergeant.'

'Let's get right to it, Mr Lambert. We've all heard about the complaints against you. Please explain to the jury what a substantiated complaint means.'

s when a member of the public, usually some criminal you've rested, says you've done something wrong. Substantiation hey believe them and not me.'

contrition would have been nice. Lambert was not helping all.

Lee looked at the document Brooks had given her. 'Both of these matters happened five years ago.'

'That's right. I had just been made sergeant. We were having a lot of trouble around the local estates then.' He paused before continuing. 'Couldn't have the police be seen to be running scared. We had to get on top of things. It was a stressful time.'

'Would you do the same again now?'

'No.' He didn't sound convincing.

'Did you attack Paul Matthews that night?'

'I didn't attack anyone that night.'

'But we've all heard the timings. The CCTV shows you speaking to his mother at the Church of God Ministry.'

'That's right.'

'Were you invited there?'

'No.'

'So what were you doing there?'

Lambert remained silent.

'Mr Lambert,' Judge Harris said, 'you must answer questions from Counsel, particularly your own.'

'I was there to get money off her,' Lambert mumbled.

'Were you blackmailing her?'

'Yes.'

'About what?'

'Some old scrote – sorry, Your Honour – I arrested for doing drugs tried to do a deal with me. He tried to give me stuff on Tony, stuff I knew about already, which was no use to me. But then he mentioned something about Tony's mum, just in passing. About her having been a streetwalker. Didn't think anything of it at first, but then . . . well, money got tight. Sergeants don't make much in London, especially for all the crap we have to deal with. And her husband – always so up himself. Used to be a custody visitor, one of those nosy do-gooders always coming round checking we were looking after our prisoners' human rights. I didn't owe him anything, or her. I knew they had money; I thought she'd give me some. With the proper persuasion.'

The jury were hanging on his every word. It was the aural equivalent of a car crash.

'Did she give you any money that night?'

'No.'

'What were you going to do?'

'Dunno. Come back again. Hadn't thought beyond that.'

'Anthony Matthews accused you of picking on him, always arresting him. So did his mother. Is this true?'

'The reason why I keep arresting Tony Matthews is because he's a drug-dealing villain. You heard about his convictions. No, I don't "pick on" him. First off, I'm not the only copper to nick him. Second, at least two of my arrests have led to him being convicted. If that didn't happen with the others – well, I can't help it if some dodgy lawyer got him off.'

'Mr Lambert,' Judge Harris warned, 'Mr Matthews's character will speak for itself. You are in no position to denigrate it further. Or lawyers, come to that.'

'I have nothing further, Mr Lambert. Please wait there.'

Brooks stood up looking confident, as well he might.

'Mr Lambert, you're not actually a serving sergeant now. You're on suspension, aren't you?'

'Yes, until this is over. It's standard procedure.'

'*If* you get acquitted. Otherwise you'll be sacked, won't you?'

Lambert shrugged. 'Probably. But that's not going to happen because I'm innocent.'

'Anyway, regarding your behaviour five years ago, you said you "had to get on top of things". Did that include getting on top of a subdued prisoner on the ground and bashing his head in with a baton?'

'That was a drug dealer who tried to knife my partner.'

'Yes, I see you said that as part of your defence at the hearing.' Brooks folded his arms and stared at Lambert. 'He didn't have a knife, though, did he?'

Lambert said nothing.

'Did he?' Brooks repeated, more firmly.

'No.'

'And was this the same prisoner you referred to as a "fucking Black bastard"?'

'Yes.'

'And the reason these complaints were substantiated was because the police discipline board found that you did in fact use excessive force, after hearing from a police officer who was so appalled that he gave evidence against you. Not a criminal, not a member of the public, a fellow police officer. That's right, isn't it?'

Lambert took his time before answering. 'Yes.'

'And the racist language, you admitted that, didn't you?'

'Like I said, that was five years ago.'

'And you've really seen the light since then.'

'Careful, Mr Brooks,' warned Judge Harris.

'You don't like Tony Matthews,' Brooks said, matter-of-factly.

'He doesn't like me.'

'And you couldn't keep him off the street.'

'Not for the want of trying.'

'That's precisely my point. All those years of trying, all those times you arrested him, and only two prison sentences as a result? You must hate that.'

'He got off some things, I know he did.'

'How do you know?'

'I just know!' Lambert shouted.

'So you thought, if the courts can't sort it out, I will.'

'No.'

'You saw a young Black man in Tony's jacket. You didn't even bother to check whether it was him.'

'That never happened. You don't think I'd know Tony, especially up close? If I wanted to shoot him, I wouldn't make a mistake.'

'It was dark, and raining, and you were blinded by hatred for Tony. In that frame of mind, one young Black man would look very much like another to you. Especially wearing his distinctive jacket with the hood up. So you attacked him. But this time not with a baton – with a gun. The one that had your fingerprint on it.'

Lee rose to object. 'Your Honour . . .'

'No!' Lambert shouted.

'No? Mr Lambert, you have shown yourself to be a violent, racist blackmailer. Why on earth should this jury believe you? I have no further questions for this witness.'

Brooks sat down. In the silence that followed, everyone in court seemed rooted to the spot. Finally Judge Harris spoke.

'Any re-examination, Ms Mitchell?'

Lee rose slowly to her feet. She looked at Lambert in the witness box, his face flushed an angry red.

'No, Your Honour. And the defence have no further witnesses.'

'No character witnesses at all? The defendant is entitled to call them now, for the jury to consider, as he has no previous convictions.'

It would be funny if the situation wasn't so grim. 'No, Your Honour.'

'Are you formally closing your case?'

'I am, Your Honour.'

'Very well. Members of the jury, it's only mid-afternoon, but you have been listening intently to two important witnesses today. Court will rise until ten thirty a.m. tomorrow when Counsel will make their closing speeches to you. I will then sum up this case, and you will retire to consider your verdict.'

34

Nine a.m. Ninety minutes before court and thirty minutes before she was due to meet Brendan. It was a ritual Lee always did – centring herself before a decisive or critical part of a big case, especially before speeches. In Lambert's case, she thought, both applied; a perfect storm, particularly after his outburst yesterday.

She found a conference room as far away from Court One as possible. It was at the end of the top floor, overlooking the river. It was the smallest, almost like an afterthought, but it was her favourite because of the view. No one in her case would think to look for her here. The next thirty minutes, at least, were all her own.

Lee closed her eyes and concentrated on her breathing, using the Box Breathing technique David had taught her. She put both palms flat against her stomach and mentally did the count in her head: '. . . *in for four – hold for four – out for four – hold for four* . . .' She tried to clear her mind but, unbidden, David's voice popped into her head, from the first time he'd taught it to her, the weekend after a very stressful case. 'This will help you more than that will,' he had said, taking a large glass of red wine out of her hand. He had sat behind her, placing his hands on her belly over her own. She remembered the rise and fall of his breathing as it synchronized with hers; how calming it felt until it changed subtly from soothing to something more intimate. He had whispered something funny and sexy in her ear, and . . . Lee smiled at the memory, then frowned as she thought of the wreckage of her relationship. So much for clearing one's mind. This wasn't helping. And it usually worked so well. Just not today.

Lee sighed and stood up. The room was so small it was less than two steps to the window, sealed in so no one could think to escape – or, from that height, to end it all. She looked out on to the Thames. Above, the sun and clouds were fighting for domination. Looking at the flowing water, however, was at least a little calming. Lee felt her breath slowing to match the gentle undulations.

David had said that she'd changed; that he didn't know her if she could defend someone like Lambert. But had she really changed that much? Ever since school she'd had something to prove, to knock down all the stereotypes about young Black girls and the limited ambitions the world had for people like her. The teachers had expected nothing from her because they thought she was nothing. But she knew different. So she fought that. When she was first called to the Bar she had thought of herself as the champion of the underdog – of people from schools like hers, from neighbourhoods like hers. More than ten years and hundreds of cases later, she knew not all defendants fell into that category. And Lambert might be an underdog in this particular case but not in the wider world, abusing his power and authority; his evidence yesterday was proof positive of that. If he was acquitted, he wasn't going to get 'woke' or see the light. Given half a chance he would beat up, fit up and abuse someone else again. So why was she fighting so hard to get him off?

She wanted to win, plain and simple. Every case she did. Always had. Tom had said as much that day back in Chambers. So had Kofi. People had a problem with that in women, but that was it. Yes, this case was different – harder and tougher in ways that went well beyond the gravity of the offence – but now she was in it she was going to work to win.

She looked at her watch: 9.25 a.m.

'You're in it now, Lee,' she said to herself. 'Get it done.' She picked up her wig and gown, and went to look for her opponent.

Ten fifteen a.m. Lee and Stephen Brooks were both seated in Counsel's Row waiting for the jury to come in. Today of all days, there was going to be a prompt 10.30 a.m. start.

'So,' Lee began, more casually than she felt. 'Big day yesterday.'

'Yes, it was,' Brooks replied without looking up. He sounded pleased with himself, as well he might.

'How long's your speech going to be? You know Harris will want to work out when he'll be sending the jury out.'

'Not long, considering. I think it's best to let the defendant's behaviour yesterday speak for itself. Yours? You don't have to tell me, of course.'

'I know that. But we're realists. We both know I've got a lot of ground to make up.'

'So, a long one, then.'

Lee could hear the court doors opening and closing behind her. She sensed, rather than saw, friends and supporters of the Matthews family filing into the public gallery. Their antipathy towards her was as tangible as it had been on day one, rolling towards her like a wave, the iciness of it making her shiver. Then she felt a gentle tug at the back of her robe. Brendan. He gave her a thumbs-up and she nodded in acknowledgement, wanting to smile but knowing how that would be misconstrued. Whatever their previous difficulties, they were in this together right to the end.

Stephen Brooks was right. His speech was short, workmanlike and to the point. A reminder to the jury of their role in this trial and other points of law, careful not to encroach on what Judge Harris would say in his summing-up. A neat encapsulation of the evidence. Nothing played up, over-egged or inflamed. He didn't have to; he was right – Lambert's behaviour yesterday spoke for itself. There were no weaknesses – except in his delivery. Lee noticed he referred to his notes rather more than usual and, each time he did, he broke eye contact with the jury. That was one thing she could not afford to do. She had rewritten and rehearsed her speech so often she knew it by heart. As hopeless as this case was, in order to have a fighting chance she had to try both to win the jury over and to keep them onside.

'Yes, Ms Mitchell,' Judge Harris said as Brooks sat down. It was her cue to speak.

Lee stood up and turned to face the jury. She scanned their faces; clearly most of them would need a lot of convincing. As she did so, someone in the public gallery kissed their teeth, clearly aimed at her. Any person of Caribbean descent would have recognized it for the contemptuous gesture it was. Lee looked at the Judge. He might have been unfamiliar with the sound, but even he recognized the disrespect. He glared at the public gallery.

'Any further outburst like that, I'll clear the public gallery. Whatever your views, both Counsel will get the same measure of courtesy in this court.'

But that person would never know how they had helped her. It was a gift; something she could use to her advantage, particularly with such a diverse jury as this. If it was intended to throw her off her stride, it failed. In fact, it gave a perfect introduction to what she was about to say.

'Ladies and gentlemen,' she began, pointing in the direction of where the sound had come from, 'I know you all heard that. And I know most – if not all – of you will know what it means. Whether it's directed at me personally, or at Jack Lambert, it amounts to the same thing. A young man's life hangs in the balance, even now, and they think he did it. Let's be real here – you're probably thinking the same. Thoughts like: *After all, he's police. He wouldn't be in the dock if he didn't do it. He could have done it; he looks the type. We all heard what he did five years ago.* Up there, in the public gallery – they think he's a racist. You probably do too.' Lee paused. 'And you know what? You're probably right. There! I've said what you don't want to say. And I'm his brief!'

It seemed like everyone in the courtroom was holding their collective breath.

'So, why bother with a trial, if that's what you all think? Why have a jury at all? Because *could have done*, *probably did*, *might have done* won't cut it. That falls far short of being sure. Proof beyond reasonable doubt: that's what the prosecution have to prove to you. And Mr Brooks has had two speeches to try and prove that to you.

'At the beginning of the trial when he set the scene, framing the events in a particular way. I don't criticize him at all for that; that's his job. But it sets your mind on a particular path, and the danger is that you view all the evidence from that perspective. And then, just now, his second speech at the end.

'I just have one chance – one – to address you directly. To remind you of your oath: to return a true verdict according to the evidence. Not according to whether you like the defendant, or think he's a thug in a uniform. According to the evidence. And what evidence do the prosecution have? When all is said and done, it's a partial thumbprint on a street weapon that has three other sets of prints on it. There are no witnesses that place him at the scene of the attack; no forensic evidence found at the scene; not even CCTV. Just a partial thumbprint.

And it's on that flimsy basis that the prosecution would want you to convict a police officer of attempted murder. The prosecution knows that, so they want you to have uppermost in your mind that Jack Lambert tried to extort money from the victim's mother, as well as his violence and racism shown years ago on the job. That has done him no favours, and neither did his outbursts in court yesterday. But is that evidence that he committed *this* offence?'

She paused, taking a breath. Next time she spoke, her voice was gentler. 'If Paulie Matthews was your son, your brother, your nephew or grandson, what comfort would it give you if the wrong person was convicted? It would mean whoever did it was still walking around out there. Of course, if after everything you've heard, including His Honour's summing-up, you're *sure* on the evidence that Jack Lambert committed this offence, then convict him. But on the evidence you've heard, how can you be? Jack Lambert may be a lot of things – a lot of nasty, vile things – but one thing he's not: he's not guilty of this offence. Thank you.'

She scanned their faces again as she sat down. Most were still unconvinced of his innocence, but she could see the flickers of doubt on the faces of at least three or four. Enough for a hung jury. The courtroom was still eerily quiet, even in the public gallery. Judge Harris took a few moments to write something down, then turned to the jury.

'Ladies and gentlemen, I am now going to begin my summing-up of the case to you, which will not conclude until after lunch. Because I do not want you to be under any pressure of time, I will not ask you to retire to consider your verdict this afternoon but rather first thing tomorrow morning, after some concluding remarks from myself. But first, some preliminary observations. However moved you might be by what you have just heard, what either Counsel has said in their speeches, both at the start of the trial and this morning, is not evidence. The evidence is what you have heard from the witness box, any statements which have been read to you with Counsel's agreement, and any other documentary evidence, including CCTV, that has been adduced in this trial. This has also been a comparatively short trial for such a serious allegation and the media attention it has generated – four days, now going into a fifth – but the length of the trial in no way undermines its seriousness, both for Paul Matthews and Sergeant Lambert.'

As Judge Harris continued his summing-up, the jury were paying rapt attention. Some were writing and taking notes. For the first time since she'd sat down Lee looked back at Lambert, but he was staring straight ahead, his face expressionless. Then Brendan passed her a crumpled piece of paper. She recognized Lambert's writing. *Speech – four stars. Five if you hadn't slagged me off.*

She wrote back, then handed the paper to Brendan. *Think I did this for you?'*

35

The next day, Lee was standing outside the court, in the nearest part to the building where she could smoke. Looking around, she could see other frustrated lawyers doing the same. She took a last drag on a much-needed cigarette as Brendan came down the steps to join her. 'Thought you'd be out here.'

'How is he?'

Brendan shrugged. 'He knows he fucked it up. He was feeling really good after you demolished Tony on the second day, but then . . .' He looked at his watch. 'How much longer do you think they'll be?'

'You know you can never tell with juries. But it's been over two hours already. I'm surprised at that.'

'Well, maybe we've given them something to think about. Your closing speech was risky, but good.'

Lee stubbed out her cigarette. 'Brendan, it's hopeless. You know that. Especially after Wallace, and then his own evidence.' She shook her head. 'I was angry; guess you could tell that from my reply to his note. Maybe I shouldn't have called him.'

'He had to explain himself, Lee. You know juries don't believe defendants unless they hear them in the box, no matter what judges tell them. He'd have been potted for sure if he hadn't.' Suddenly he laughed. 'This is all very strange, you critiquing your performance, especially as you never wanted it in the first place. That was always the thing about you. Once you took it on I knew you'd go for it, right to the end.'

'You weren't worried that I'd deliberately try to sabotage it? I considered it, you know.' Lee thought back to her conversation with Ray, that night outside Chambers. 'And with this case, there were ways I could have done it and no one would have known.'

'We all think that occasionally, Lee. But I know your reputation means more to you than gutting Lambert. This is just another case. And at least we're talking again. I know, I know – not like we used to, but it's a start? Maybe?'

Lee gave Brendan a half-smile. She was just about to light up again when the court usher came out, flustered.

'Ms Mitchell, Mr Donnelly. You know you can't hear the tannoy from out here. The jury's back.'

Lee looked at the jurors as they entered the courtroom. Of the twelve, not one of them would look either at her or at Lambert. That could only mean one thing.

When they were seated, the Court Clerk stood up. 'Madam fore-man, would you please stand?' The woman seated nearest the Judge stood up.

'Will the defendant please stand? Members of the jury, have you reached a verdict?'

'Yes, we have.'

'On the count of attempted murder, how do you find the defendant?'

'Guilty.'

There was a burst of spontaneous applause from the public gallery. 'Yes!' someone shouted out. Reverend Matthews put his head in his hands. Hugo Cunningham slapped him on the back, seemingly oblivious to the fact that this was not a moment of triumph for the older man.

Lee turned back and looked at Brendan. He shrugged. 'Well, we tried.' But Lambert's face was ashen. He sank back into the dock between two custody officers, looking completely shell-shocked, as if he couldn't believe what he had just heard. Even after she had overcome her reluctance to take this case and had begun to fight to get him an acquittal, it was professional pride that motivated Lee, not belief in his innocence. She had always thought he was guilty; looking at him now, though, she wasn't so sure.

'Quiet in court!' Judge Harris said. 'John Alfred Lambert, stand up . . .'

But Lambert was paying no attention to him. He was looking at the jury. 'What have you done?' His voice rising.

'Mr Lambert, I warned you yesterday about your conduct. I won't do it again.'

'You know what you've done? You?' Pointing to the jury. 'And you?' to the Judge. 'Me, a copper in prison? You've written my fucking death warrant! I didn't do it!' Flecks of spittle were flying from his mouth, which he wiped away with the back of his hand. Some of the jurors shrank back from the force of his words.

'You got what you deserved, you racist bastard!' someone from the public gallery cried out.

'That's enough! Take the prisoner downstairs. Madam usher, clear the public gallery.'

Lambert was forcibly held by the custody officers and was taken down to the cells, struggling, his shouting and expletives echoing back into court. The friends and supporters of the Matthews family were only a little less noisy, some of them shouting 'Thank you!' to the jury as they left.

Once they had all gone, the courtroom was eerily quiet. Judge Harris was clearly angry, which Lee thought strange. Outbursts like this were rare, but they happened. As an experienced judge, surely he couldn't have been dealing with this for the first time. It was several minutes before he spoke again.

'Ms Mitchell, I see no reason why, once the defendant has calmed down, I cannot proceed to sentencing today. I really don't see how pre-sentence reports can assist me. Are you ready to mitigate on his behalf?'

Judge Harris was right. For an offence as serious as this, custody was certain. But even if he didn't order the reports, the last thing Lee wanted was for him to sentence Lambert affected by what he had just seen. 'Your Honour, as a police officer, the defendant will know as well as you or I that custody is inevitable. That said, he's a man of good character.' Lee remembered the police complaints and corrected herself. 'I mean, he has no previous convictions, and has been a police officer all his working life. Your Honour knows that before a first sentence of imprisonment it is both usual, and recommended, that pre-sentence reports are obtained, even where there is only one possible sentence. These will tell you more about the defendant's personal background and work history. In addition,' she added, hoping against hope Brendan might drag some up, 'despite not doing so during the trial, the defendant may yet wish me to call character witnesses on his behalf, none of whom are here today.'

She hesitated, considered what she was about to say, and decided she had nothing left to lose. 'It has been an emotional day all round. Ordering reports would give Your Honour the time and space to consider sentencing in a frame of mind where reason and logic prevail.'

She was sailing dangerously close to the wind, and she knew it.

Branding a judge as a hothead in front of his jury was risky, and from the look on his face she was sure he would have reprimanded her if they had not been present. Instead, he gave her an icy stare before turning to the prosecution. 'Do you have any representations, Mr Brooks?'

'The Crown is neutral on this point, Your Honour. However, on the matter of bail . . .'

'Oh, there's no chance of that. Ms Mitchell, I hear what you say. I am only just persuaded by your argument. Sentencing in twenty-eight days. Pre-sentence reports to be ready by then. As a convicted man, the defendant's bail is revoked and he will remain in custody until then. It only remains for me to thank you, members of the jury, for your diligence in this matter. Some of you may be at the end of your period of jury service. For those of you who are not, there may be more work for you. Court will rise.'

As soon as the jury filed out, Lee turned round to face Brendan. She looked at the empty dock. 'Well, I guess we'd better go down and see him.'

'Ms Mitchell.' It was Marlon, the head custody officer. 'The prisoner Lambert doesn't want to see you, or Mr Donnelly. He's going to Brixton tonight. He'll probably stay there until sentence. There's a van going back any minute now; he'll be on it.'

'Don't worry, Lee,' Brendan said. 'I'll go and visit him in Brixton. See if he still wants to appeal.'

It was the longest conversation Marlon and Lee had had since his own revelation about Lambert. 'Okay, thanks, Marlon. Nice of you to come and tell us this yourself.'

'Oh, I was up here for the verdict. Wouldn't have missed it for the world. Justice at last, eh?'

*

It was two days before Brendan was able to go to Brixton prison. A good two days for him, as it happened. Jason, his young whipper-snapper boss, wasn't bothered about the verdict; he expected nothing else. But he had noticed the graft he had put in and was even talking about making him partner. Only junior partner, in the firm he used to own. Still, it was a start.

The same two days hadn't been as kind to Lambert. When the guard brought him in to meet Brendan in the tiny consultation room at the prison, he had a black eye, a cut to his lower lip, and his right cheek was bruised.

'Jesus! What happened to you?'

'I tripped,' Lambert replied through swollen lips.

'Like fuck you did!' The guard was standing back, looking slightly sheepish. 'You know about this?' When the guard said nothing, Brendan said, 'Wait outside. Just leave us alone!'

Once he had gone, Brendan asked Lambert again. 'Who did this to you, Jack?'

'I told you, I tripped. And that's the story I'm sticking to for as long as I'm in here.'

'Remand is one thing, but it doesn't include having the shit kicked out of you. You want me to make a complaint? Speak to the Governor?'

'No! Bad enough I'm being kept away "for my own protection" with the grasses, the nonces and all the other perverts. Let's just get down to business and why you've come here. You want to know if I still want to appeal.'

'Yeah.'

Lambert pointed to his face. 'What do you think?'

'You still want Lee Mitchell to do it? I know you said that before.'

But Lambert surprised him. 'You know what? I really don't care now. One brief's the same as another. Don't suppose I can insist after my evidence, anyway.'

'I'll ask her to advise on appeal, at least. See whether we have a chance, though that'll have to wait until after sentence.' Brendan stopped taking notes. Putting down his pen, he looked at Lambert. 'Why didn't you tell us about the complaints, Jack?'

Lambert shrugged, wincing as he did so. 'Didn't think the prosecution would find out. They don't always. Five years is a long time. And if you knew, I wasn't a hundred per cent sure you could put me forward as a man of good character. She might even have withdrawn from the case. I knew she wanted to, and this time I wouldn't have been able to stop her. Anyway, people can change.'

'And have you, Jack? Changed?'

Lambert didn't answer. He stood up, gingerly, signalling the end of their meeting. At this, the guard came back into the room. 'You know what I want. And character witnesses? Don't bother; there aren't any. I'll see you when I'm sentenced.'

Three nights later, Brendan was in bed when his work mobile rang.

'Bloody hell, Brendan,' his wife muttered. 'It'll wake the baby. Why didn't you turn the thing off? You're not even on call.'

'Shit! Shit!' Brendan scrambled around to try and find it, bleary-eyed from sleep. He answered it on the last ring before it went to voicemail, not even checking the number. 'Hello?' he mumbled.

'Mr Donnelly?' It was a voice Brendan didn't recognize. 'It's the medical wing, Brixton. It's your client. We've got a situation here. We've called an ambulance. It's serious.'

36

Hugo had just seen off the last person at his regular surgery. It was the first time he had been there since the trial. He wondered, for all the good he was able to do, if he'd even been missed.

The door between his office and the waiting room was slightly ajar. Norma peered in. 'Okay if I go, Mr C? There's no one else waiting. Or would you like me to lock up?'

'You go on, Norma. Don't worry, I'll do it.'

'Well, don't forget to switch on the alarm. Goodnight.'

He heard the main door shut. He yawned, stretched, then ambled out into the reception area. It was tidy – Norma always saw to that. The chairs were neatly lined against three sides of the room. He looked at the carpet. God knows how long that had been down. He had wanted to replace it ages ago but didn't want to be accused of wasting public funds. It was now so threadbare and grimy it was becoming a health hazard.

A stack of newspapers left behind throughout the day was piled up neatly for recycling. He picked one up. Reading a tabloid was a guilty pleasure, especially one that was right-wing even by Tory standards. Same story that had kept war and terrorism off the front pages for the last few days, just a different headline: *Race Cop Fights for Life*. He was still reading when he heard someone banging on the front door.

'We're closed,' he shouted out, and carried on reading the article.

But the banging persisted. He went to the door. 'Sorry, you're too late. I –'

Fee Smith was standing outside, panting. She peered up at him, her curly blonde hair clinging limply to both sides of her face. 'Thought I'd just make it,' she said, slightly out of breath. 'Got something from Mrs Appleby.' She started to rummage through a big rucksack.

'Fiona? No, don't do that out there. Come in.' He quickly threw the paper on a chair, stood aside and allowed her to enter. She moved past him and sat down.

'We can go into my office, you know,' he said as he locked the door. 'It's more comfortable.'

'Don't worry, I'm not staying.' She finally found what she was looking for. She handed him a brown manila envelope that had been used before. 'It's about her rent arrears. She said you'd know what to do.'

'Oh. Yes, of course. How do you know Mrs Appleby?'

'She lives on my estate. She doesn't know you're my cousin. And I want to keep it that way.' Having got her breath back, she looked around the room properly for the first time. 'Good to see you're not wasting taxpayers' money, at least. Or is it all going on your private office?'

'You always did like to make assumptions about me. Why don't you go in and see for yourself?'

'I told you, I'm not stopping. Though I admit I was surprised to see you at the trial. Didn't think you'd come, or stay past the first day. Thought it would have been a bit too gritty for an aspiring Tory MP.'

'Tories care about social justice too. At least, this one does.'

She looked at him. 'Is that the reason you got involved, Hugo? The *only* reason?'

His heart hammered in his chest. 'What the hell do you mean?' he asked aggressively. 'I didn't see *you* past day one, shouting your mouth off outside court, as always.'

'I stayed for Mrs Matthews's evidence. I left before Tony went up. There was nothing I wanted to hear from him. He may lose his brother, but he's everything they say about him. And worse.' She saw the paper Hugo had discarded and picked it up. Pointing to the story about Lambert, she continued, 'But at long last *he's* getting his just deserts.'

'That would be a sentence of imprisonment from a judge, not to be beaten to a pulp by a gang of thugs in prison. They don't even know when he'll be well enough to be sentenced.'

'Well, at least he wasn't shot in the face. Don't expect me to feel sorry for him.'

'Come on, Fiona. I thought you didn't believe in corporal punishment. Anyway, what about *his* human rights?'

'But he's not human.'

Hugo had no time for Lambert, but he was shocked by the coldness in her voice. She always said he didn't know her. Maybe she was right.

Fee calmly continued reading the article, oblivious to him staring at her. When she'd finished, she said, 'Anyway, just in case you think I'm anti-police, the same should happen to Tony. He's a drug dealer. But then, you know that already, don't you?'

Hugo could feel cold sweat breaking out on his forehead and a trickle running down his back as she continued. 'I'm just surprised it wasn't him who was attacked that night. And the drugs in the jacket pocket – the rock, the coke . . .'

His mouth went dry, and his stomach lurched as if he were about to vomit.

'Fiona . . .' His voice was hoarse.

'Don't call me that!' she snapped.

'Fiona, how did you know about the drugs?'

'What drugs? Everyone knows Tony's a dealer.'

'But that night? On his brother? How did you know about those?'

'It came out in the trial.'

'You just said you weren't there.'

'One of the others told me. Why are you quizzing me about this?'

'Don't lie to me. None of that detail came out. And Tony rarely does rock; says it's too low class for him. It's mostly coke with him.' He paused, about to confirm what she already knew. 'And yes, I do know that because he's my dealer.'

Finally, it was out in the open. The first time he had admitted it to a living soul.

Neither of them said anything for a long time. The most surprising thing to Hugo was how calm Fee was – unnaturally so. Then she spoke.

'I always knew you were an occasional user, but I could tell when it was escalating, when you were really getting hooked. Granny's ninetieth – do you remember? I saw you doing lines in the bathroom. You were so desperate; you didn't even close the door properly. So I made enquiries. Thought it might have been one of your old Eton chums again, the ones that got you started, but all roads led back to Tony. You know I was fucking him.' The statement was as casual and lacking in emotion as if she were discussing the weather. On seeing the look on Hugo's face, she added, 'You really didn't know? God, that's a surprise. He didn't strike me as the discreet type when it came to women. I thought he'd have told you, at least. You know, sticking it to the upper classes, like yourself. Literally. What's so shocking? The fact that he's Black, or that he's a dealer? Your dealer?'

'The fact that you hated him. Or so you said.'

'Oh, but I did. And do. That hasn't changed. It was just sex. And the fucking is better when you hate them. It's intense. You should try it.' She shrugged. 'Besides, we were both curious. I even wondered whether he'd found out about us being cousins.'

Hugo shook his head. 'He didn't find out from me. And what you do with your life is your business.'

'Anyway, once or twice was enough to get that particular fantasy out of my system. You men are all the same. None of you can think straight when your cock is involved, not even someone as streetwise as Tony.'

'A social experiment, then, was he?'

Hugo's sarcasm was wasted on Fee. 'If you like. But I also knew that effect wouldn't last forever. So when I found the gun I had to take my chance.'

'He must have known you had it,' Hugo said slowly. 'You'd have been very, very sorry when he found out.'

But Fee just laughed. 'All his clients are people like you. He doesn't need to carry a gun. That's for his runners – if he lets them. Besides, you think he only has one? You're such a fool, Hugo.'

She got up and walked across to a photograph of Hugo and other local dignitaries hanging on the wall. 'It's true,' she said, thoughtfully, 'you do look a bit like David Cameron in this one. Never noticed it before.'

'How did you do it, Fiona?' Even to Hugo's ears it sounded like a stupid question. Clearly, his cousin thought so too.

'What do you mean, how did I do it? I shot him, Hugo. What part of that don't you understand? Or at least, I shot someone I thought was him. No one seemed to be able to stop him destroying people's lives. It was sickening. So I just waited. Waited, biding my time. I didn't think my chance would come so soon. I'd had the gun less than twenty-four hours. That night, I followed him. I knew his mother still let him stay with them sometimes even if the father didn't like it. I saw Tony leave, wearing that jacket he was so proud of. It was easier in the rain; he wasn't paying as much attention as he normally would to people following him. And so I did. Then he stopped by the alley near Havant Road, to do some deal on his mobile, or so I thought. I saw my chance and I took it. I had years of hate built up in me. Hate gives you strength.'

'Listen to yourself! That wasn't Tony, that was his brother. He didn't do anything.'

'Yes. That was unfortunate.'

'Unfortunate?' Her matter-of-fact tone was almost as chilling as what she had just told him. He sat down, pulling his chair away from her. 'Why in God's name did you do it?'

'You weren't the only person he was dealing to. You should see my estate. At least you're an adult . . .' She paused as she thought of the little girl with the rucksack. For a moment, Hugo thought he saw a glimpse of real emotion on her face, but it was so fleeting compared to her icy demeanour that he'd probably imagined it. When she spoke again it was in the same matter-of-fact tone.

'It did get a bit more personal when I realized you were involved. Even I was surprised; I didn't think I'd care that much what you did. I suppose blood is thicker than water, after all. Anyway, after I shot Tony –'

'Paul,' Hugo corrected her.

'– whatever, I thought I might have made a mistake. I had a very small amount of stuff Tony had given me when he thought I was a social user, so I put that in the jacket pocket while he was on the ground. I don't know what happened to it. Maybe one of the cops took it. After all, it wouldn't be the first time that happened round here, and Paul wasn't going to say anything.

'Afterwards, on my way back to the estate, I saw that idiot, JT. I was almost sorry for him, he looked so pathetic. He was about to piss himself, he was so frightened. Do you know, when I took that gun out of my bag and gave it to him, telling him I had it for protection but he could use it if he was really scared, he actually believed me?' She shook her head, incredulous.

Suddenly, she held up her hands. Hugo had forgotten how pale and thin they were. He could see the veins threading their way under the skin, pale blue beneath the harsh fluorescent light. The hands of an old lady – or of a Lady. 'I had every excuse for wearing gloves – little me, in the cold. So I knew it was unlikely my prints would be on there, and even if they were, I don't have a criminal record. Nothing for the police to check against. JT, however . . . I told him I wanted it back, but early the next day he came round in a state and said Lambert had found him. That's why he'd been so scared. And he had taken the gun off him. Then two weeks later, he was dead. Don't know who did that; could have been Tony. Or Lambert. But it saved me from having to sort that out too.'

'An innocent man is in prison for what you've done. Do you honestly think he'll live long enough to serve out his sentence?'

'Lambert innocent? Don't give me that shit. He didn't do this one, but he's not innocent. I don't care about him. I also have no particular feelings one way or another about Paul Matthews, though I would prefer if he didn't die . . .'

'But all those things you said? About what happened? Leading the protests?'

'Politicians lie all the time, Hugo; I shouldn't have to tell you that. This might be grass roots but it's politics too. And if I stayed involved, I could hear things. See if there was anyone else in the frame besides Lambert.'

Hugo looked at her. 'God, you're an evil bitch.'

She shrugged. 'Say what you like. And if you're about to appeal to my better nature about going to the police to confess, don't. Why do you think I'm sitting here calmly telling you? I'm not going to the police and neither are you. Because they might have gay – oh yes, I know about that too – drug-using Tories already in Parliament, but it will be a cold day in hell before you get there on that ticket. Be a national disgrace? To our illustrious family? You won't do it, to you or them. You've got too much to lose over a bent copper.'

Hugo buried his face in his hands. Fee patted him on the head in an almost maternal manner. 'Don't worry, Hugo. I'm not. But,' she added, looking at the paper with the lurid headline, 'stop reading that rubbish. I'll let myself out.'

37

Silence.

It was dark outside. The only sound was the rain, not that loud but, in the yawning absence of noise, rapping like hailstones as the drops hit the bedroom skylight.

'I didn't want to tell you on the phone –'

'I'm going for a run,' Wallace interrupted. He didn't want to hear any more. His voice sounded strange, even to him.

'What? Now?'

Wallace said nothing. He turned his back and grabbed his things. His companion watched silently as he dressed, not knowing what else to say.

As Wallace sat on the bed and bent over to lace up his trainers, he felt a tentative hand on his shoulder. He angrily shrugged it away. He didn't trust himself to say anything more. He stood up and walked out, not bothering to close the door behind him.

The street was deserted save for the occasional lone vehicle, its headlights picking him out, a tall Black man in faded sweats. A lone figure on an empty street, running into the night. He knew that this fact alone would make him a suspect in the eyes of many. Someone leaving the scene of a crime, not just a jogger. He was a cop; he knew what they thought about Black men running at Miller

Street. Always the criminal by default. Never the victim. Never the pursued.

Different thoughts and images were flashing through his head now like a kaleidoscope. His time in the Army when not a week would go by without hearing ever more inventive ways of calling him a nigger, under the guise of 'banter' – until he put the worst offender in the hospital. The police when he worked in close protection – believing themselves to be an elite cadre above such things, but they still thought it. And now Miller Street. His rank and seniority protected him personally, but he still overheard things said about others who looked like him. What they probably even thought about men like Reverend Matthews despite his work in the community. And about Paulie Matthews, not even a man – just a teen who sang in his dad's choir. Some probably thought he deserved what had happened to him, that he had it coming. He couldn't possibly be innocent, a victim. He was Black, wasn't he?

He felt pursued tonight, trying to outrun his own thoughts. He didn't even bother with his usual warm-up pace before getting into his stride. As soon as he hit the pavement, he was running as fast as he could. Across the road. Down the empty streets. Along the path through the Common, the trees looming darkly on both sides. No one from the station came down here alone. They were always double crewed. Wallace didn't know what he would find here or who he would meet, and he didn't care. Adrenaline and rage had his lungs burning with exertion, his heart pounding so hard it felt as if it would jump out of his chest. Doggers, muggers, drug dealers, gang members – let them all come. He was so angry that he would take them all on. Just let them try. If anyone stepped to him he would give them what he had wanted to give Lambert for so long. He would beat the living shit out of them, then claim self-defence. They'd believe the badge, even if the holder was a Black man.

But then, that was just what Lambert would do, and had done.

Wallace collapsed against a tree, breathing heavily. He tasted bile in his throat. He had been wrong. He, who was always aware of all the angles. All his life he had needed to be that way. Never let yourself be caught slipping. And yet here he was. How had he not let himself consider any other possibility?

He could just imagine Superintendent Reid's face when he found out. The mutterings around the station. '*This is what happens when you overpromote them.*' '*Positive discrimination gone mad.*' People doubting his competence. The disappointment in the eyes of the only other Black person in the station, because his failure wasn't just his own: it was every Black person's.

Worst of all, Paul's parents. What could he possibly say to them?

He could just bury it; pretend he didn't know . . .

'You could just pretend you didn't know. I won't say anything.'

Wallace was back now. He was looking at, rather than seeing, his companion, but he could hear the words. They echoed the very thoughts he'd had. He had thought of nothing else on the long walk back.

'After all, Lambert's a disgrace to the uniform. And a racist. Everyone's known it at Miller Street for years. He just got caught for this.'

'But he didn't do it,' Wallace said, his voice quiet.

'So what, Danny? What about the others? The ones he got away with?' Adding softly, 'And what about you, and your career? That's really what I care about. What do *you* want me to do?'

'I hate the man, but there's only one thing you can do.'

298

'I don't suppose telling you counts?'

Wallace leaned over and kissed Hugo full on the mouth. 'Not like this. First thing tomorrow, go to Miller Street and ask to speak to Superintendent Reid.'

'I won't mention you.'

'Don't. Not if you want to see me again.'

38

Six weeks later

The cameras whirred and clicked. Dozens of microphones were being thrust forward, and everyone was speaking at once.

Ray stood back, watching.

The demonstration was being kept well away, the police line holding, but only just. They were across the street from the Court of Appeal. One or two more determined protesters managed to break away, dashing into the road, causing traffic to screech to a sudden halt. Both times they were brought to the ground by police. Even from where he stood he could see and hear one of them, whose ginger hair was the same colour as his trainers, taunting and goading the police, so when he made a run for it towards Lambert, they were grateful for the opportunity to rugby tackle him firmly on to the hard concrete. When he was brought to his feet Ray could see blood pouring from his nose and mouth, blood smeared across his teeth where one was now missing. He spat a gob of saliva and blood in Lambert's direction, but he was too far away. The cameras noticed that, though. It was the only time they had turned away from Lambert, but not for long. There was only one story here today.

'Mr Lambert! Mr Lambert!'

'*Sergeant* Lambert to you, son.' Standing on the steps of the Court of Appeal, he might be using a walking stick and had his arm in a sling, but Lambert was as belligerent as ever.

The young reporter looked sheepish. 'Of course. Do you want to go back to your old job now this is over?'

'Why not? It's all I've ever done.'

'Still happy to go back to your old station?' another reporter asked. 'Everyone associated with this case still lives in the area. Don't you think it might be a bit insensitive?'

'Well, Fee Smith won't be getting out any time soon. And Hugo Cunningham's given up politics. So why shouldn't I go back? I've done nothing wrong.'

Ray looked at Lambert's smug expression and could feel his hands instinctively balling into fists. He wanted to go back to Miller Street, and his old life, as if nothing had happened – and he'd probably try to even if they didn't want him, just to prove a point. He would be walking around the same area as JT, except JT would never be on those streets again and no one was doing fuck all about it. As far as murders went, JT was so low priority he'd fallen off the edge of the list. After all, he had no family to speak of, especially not a dad like Reverend Matthews with access to the great and the good. There had been no marches or protests for him. As far as the police were concerned he was just some small fry drug-dealing scum who got what he deserved. His only use to them had been as Lambert's informant. Ray remembered what Wallace had said at Satyr about investigating his murder; even he didn't sound convinced.

He didn't have anyone sticking up for him, the little runt, Ray thought. That used to be my job. Still is.

Brendan Donnelly, Lambert's solicitor, was standing next to him on the court steps. Even here, after his successful appeal, his client was capable of snatching defeat from the jaws of victory, losing whatever goodwill had been generated around his false conviction, particularly in light of the attacks he had suffered in prison which, as it turned out, had been inflicted on an innocent man. Innocent. That word would always sound strange when used in relation to Lambert. Best if he stepped in now.

'My client is very happy indeed that justice has at last been done, and that he has been completely exonerated. Of course he wants to contribute to the Metropolitan Police in the position he loved, and at the station where he has given such extraordinary service to the local community, but he appreciates where he will end up is within the gift of the Metropolitan Police. After he has finished his convalescence, he will continue to be a dedicated and loyal officer wherever he is posted.'

Ray could see Lee about two hundred yards away from him, separated by the protests neither of them were taking part in. He could always spot her in a crowd. She gave him a half-nod of recognition before turning away.

Lee was just one of many onlookers across the road. She could see Lambert was wearing the shirt she had bought for him, on the day he gave evidence at his trial.

There had been no actual hearing. After Hugo had told Superintendent Reid about Fee, it was only a matter of time before she was arrested, and Lambert was brought to the Court of Appeal and formally acquitted. However, due to his injuries, it had been a long time between Fee's arrest and Lambert's release. He was revelling in it now, though, for once his perennial sense of grievance entirely justified. Lee was glad she was well out of it. She hadn't seen him since the trial and had often wondered whether he would have kept her locked into this case right through the appeal process if things had been different. Luckily, she had never had to find out.

Just then her mobile rang. It was David. Though he had called her since Lambert's conviction, it was still infrequent enough to be a pleasant surprise. He hadn't moved back in – but at least they were talking.

'You're out there watching it, aren't you?'

'Yes. He is now officially a free and innocent man.'

'Free to go back to being a police officer? Doesn't sound like justice to me. Anyway, I've finished early.' He paused. 'Want to meet up?'

'What?' She wasn't expecting that.

'Don't get it twisted, Lee. I don't know if I'll ever be able to get past you taking Lambert's case. I still can't get my head around that, and I'm still angry at you, to be honest. But I miss you. I know you miss me too. And we're big people; we should at least talk, face to face. No law against that, is there?'

It was a start. Lee smiled. 'No, no law at all.'

Wallace sat in his car in the secure car park listening to the whole thing on the radio. He knew they would be watching it inside the station. This was not a moment he wanted to share.

As it turned out, the more experienced members of his team were sympathetic. '*You win some, you lose some. On to the next.*' '*At least the boy was still alive, even if just. We've got real murders to deal with.*' And the ones who thought they could do better – he could deal with them. But he couldn't bear to watch Lambert walk free.

Someone tapped on the window, startling him. It was Bill Roberts, almost old enough to be his father. The first person who had befriended him when he arrived at Miller Street. The one who was with him when they first went to Lambert's home all those months ago. It seemed fitting that he should be here at the end.

'Guv . . .'

'I know, Bill. The boss ready for me now?'

Roberts nodded. Wallace fished his jacket out of the back seat and put it on. A formal meeting required formal attire, after all. Then he stepped out of his car and into the professional unknown.

39

Lambert came out of the front door, stood on the step and looked around him, the same thing he had done a month ago. He had looked around in triumph then. He'd shown them. No one had believed him? Fuck them!

But tonight, he was doing it for his own protection, especially now. All day the news had been reporting that Paul Matthews's life support had been switched off. In court, Tony had threatened to kill him and now, with his brother's death, Lambert had no doubt he would try. Despite his acquittal, he knew there were some people who would never see him as anything other than a racist murderer in a police uniform. Typical liberal media bullshit. Obviously they cared more about some brain-dead Black kid who wouldn't have had much of a life anyway even if he'd lived than about the fact they were jeopardizing his right to life every time they ran that story.

The one loose end was the gun. The same gun that had been submitted in court as the weapon used to shoot Paul Matthews. He hadn't told a living soul that he had kept it in his house for days without handing it in – not his Super, and definitely not his lawyers. Only JT knew that it had been in his possession at all and he wasn't alive to say anything. As far as Lambert was concerned, he had been right to keep *schtum*. Once his brief had successfully cast doubt on its link to him, there had been no need to say anything, anyway.

That was always the way to feed information to lawyers, even his own – on a need-to-know basis only. His first loyalty is, was and always would be to himself.

But someone had got into his house – a place he had thought so impenetrable, with its many locks and burglar alarm, that he had only bothered to put the gun in the most obvious of hiding places, under the mattress. Whoever did it was a professional. At this point it didn't matter who; despite living here for years, that, plus Tony out for revenge, meant he would have to move. Within days.

He hobbled down the garden path. The weeds either side were starting to choke the narrow strip of concrete leading to his front gate. Not that he cared. He couldn't pull them out even if he wanted to now, not with his leg. He'd never be able to bend it properly again, according to the doctors. But he'd show them. The Met were using it as an excuse to get rid of him – or worse, give him a desk job. Bollocks to that!

It was painful to walk, even with a stick. It didn't help that it was surprisingly cold for early August. Every chill blast of wind made his leg hurt. But he'd go mad if he had to stay in one more night. Now he was on indefinite sick leave, he could go days without seeing or hearing from anyone if he didn't get out of the house. Good thing the Flag wasn't far. He kept his head down against the wind and pulled his clothes around him like a modern-day Steptoe.

It wasn't that late, but there were fewer people on the street than he would have expected to see, especially on a Friday night. But then, it was the kind of night where you wouldn't be out unless you had to. Walking into the wind made his progress slower. He could just see the lights of the Flag at the end of the road when . . .

Lambert didn't realize what had happened at first. People were always taking a short cut through that alley. It happened so quickly

306

he didn't see who it was, but it had to have been a man to hit him hard enough to make him lose his balance. He staggered back against the wall, his stick clattering to the ground. The man kept moving, not running – in fact he'd slowed down – but moving away just the same.

Fucking bastard. Lambert opened his mouth to shout the words, but it hurt to speak. He must have been more winded than he thought. He put his hand to his stomach. His coat was damp. He took his hand away and stared, fascinated at the sight of his own blood. He felt oddly light-headed. Now he needed to lean against the wall. He put his hand under his clothes on to his belly. A puncture wound, just above the navel. Tony?

He always knew he wouldn't make old bones.

He felt himself sliding down the wall on to the pavement. He looked up the road. No one was coming. He wondered how long it would take before someone came across him, before someone realized that he wasn't just another drunk who'd stumbled out of the Flag and collapsed in the street. And he wondered how long that would be after he was dead.

Who knows, he thought. It might even be coppers from Miller Street who found him. You had to laugh . . .

The man who had stabbed Lambert didn't have to look back. If you went for the belly button, that was it. Good. JT got some justice too. For an instant, the street light glinted on the bloodstained knife Ray held in his tattooed hand just before he put it in his pocket.

Acknowledgements

First, to everyone who is going to read this book – and I'm counting on that being very large number! I write because I have something burning inside me to get out, and because Lee Mitchell, as a character, won't leave me alone. But I know a reader is at the other end of the seesaw. I'll never forget that.

More specifically there are some people who I have to name who are directly connected to the writing of this book:

To Susan McFarlane, who invited me to an event on a cold rainy night which has become a real-life 'sliding doors' moment for me.

To Bernardine Evaristo, who I met that night, for bringing my first book, *Without Prejudice*, back to life, renewing interest in Lee Mitchell and leading ultimately to my new home at Penguin.

To my editors at Penguin – first Hannah Chukwu, now spreading her wings in pastures new, for being both brilliant and patiently dealing with my many questions, and now the wonderful Simon Prosser. Together with my amazing agent Jonathan Ruppin of The Ruppin Agency, who helped so much with the book before it even got to Penguin and effortlessly smooths out issues for me, I think we did good!

To Ayo Onatade, my friend; super bright, super funny and one of the best crime fiction reviewers in the UK, as well as having a seriously important day job. If you ever write a time management book I will be first in line to buy.

To Brenda Hale, Baroness of Richmond – your letter served as an

309

encouragement to me just when I needed it, proving that your kindness is as expansive as your legal mind.

Special shout out to the Well Read Book Club who invited me to do a reading and then let me become a member. Unusual both in the breadth of books discussed and the fact that they have an equal gender balance when most bookclubs are predominantly female. Discussing books, plus great food, plus jokes and all in my neighbourhood. Who knew? Every time I have attended I've always enjoyed it.

To all my family and friends which I'm very fortunate to say are too many to name (and some of whom would prefer not to be named; I respect their privacy), thank you for your support even though I'm sure some of you thought I was mad to take so much time away from judicial and other duties to focus on this! On paper it might not have been a sensible choice but it was absolutely the right choice for me.

And finally to people I have lost during the writing of this book: Stephen Isaacs, Alice Jackson, and of course Tony. You live on in these acknowledgements.